PERILOUS FALLS

⚬⚬⚬

est. 1899

G.L. Shoe Repair

Morning
Star Bank

Bobbit's
Bestiary

Gall Lane

dePlancy Cemetery

High Street

Simon
Blabbingdale's
house

Phosphorus Way

Karnak Center

Dura Street

Gabbatha
Place

Phosphorus Way

Heinrick Crinshaw's
house

Mayor Lynch's house

Rapids Lane

Will
Wilder's
house

Dorcas Drive

WILL WILDER
THE LOST STAFF OF WONDERS

ALSO BY RAYMOND ARROYO

Will Wilder: The Relic of Perilous Falls

WILL WILDER
THE LOST STAFF OF WONDERS

❖ BOOK II ❖

RAYMOND ARROYO

CROWN BOOKS
FOR YOUNG READERS

NEW YORK

Text copyright © 2017 by Raymond Arroyo
Jacket art and interior illustrations copyright © 2017 by Jeff Nentrup

Visit us on the Web! randomhousekids.com

Educators and librarians, for a variety of teaching tools, visit us at RHTeachersLibrarians.com

Library of Congress Cataloging-in-Publication Data
Names: Arroyo, Raymond, author.
Title: The lost staff of wonders / Raymond Arroyo.
Description: First Edition. | New York : Crown Books for Young Readers [2017]
Series: Will Wilder ; 2 | Summary: "Twelve-year-old Will Wilder is back to protect the town of Perilous Falls from another ancient evil—the fearsome demon, Amon"—Provided by publisher.
Identifiers: LCCN 2016012966 | ISBN 978-0-553-53967-7 (hardback) | ISBN 978-0-553-53968-4 (glb) | ISBN 978-0-553-53969-1 (epub)
Subjects: | CYAC: Supernatural—Fiction. | Demonology—Fiction. | BISAC: JUVENILE FICTION / Action & Adventure / General. | JUVENILE FICTION / Family / General (see also headings under Social Issues). | JUVENILE FICTION / Religious / General.
Classification: LCC PZ7.A74352 Lo 2017 | DDC [Fic]—dc23

Printed in the United States of America
10 9 8 7 6 5 4 3 2 1
First Edition

Random House Children's Books supports the First Amendment and celebrates the right to read.

For Rebecca, who first read our children stories,
and to Lynda, who first read them to me

CONTENTS

Do not plunge thyself too far in anger,
lest thou hasten thy trial . . .

—William Shakespeare,
All's Well That Ends Well

WILL WILDER

THE LOST STAFF OF WONDERS

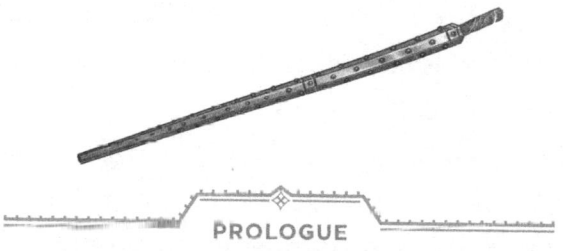

THE BROTHERS' STAFFS

Axum, Ethiopia
April 23, 1939

The Guardian bounded across the dusty church toward a soldier clutching the doorway's edge. A square silk hat bounced atop his head as he ran, golden fabric trembling around him.

Kicking dirt from his boots, the lean American soldier in the pith helmet wore a scowl. He clearly hadn't come to pray.

"We asked the Brethren to send you months ago, Wilder. Months ago!" The bearded man with skin like caramel and a heavy Ethiopian accent tugged at the soldier's arm. He pulled him inside St. Mary of Zion Church. But within a few steps, he released the soldier as if he had just clutched a sizzling coal.

"You have such anger, son. Such rage." The small man's eyes searched the soldier's sculpted face for answers. "What is the matter, Wilder?"

"I couldn't get here any sooner," the soldier seethed, removing his helmet, not making eye contact. "I was in Hong Kong. I lost the last two Chinese *collaborators*. Their son got out with me, but—" His lips trembled. "The *Sinestri*. They released four or five *Yaoguai* into the house and—" He clenched the brim of his pith helmet hard enough to snap it in two.

"Nah, nah, nah." The Guardian gently patted the soldier's forearm and drew close. "You saved a life. You did your best. We will conquer the *Sinestri* with hope. Not with regret or anger." In a cracked voice, he whispered intensely, "A German—an archaeologist—has been here for three days. He has been asking questions and looking, looking everywhere."

"For the Ark of the Covenant?" the American asked, dabbing his eyes.

"No, no. The security of the Ark does not trouble us. The sacred Tabot can fend for itself." The Guardian yanked his silken robes to his body and leaned in. "Edmund Kiss is the man's name. The Italians tell me he was sent by some Nazi commander—called Himmler—to collect 'powerful objects.'" A devious smirk suddenly cut across his face. The man's ghostly blue eyes flickered with glee.

"What's so funny?" the young soldier asked.

"You should see his face, Wilder." The bearded man revealed a mouthful of blinding white teeth. "This Edmund Kiss went near the Holy of Holies." He pointed toward the crimson silk curtain to his right, surrounded by hand-painted murals of saints and the Virgin holding the Christ Child.

"Did he make it inside?"

"He got past the first curtain. But no farther. Only the Guardian is permitted to enter here—to even approach the Ark. Only I, Wilder."

"So what happened?"

"We heard screaming inside. Moments later Kiss is running out through the curtains, hands over his face." The Guardian lifted a bleached hand to his mouth, concealing a giggle. "Screaming—yelling, 'Help me! Help me!' There was smoke coming off his head. When he pulled his hands back—oh! Blisters. Tumors all over his face. Everything exposed was blistered. He won't be back for the Ark." The Guardian's hoarse snicker filled the sanctuary.

Jacob Wilder shot a worried look toward the curtains hiding the Ark of the Covenant. He sidestepped away from the radiant drapes, dragging the Guardian along with him.

"Abba Azarius, the Brethren told me you were concerned about the safety of something precious and that I should retrieve it. It isn't the Ark, I hope."

"No, Brother Jacob. Since the time of Moses, the Ark

has slain armies and reduced men to dust. It has been in Ethiopia for thousands of years—snatched from Jerusalem by the son of King Solomon and the Queen of Sheba. It will take more than the efforts of the Italians or the Nazis to possess it. We are concerned about *the contents* of the Ark."

"You mean the tablets bearing the Ten Commandments?" Wilder asked.

"No. The tablets are safe inside, as is the jar of manna—the bread God gave the Israelites in the desert. But there is another item—"

"The Staff of Aaron. Moses's brother's staff?"

"You know the Old Testament, Wilder. Many centuries ago, the brothers here in Axum used the power of the staffs for protection. Later, fearing that invaders might steal them, we took precautions." The Guardian walked over to a mural of brightly colored monks raising their hands in prayer. Then pushing his hands against those of a monk in the mural, the part of the wall he pressed receded several feet into darkness. The Guardian stepped into the slight opening in the wall.

He descended a dimly lit flight of stairs, followed closely by Jacob. "You have both staffs? The ones belonging to Moses and Aaron?" Jacob whispered.

"We hid the Staff of Aaron, but these barbarians are very close to discovering its location."

The Guardian spun around as he reached the last step. "In the obelisk field, the one with the granite pillars across the way"—Abba Azarius dropped his voice—"Aaron's rod is there."

"Above the underground tombs where I entered? In the field?"

The Guardian cackled. "Inside the first obelisk to the left." The little man walked to the corner of what appeared to be a low-slung storage room. He lifted his garment at the knees and began dancing a peculiar jig. Stamping his feet in rhythm on the sandy stone in the corner, he never stopped talking. "Aaron's rod is far more powerful than Moses's staff. But you must take both back to Monte Cassino. They are not safe here."

The Guardian stopped his footwork and joined Jacob in the middle of the room. He intently watched the stone in the corner, caressing his chest-length beard. The crunch of rock grinding on rock echoed as the stone he had danced upon slid beneath the nearby wall.

From the opening in the floor, a dark blue rod flew into the air, then hung in suspension. The Guardian lifted one arm, his hand wide. The thick rod hit his palm with a smack. "Behold, the Staff of Moses. The staff of God."

Jacob Wilder was speechless. His green eyes darted over the rod. The sapphire surface held an ethereal glow, as if it possessed an internal light. Etched up and down the shaft were Hebrew letters. Jacob reached for the rod.

"Mr. Jacob . . . Mr. Jacob," a high-pitched voice screeched from the stairwell behind them. A long shadow crept down the wall.

The Guardian aimed the thick end of the staff toward the staircase. "Come no farther!" he yelled to the approaching figure.

Jacob leapt in front of the staff. "Everything's fine. He's with me. It's the boy from Hong Kong. The cooperators' son. You can come down, Tobias," he said over his shoulder.

The worried face of a small Chinese boy, all of six, leaned around the visible part of the stairs. "You told me to call if there was trouble. Well . . . there is trouble, Mr. Jacob. Big, big, big trouble . . ."

The Guardian passed the staff to Jacob. "What trouble, child?"

"Troops. Soldiers. I saw lots of soldiers coming here. To the church," Tobias said.

Without a word, Abba Azarius slipped past the boy, up the staircase. Soon the gentle scraping of the wall being pushed back into position could be heard from above, followed by the footsteps of the Guardian returning.

"Who is the guy in the funny hat?" Tobias asked, scrunching up his face.

"Keep it down," Jacob said as the Guardian reappeared. "Abba, is there another way into the obelisk field?"

"There is always another way, Wilder." The Guardian opened a woven chest beneath a table lined with brass lamps. He pulled out folded linen robes, which he threw onto the table. "Wear this. You too, boy. Hide the helmet under your vestments, Wilder." The Guardian tossed Jacob a black linen pillbox hat, which he pushed onto his head.

"There is a tunnel here," the Guardian said, pointing to a wall behind them. "It leads to the royal burial chambers where you entered. Directly under the obelisk field." From his robes, the Guardian pulled out three elaborate metal disks emblazoned with crosses. He jammed each one into a distinct slit in the stone wall. Like circular saws, the metallic disks madly spun up and down, side to side, along the space between the stones. When they stopped, the Guardian gave the wall a shove and a square passage presented itself.

Lighting two brass lamps, Abba Azarius led the way. Jacob, carrying the sapphire rod, followed.

"You see the marking on the knob of the staff? The serpent with the straight tail?" the Guardian asked as they moved. "On the obelisk outside, you will find the exact same marking next to a false door. *Gently* press the knob of Moses's staff to the marking on the granite and Aaron's rod will appear. If you are the 'chosen one,' you should be able to claim it."

According to a prophecy revered by the Brethren, Jacob Wilder was "the chosen one" among them—the key to defeating the *Sinestri* and resisting the *Darkness*.

The Guardian stopped suddenly and clutched the staff in Jacob's hands, his tone grave. "This staff is capable of wonders, Wilder. It called down the ten plagues upon the Egyptians. It transformed into a terrible serpent. Throw it to the ground with enough force and it may do so again. Remember, the tail of the thing will remain as you see it here. Clutch its tail and it will become a staff once more. Protect it. If the rod of Moses ever fell into the hands of the *Sinestri*—"

"I understand," Jacob snapped, pulling the staff away. "I've got it."

"I hope you do, Brother Wilder. Be quick, but remember the sin of Moses: defiance! Anger! Do not allow your wrath to deceive you. It can blind even a *Seer.*"

Jacob nodded and raced down the passage.

The Guardian blessed the head of Tobias and sent him down the dark passageway as well. "You will see the light up ahead," he called out. "Remember, just *touch* the staff to the obelisk marking. I will distract the soldiers in the church. You will need the time. God go with you."

Jacob focused only on his task: find the obelisk, seize Aaron's staff, and get out of Axum. Catching sight of the orphaned boy trailing him in and out of the shadows, sadness ambushed him. Had he arrived a few minutes earlier—struck faster—he might have saved the boy's parents. They hadn't seen the skeletal demons coming, but Jacob Wilder had. By the time he burst through the door of the home, the *Yaoguai* held Mr. and Mrs. Shen by their throats. Tobias crouched under a table screaming for his parents. The winged beasts carried the couple up to the ceiling of the main room and in seconds had pressed the life out of them. Jacob's jaw muscles twitched with fury.

"Tobias," he said with more force than he intended. "Stay near the sarcophagus." He indicated a side chamber with three stone caskets. "I'll be back in a few minutes. If anyone comes, get in that one—with the cross on it. You know the formula."

For centuries the Brethren had traveled via sarcophagus in a pinch. Jacob and his allies were no exception.

Tobias nodded, fear in his eyes. "Careful, Mr. Jacob."

"It's a deal." Jacob charged up the stairs into the purple twilight of the field. Within seconds he was in the shadow of the enormous central obelisk. Slim granite pillars reaching into the sky surrounded him. The elaborate towers indicated the tombs of the Axum royalty. After a quick search, he found the pillar with the carved door but had trouble locating the "serpent" marking.

Where is it? Where is the mark—

The distant approach of footsteps distracted him. Leaning around the edge of the obelisk, he could see soldiers emerging from the fortress-like church across the field, about four hundred yards away. They were headed in his direction. Time was running out.

On a circular emblem next to the granite door, he discovered the faint etching of the stiff-tailed serpent. Raising Moses's staff, he aligned the marking on the top of the rod with the granite emblem and gently pressed them together. *Nothing.* His heart pumping faster, Jacob repeated the action. He could hear the soldiers drawing near.

Once more he touched the rod to the emblem. His breath quickened; his mouth went dry. In frustration, he smashed the sapphire knob into the granite. *CRACK.* It was a hollow space. The granite gave way. *CRACK*. He hit it again, hard, and a three-foot area of the granite face dropped like broken eggshells to the ground. Inside stood a tangle of blooming vines connected to a central shaft.

"What am I supposed to do with this?" Jacob asked himself. At first, he felt for his knife. Then recalling what the Guardian had said, he reached into the opening for what looked to be the slender trunk of a sapling. There were Hebrew letters carved into the bark. The moment his hand made contact, the white blooms retracted and the vines slithered into the shaft as he held it. He easily pulled the wooden staff from the obelisk.

"Quite a trick," Jacob said, marveling at the two staffs in his hands.

"Quite a trick indeed," a slurred, German-accented voice spat from behind him.

Jacob stiffened. When he turned, there was Tobias, a Luger pointed to his small head. Holding the gun was a portly figure in khaki, his face full of raised boils, some of them oozing.

"I have paid a dear price for those sticks. Give them here"—he cocked the gun's hammer back—"or the boy dies."

Tobias flinched as the hand, covered in red, open blisters, tightened its grasp on him. Seeing the boy once more in distress, something snapped inside Jacob Wilder. He had but one thought: *Protect Tobias*.

"Of course, Mr. Kiss. Here are your sticks." In one fluid

movement, he smacked Kiss on each side of his head with the two staffs and kicked the gun from the man's hand. Wilder positioned himself between the boy and the blistered archaeologist. Before the German knew what was happening, Wilder turned him around and pinioned him against the obelisk, the staffs holding his neck in place.

"Help me! I'm here behind the obelisk," Kiss yelled to the Italian soldiers entering the field. "The staffs are here. I have the sta—"

Jacob punched him in the face, which quieted the German. He wiped the back of his sticky hand on Kiss's shirt.

"Tobias, don't let anyone get this." Jacob handed the plain wooden staff, Aaron's rod, to the boy. "Hold it tight. Run straight to the sarcophagus. Get in and go."

Tobias immediately obeyed and had disappeared down the steps to the tombs in moments.

"You have a problem, sir," Edmund Kiss wheezed, standing with his back to the obelisk.

Jacob Wilder turned to find Kiss's grotesque mask of red and white hives. Even his eyelids and lips were covered in pustules. He aimed a small pistol at Jacob's belly.

"I'll take that one now," Kiss demanded, ogling Moses's staff. Soldiers were filling the obelisk field.

Jacob couldn't take his eyes off of Kiss's face. For several seconds the German's features were obscured by a mad night bird, snapping a beak filled with sharp teeth. Jacob startled at what he saw.

The guy's possessed.

Without hesitating, Jacob hurled the staff at the big man's feet. The tip of the rod instantly swelled into a sparkling blue snake with a head as big as a bison's. Kiss dropped the gun, releasing a scream that ripped the sores at the edges of his mouth.

"Aaaaaah! Aaaaah!"

The snake's twelve-inch fangs slashed at Kiss, who raised his arms to defend what was left of his face. Terrified, the German shoved part of his rear end and one leg into the opening of the obelisk, where Aaron's rod had been hidden. The soldiers clamored up the steps on the backside of the obelisk.

Jacob reached down for the serpent's rigid sapphire tail. The second he grasped it, the snake withdrew into the knob of the staff as if it had never been there.

"Kill him and find the boy!" Kiss yelled to the soldiers, trying to wriggle free of the obelisk hole. "Don't let the boy escape!"

"You may kill me, but you'll never touch the boy," Jacob whispered, jamming the knob of the staff into Kiss's gut. The ferocity of the move shoved Kiss farther into the obelisk, causing the entire structure to quake. Looking up, Jacob could see the pillar swaying. Then the undulating obelisk, with Kiss still in it, toppled backward.

Hundreds of feet of solid granite fell to the earth, crushing stairs, grass, and several Italian soldiers. Wilder didn't wait for a casualty report.

He broke into a long stride, running toward the underground tombs, a smattering of gun-toting soldiers in pursuit. Entering the tombs, Jacob yelled for Tobias. Satisfied that the boy was gone, he ripped off the linen robe and threw himself into a sarcophagus. Lying flat, Jacob pulled the strap of his pith helmet under his chin and wrapped his arms around Moses's staff. *"Morte in vitam,"* he said.

Eight Italian soldiers crashed into the burial chamber. They fired their guns into the sarcophagus where they had seen Wilder take refuge. When the smoke cleared, one officer extended his pistol and tentatively advanced to check the body. Reaching the casket, his eyes wide, the soldier lowered his gun with a shrug. Inside were spent bullets and dirt. But Jacob Wilder and the Staff of Moses had vanished.

CHAPTER 1

THE FLYING DEMON

Few of the residents of Perilous Falls knew that their town's museum housed much more than relics and antiquities. Rising up like a mountain of spires and domes at the high end of Main Street, the museum could be seen from anywhere within the city limits. Assembled from bits of demolished European castles, monasteries, and churches, the small village of stone buildings on the hilltop was officially known as the Jacob Wilder Reliquarium and Antiquities Collection. Wilder himself dubbed it "Peniel," for reasons no one could quite recall. But everybody in town simply knew it as "the museum." Most had no idea that a mysterious community lived within its walls, hidden from public view.

Along a stone hallway, deep within the recesses of Peniel, twelve-year-old Will Wilder dashed from door to door. He yanked at the ringed handles, peering into the darkened rooms, manically searching.

"Abbot Athanasius? Abbot Ath—Oh, come on!"

Another empty chamber.

He slammed the heavy door in frustration, stomping down the hall to try another. His "Discernment of Spirits" training session was to have started forty minutes earlier. But when he appeared at the huge chamber on the north side of Peniel, where he had been meeting the abbot every weekend for months, it was vacant.

"Abbot Athanasius?" Will pushed open the last door at the end of the hall. The smoky lighting of the chandelier in the windowless room made it hard to see. Once his eyes adjusted, he caught sight of a figure seated on a high-backed chair in the middle of the room. Its back was turned to the door.

AH-CHOO! Will sneezed.

Tentatively he entered, taking his pith helmet in hand, wary of the situation given the—AH-CHOO!—sneezes.

"Abbot?" When Will touched the shoulder of the figure, it collapsed to the ground. He kicked the mannequin in disgust. "Where are you?" he yelled.

"*Look.*"

Will spun around, trying to locate the voice.

"*Look closely.*"

AH-CHOO! AH-CHOO!

A shadowy form stood in the corner of the room. The faint light from the chandelier twenty feet above made it impossible to say for sure who or what was there.

"Abbot, is that you?" Will whispered, inching toward the dark corner.

He grabbed the arm of the thing lingering in the shadows. Another dummy. Will hit the midsection of the figure with his helmet.

"What is this?" Will asked.

"What do you see?" a screechy voice echoed from the opposite corner.

Will turned quickly.

He could feel heat gathering on his face. He was so annoyed by the mannequins he felt like kicking in a wall or breaking something. Still he walked toward the dark corner, his dread increasing with every step.

"What do you *see*?" the voice demanded.

"I can't *see* anything." AH-CHOO! "It's too dark," Will huffed.

Someone was in the corner. Maybe Abbot Athanasius. Maybe another dummy. He had to figure out which it was.

Zzzzzzzzzzzzzzzzz.

A buzzing sound from above forced Will's eyes upward. From the chandelier, a withered creature in black robes descended. Deep wrinkles covered its face, a cruel look in its beady eyes. Two claws reached for him.

Zzzzzzzzzzzzzzzzzzzz.

Will scampered back toward the nearest wall. The creature touched the ground, closing in on him.

"What did you *see*?" it demanded.

"I . . . I . . ." Will inched along the wall toward the door. "Get away from me!"

The creature tore at the wrinkled flesh of its neck. As it got closer to Will, the shredded flesh revealed pale white skin beneath. Once half of the wrinkled latex was peeled away, steel blue eyes and a short beard emerged. The creature's fake claws were dramatically thrown aside. It was Abbot Athanasius Poeman standing like a matador who had just slain a bull.

"Why did you converse with what might have been a demon, Will?" Athanasius asked, removing the tattered robe from his lanky frame.

"But you're not a demon."

"You didn't know that," Athanasius said, unhooking a vest connected to the cable on the ceiling. "Your impatience will be the death of you."

"My impat—Why were you hiding?" Will's worry gave way to irritation. "I've been looking for you all afternoon."

"It was a test. The patient man abounds in understanding, Will. The impatient one becomes the devil's plaything." Abbot Athanasius began to leave the room, his long black habit making him appear to levitate across the floor. "You should have been more attentive—studying the room, considering all angles before you entered."

"I didn't think my training was going to be a forty-minute game of hide-and-go-*shriek*." Will pursued the abbot down the hall.

"The sneezes should have been a warning to you—as

they were for your great-grandfather. While not conclu-sive, they do offer some early indication that evil is pres-ent."

"Or that the place needs a dusting." Will smirked.

"Keep joking. There were dark objects concealed in each of the mannequins in that chamber. Objects you failed to perceive." Athanasius stopped walking. "They could have injured you and should not have been handled."

"That was my training? I gave up my friends—half the day—to dodge dummies and watch that evil Batman rou-tine?"

"If only the cable had not buzzed during my descent . . . it would have been perfect," Athanasius said offhandedly. "Perhaps next time."

"I'm not sure I want a next time." Will slammed his pith helmet onto his head and marched down the hall in the op-posite direction. Embarrassed, he felt as if he'd been tricked by the abbot and played for a fool. But when you're twelve, feelings are powerful things and difficult lessons are often the easiest to resist.

"WILL!" Athanasius bellowed in a deep tone that filled the hall. The boy stopped cold. When the leader of the Breth-ren raised his voice, which he rarely did, everybody froze in place. "Whether you train or not, the *Sinestri* know who you are. They will pursue you. Unless you refine your sight and learn to distinguish deceptions from reality, darkness from light, you'll be no good to this community or to yourself." The abbot faced Will with a look of disappointment. "The training cannot progress until you learn to control your emotions—to master yourself."

"I was trying." Will's brows knit together as he glared at Athanasius. "But after searching the *tenth* room, even an angel would start growing horns."

"Silence! Do you hear yourself, boy?" The veins on the side of the superior's balding head pulsed. "Always an answer. Always the last word." He paused for a long moment before he continued. "I want you to go down to the museum. Polish the display cases."

"Not again." Will's head and shoulders slumped.

"Again and again and again and again until you are self-composed enough to take direction."

"My brother, Leo, has a karate meet that I told my family—"

"After you clean the cases in the Egyptian Gallery, you may go to your event."

"I promised Leo that I would—"

This time an icy glance from Abbot Athanasius was enough to quiet Will. He walked over to the boy and in a kinder tone added, "I am doing this for your own sake, Will. The prophecy says that you may one day lead the Brethren against the enemy. To lead, you must first be a servant. Attend to your duties and be here at the usual time tomorrow." His blue eyes bore into Will.

Before he could say anything he might later regret, Will descended a slightly bowed spiral staircase and ran toward the museum in the front, public section of Peniel.

The prophecy. The prophecy. All I ever hear is the prophecy.

Had he not borrowed a relic a few months earlier, Will might have been playing with his friends on that Friday afternoon. But when he snatched a saint's finger bone from a local church, things sort of got out of hand. Will had befriended a riverboat captain who turned out to be a major demon. Though he didn't realize it at the time, Will was the only person who could see the beast. The demon deceived Will, stole the relic, and the whole town was soon beset by floodwaters and terrifying monsters. That was when he first read the prophecy. According to this old book, protected by Will's great-aunt Lucille, a firstborn son of the Wilder family would be a *Seer*—one possessing the ability to see demons. Sure enough, Will could spot the horrible creatures, but he hoped he would never have to see another one—and he hadn't for many months.

"Your gift must be honed," Lucille would say. So several times a week, Will dutifully showed up at Peniel to undergo training by members of the Brethren, a secret order that had been fighting demons for centuries. They lived in community in and around the museum, which they often called an archabbey since it was the most important monastery in the region.

On the ground floor of Peniel, Will rushed past ancient columns and a row of Gothic windows. In the courtyard garden outside, overrun with vines and pink sprays, a chubby man in a black habit with a bright green apron caught his attention. Brother Ugo Pagani, the gruff herbalist and chemist for the archabbey, pinched leaves off a bush. He placed each one in a basket looped over his forearm. From the way he handled the leaves, one would have sworn he were collecting rare butterflies. "If he only treated people that way," Will said under his breath.

Ugo was known for his caustic humor, hair-trigger temper, and for occasionally hurling things across rooms at great speeds. Though you'd never know that from the gentle Ugo in the garden. He could have been mistaken for an oversized Girl Scout rescuing a wounded cat from a tree. That was until Ugo saw Will staring at him through the glass. He quickly assumed his natural attitude, scowling at the boy and poking a finger to his right, indicating that Will should move along. He did as directed.

No matter how many times Will wandered the halls of Peniel, he could not fathom how his great-grandfather Jacob Wilder had managed to construct the place. It was as if one ancient castle opened on to another—a mix of Gothic halls giving way to Romanesque chambers, leading to Byzantine anterooms and filigreed chapels. There were so many passages and stairways he had yet to explore, like the one he passed leading down to the vaults. The sudden mention of his name and a pair of intense voices within the darkened stairwell forced him to stop.

". . . Will Wilder is making no progress at all," a resonant male voice intoned in the darkness. "He's barely trained."

"There *is* the prophecy. He's the only one that can see the *things*," an Irish-inflected voice responded.

Will inched down the stairs.

"Untrained gifts do little good. He is not a leader. He's a *boy*. And who of us have read the prophecy?"

A languid female voice interrupted them. "I have, actually." It was Will's great-aunt Lucille. No one said a word. Will moved farther down the stairs for a clear view.

"Close up the vault, will you? If you have concerns, Baldwin, you should bring them to the council," Aunt Lucille advised. "Gossip can be so destructive." She walked through the rounded opening of some Old World safe, a gold wooden box topped by glass in her hands. Will mistook it for a shallow birdhouse. From the white gloves, he knew Aunt Lucille must be transporting a relic or some other precious treasure up to the museum.

Baldwin, a thick-necked brother with thinning blond hair, closed the vault door with his considerable brawn. "I meant no harm, Lucille," he said, dropping his haughtiness as the locks automatically engaged. "We all want what's best for Will . . . and the order."

"I'm sure you do, Baldwin. And as vicar of the community, you should keep an open mind." Aunt Lucille headed to the stairs, spotting Will on the landing. "Look who's here."

Baldwin turned his hawk nose in Will's direction, stiffening to his full height. "How are you progressing, young man?"

"Okay, I guess." Will narrowed his eyes. "I mean for someone barely trained and all . . ."

Before anyone could say another word, Brother James, the slight, thirtysomething, red-bearded man with the

Irish brogue, wrapped a thin arm around Will. "I want yuh ta know, I defended yuh. I believe the prophecy, I do." He blinked a lot when he spoke, which always made Will smile.

"James, why don't you join the others at the chapter meeting in the Perilous Chapel?" Baldwin suggested.

"Right away, Vicar." James gave Will a pat on the arm and blinked out his supportive Morse code. "Good day to yuh, Will. Keep at it. I believe in yuh, I do," he whispered before shooting up the stairs. Baldwin nodded to Aunt Lucille, then to Will and silently followed James.

"Where are you headed?" Aunt Lucille asked Will, her blue eyes traveling to the ornate box in her hands.

He quickly got the message. "Do you need me to carry that?"

"Thought you'd never ask." At the top of the stairs, she placed the box on a nearby chair, gave Will her gloves, and led him down the hall.

At sixty-six, Lucille Wilder was used to leading the way. She had spent her life in the walls of the museum, working with her father as a young girl here and in the decades since as its director. Whether tending to artifacts or curating exhibits, calming the factions within the Brethren, or overseeing the training of her grandnephew, Lucille's strawberry-blond curls were bouncing all over Peniel. Time seemingly had no effect on her. In fact, Aunt Lucille moved with such verve through the halls, she left Will short of breath.

"Come on, catch up, dear. Help me deliver that to my father's office in the tower; then you can run along to Leo's karate meet."

"I wish I could. Abbot Athanasius ordered me to clean the display cases *again*. This time I'm scrubbing down the Egyptian Gallery," Will complained.

"The training mustn't have gone well. How bad was it?"

"I kinda snapped at him. He was hiding from me. . . ." Under the glass top of the box in his hands, Will could see a piece of silk, tanned and spotted by age. "Hey, what is this?"

Aunt Lucille pulled at the high collar of her powder-blue jacket and turned to her nephew. "You've got to watch your tongue with the abbot—with all your instructors. Obedience is the only way you'll learn anything, Will. Much depends on your progress."

"I understand," he said. "So what's in the box?"

"Oh, that is quite a relic. The veil of the Virgin Mary." Aunt Lucille tapped a finger on the glass. "Careful with it, dear. That's the original. We sent a facsimile to Chartres Cathedral in France. The *Sinestri* have been attempting to steal it. They even started a fire in the cathedral last week as a distraction. The Brethren there were so concerned, they transferred it to us for safekeeping. It'll be quite secure in my father's office. Bartimaeus and I have the only keys."

"What can it do?" Will asked as they approached the private door that led to Jacob Wilder's personal hideaway.

"It is believed to have protected the town of Chartres from invaders back in the year 911. When it was shown to the soldiers, their energies surged and they repelled the

Normans. The veil has quite an established history. It once belonged to Charlemagne and has been in the possession of the cathedral there for more than a thousand years."

"So it can protect people?" Will asked.

"Yes, the Voile de la Vierge can stir the faith of those seeking protection. Some have said it can even calm tempers and bring the peace the Virgin experienced to those who touch it. I'm sure they're right." Aunt Lucille opened her hands and reached for the box as Will stared at the silk. "I can take it from here." She retrieved both the veil and her gloves from Will. "Better run along and start polishing or you'll miss your brother's competition." She gave him a peck on the cheek. "I'll see you tomorrow morning for sight training upstairs." In seconds, she disappeared behind the door marked PRIVATE.

Will found himself alone in Bethel Hall, the grand entryway to Peniel. Dying sunlight cast a pink glow through the stained-glass Gothic windows. Will dodged the display cases spread throughout the room and headed to the corridor that led to the Egyptian Gallery. What he saw on the far edge of the red jasper and marble floor made his blood run cold.

The passage leading to the Egyptian Gallery was choked in silky black feathers, a few of which had tumbled out onto the floor of Bethel Hall.

AH-CHOO! AH-CHOO!

This could be a problem, Will thought. He stood before the mouth of the entryway, unmoving—too fascinated to turn away and too frightened to press on.

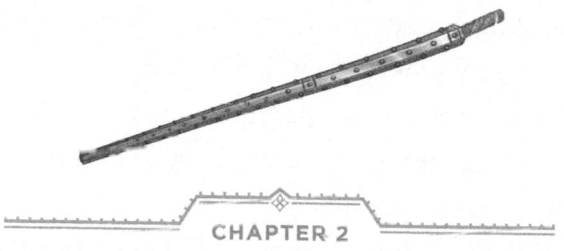

CHAPTER 2

BLACK FEATHERS AND BLACK BELTS

"Those cases ain't going to clean themselves," a familiar low voice echoed in the hall behind Will. "The abbot told me he's making ya——"

Will spun around, worry covering his face.

"What's wrong, son?" Bartimaeus Johnson, a black man with tinted glasses, balanced on a pair of wooden crutches. He shambled toward Will as quickly as the crutches could carry him.

"The floor. There're black feathers all over the floor," Will sputtered.

"Easy, Will. It's okay." Bartimaeus squinted, throwing his unresponsive right leg forward as he shuffled closer. He calmly spread his hand wide. "Oh yeah, I can feel the *Darkness*." He scanned the floor of the passageway before him.

"I know my sight ain't what it used to be, but I don't see no feathers, Will. Look."

When Will turned back to the entryway, the feathers were exactly where they had been moments earlier—clogging the hallway and spilling into Bethel Hall.

"They're right there, Mr. Bart. They're everywhere." Will bent down to pick one up.

"Don't do that!" Bartimaeus said. "I wouldn't touch 'em. Tell me what they look like first." Bartimaeus slowly reached inside his tweed jacket.

"They're black feathers. They're dark and shiny. Can't you see them?" Will asked, squatting low to the ground.

Bartimaeus held a small clear bottle in his hand. "Step aside there and tell me what happens to the feathers when I do this." He flung droplets of water from the vial.

Will's eyes widened as the moistened feathers crumpled in on themselves and dissolved into a smoky mist. "They're evaporating. I mean the ones you hit with the water are evaporating." AH-CHOO!

"Somethin' isn't right. I been gettin' bad sensations all day," Bartimaeus said, almost to himself. The old man was a *Sensitive,* one who could intuit events before their arrival and feel the vibrations of the supernatural. Years of working alongside Jacob Wilder to evaluate and "clear" dangerous locations and decades as Lucille's assistant had sharpened his skills. He bit his lower lip. "Will, look real close at those feathers. Your great-granddaddy used to say he could see a glow around paranormal things—particularly the dark ones. So what color do ya see around the feathers?"

Will got down on all fours and studied the plumes, which he now realized were hovering just above the surface of the floor. "There's a dark outline, like a shimmery purple cloud around the feather's edges," Will said.

"Definitely don't touch them. Better step back here." Bartimaeus liberally splashed the water up and down the hallway. Will watched as nearly all the feathers vanished from sight. A rotten smell, like year-old Cheez Whiz, suddenly permeated the hall, followed by a blast of icy air.

"Do you feel that?" Will asked with a shiver.

"Felt it my whole life. First time I've ever felt it—or smelled it—in Peniel, though." Bartimaeus slipped the holy water vial inside his breast pocket. He scratched the side of his gray head. "This is hallowed ground. A demon couldn't enter here without assistance. But *somethin'* is definitely among us and it sure ain't friendly."

"A demon? You think it's a demon?" Will asked, wiping his nose with the back of his hand.

"Well, it's not Santa and his elves. It's some kind of dark force." Bartimaeus's milky eyes darted from side to side. "Could be someone oppressed or possessed by a demon. I don't know for sure. But the vibrations of *Darkness* are unmistakable."

Will's chest tightened. Visions of Leviathan flooded his mind—the horrible demon with seven heads and deadly tentacles that he and Aunt Lucille had battled in its lair only a few months before. The demon wreaked havoc on Perilous Falls, drowning boats and yanking souls beneath the rising river waters. After it snatched the relic from Will, it released a series of monsters that nearly devoured him, his family, his friends. . . .

Not again. I can't do this again. I can't see another one.

"Will, you all right?" Bartimaeus asked the clearly agitated boy. "Let me walk ya down to the Egyptian Gallery. I'll go talk to the abbot and Lucille about this once I get ya settled. We'll figure it out." He squeezed Will's arm. "Don't be afraid. If we all hang together, we got this covered."

"What does *it* mean? The feathers? The shadows around them?" Will fanned himself with his pith helmet.

"No telling. It's clearly some kind of sign. But darned if I can understand it." Bartimaeus propelled himself into the Egyptian Gallery and Will followed.

Will always felt he was walking inside a pharaoh's tomb when he entered the room. Dimly lit yellowed stone blocks lined the walls. Huge clay jugs, a pair of skinny black dog statues, and a bronze serpent on a pole populated the edges of the gallery. At the center of the room was a pair of large display cases.

Valens, a twenty-seven-year-old British protégée of Aunt Lucille, bent over the first case. He wore square goggles and a surgical mask over his mouth. In one hand he held a brush. The other wielded the pointed nozzle of a special museum-issue vacuum. At Bartimaeus and Will's approach, he killed the vacuum's motor. "You caught me giving Tuthy his yearly dusting," Valens laughed, laying aside his instruments.

"Tuthy?" Will asked. The dry mummy in the case could have been made of coal. Its withered crossed arms riveted Will's attention.

"Tuthmosis the Second was an important pharaoh," Valens said in his High English accent, indicating the mummy whose loose gossamer linens barely held it captive. "His wife Hatshepsut was the real power behind the throne. You know what they say: behind every great pharaoh . . . is a great pharaoh." He guffawed at his joke, exposing a set of perfect white teeth. "The wife controlled everything, eventually naming herself pharaoh and expanding worship of the great Egyptian god Amon." Valens removed the magnifying goggles and surgical mask, pinching his chiseled chin. "What I could never figure is why your great-grandfather kept Tuthmosis's mummy here. Do you know why, Bart?"

"Beats me." Bartimaeus shrugged. "Been here long before Jacob brought me over from New Orleans."

"Now there's something for you to investigate, Will. Let me know if you find any answers." Valens closed the glass lid on the mummy, turning the locks with a key. He collected his equipment, placed it onto a rolling cart, and tucked his neon orange tie into a linen vest. "What brings you down here, Will?"

"Abbot chores," the boy droned. "I have to clean the cases."

"You're in luck." Valens reached for the lowest shelf of his cart, producing a soft gray towel and a spray bottle. "Peniel-approved glass cleaner," he said, extending the articles with a blue-eyed wink.

Will accepted them with something less than excitement.

Bartimaeus hobbled over to a pair of panels on the wall near the entrance to the gallery. "I was going to put the alarm back on, but with you rubbing on the cases, I'd better turn them both off." He punched some numbers into the keypads, disabling the alarms on both displays in the center of the gallery.

"Aaah, the Peniel brain trust," Baldwin announced, filling a doorway of an adjoining gallery. Given the vicar's sudden appearance, Will figured he must have traveled by sarcophagus—several of which were in the next room. Baldwin turned his hawkish nose in Valens's direction. "Aren't you done? I didn't expect you'd still be here with the chapter meeting under way."

Valens, also a member of the community, lowered his head slightly, his usual jauntiness dissipating. "I was just cleaning up, Vicar. Heading to the meeting immediately." He gave Will and Bartimaeus a sheepish smile and quickly pushed his cart out of the gallery.

"Without duty and order, a community crumbles," Baldwin said evenly to justify his intrusion. He then looked Will up and down as if mystified by him. "I assume you will look after Mr. Wilder, Bartimaeus. Industry does not seem to be his strong suit."

"I was kind of thinkin' he could look after me." Bartimaeus chuckled. "But whatever you say, Baldwin. Whatever you say."

"Keep a close eye on him." The vicar continued staring at Will for several awkward moments until he folded his massive hands, inspected a few cases, and ever so slowly crossed the gallery toward Bethel Hall.

"That was weird," Will said.

"It's looking like a day for weird. I'm going to go lock up the museum. Why don't ya get to scrubbing those cases?" Bartimaeus hobbled toward the same hallway Baldwin had just passed through. "When you're finished in here, Will, make sure to put those alarms on. You know the code—don't share it with anybody. I've got to get myself to the archabbey. Scoot out the front door when you're done and we'll see ya tomorrow."

"Sure thing," Will said, and Bartimaeus left him to his work.

It was nearly five-thirty, the time Leo's peewee karate tournament was set to start a few blocks away. Will hastily sprayed blue liquid atop the mummy case, smearing the soft rag over the surface. He then made his way to the next case, the one holding the Staff of Moses.

He was about to spray the cleaner onto the rectangular glass, but with no one around, Will couldn't help but stare at the object glinting in the spotlight: the gold, jewel-encrusted rod with a slight curvature near the top. Aunt Lucille had explained to him that the gold exterior was an ornamental sleeve that held the true Staff of Moses. A few inches of the staff's knobby sapphire head were visible above the edge of the gold container.

Will absently ran the cloth over the display case as he read the brass plaque inside:

ACCORDING TO THE HEBREW BIBLE, GOD
TOLD MOSES TO "TAKE THIS ROD IN THY HAND,
WHEREWITH THOU SHALT DO THE SIGNS." MOSES
RETURNED TO EGYPT CARRYING THE ROD OF GOD
IN HIS HANDS.

Will started to clean the sides of the glass case, but his attention now drifted to the slanted plastic information cards surrounding the display.

They were titled THE TEN PLAGUES OF EGYPT. The first panel showed a picture of a bearded Moses standing beside another man who held the sapphire staff over a blood-filled river. A few panels down showed an angry Moses clutching the rod, calling down "fiery hail." Others held images of frogs and dead cattle, locusts, and dark clouds moving over the land of Egypt.

Will tried to force himself to resume cleaning the other side of the case, but after a few rubs, he was distracted by the display labeled OTHER MIRACLES OF THE STAFFS. These depicted Moses pulling the rod from his father-in-law's garden, parting the Red Sea, and striking his staff against a rock to produce a gush of water.

One particular illustration captivated Will. It showed Moses standing behind a man reaching for the tail of an enormous snake. Fleeing the giant viper was a terrified pharaoh and some black-robed men with tiny snakes at their feet. Will put down his rag to read the museum's description:

The Staff of Aaron

Moses and Aaron went to Pharaoh and did as the Lord had commanded; Aaron threw down his staff before Pharaoh and his officials, and it became a snake. Then Pharaoh summoned the wise men and the sorcerers; and they also, the magicians of Egypt, did the same by their secret arts. Each one threw down his staff, and they became snakes; but Aaron's staff swallowed up theirs.

—Exodus 7:10–12

The staff in this exhibit is not the staff of Aaron, but the staff of Moses, which also turned into a serpent.

The reading elicited a raised eyebrow from Will. He took up the cleaning towel again and began to polish the smudged display glass. When he saw that it was nearly six o'clock on his watch, he raced around the room, wiping the towel along the fronts of all the cases as he passed.

"Got every one," he proudly announced to himself after circling the gallery. They were clean enough.

He hid the spray bottle and towel behind an engraved column of hieroglyphics and made for Bethel Hall. Like crooked fingers, the shadows of the trees outside touched the hall's marbled floor. He ran through them into the outer library, past the delicate brass grate protecting hundreds of books, and out the front door. Will checked that it locked behind him. It did.

Outside Peniel's main gate, he crossed High Street and dashed into Azal Alley. It was a narrow passageway that Will knew well, a quiet lane that allowed him to run behind the shops of Main Street as far as city hall. He pounded the cobblestones, dodging stray cats and puddles of stagnant water. Every so often, movie and show posters appeared on the dingy brick walls of the alley. One poster seemed to be everywhere that day. It was so common, Will couldn't help but notice it.

A man with hypnotic eyes that seemed to be lined with charcoal stared out from the posters. His trimmed mustache and beard reminded Will of a magician he had once seen at the old Genesius Theatre downtown. The tanned man in the poster wore a silk ascot at his throat and extended an open palm to the viewer. Above his face, the blue lettering read:

The Karnak Center for Regeneration
and Creative Therapy
Grand Opening Celebration
All Are Welcome to See and Hear
POTHINUS SAB, Founder
At the Perilous Falls Bandstand,
Saturday, August 13, 10:30 a.m.

Will rolled his eyes before resuming his gallop to the Karate Kove, the storefront martial arts studio where his eight-year-old brother, Leo, studied. It was packed with parents, their backs to the big front windows. Behind the fighting dragons stenciled on the glass, Will could see his mom and dad flanking Leo. They were up against the wall on the right side of the studio, near a broom closet. His brother wore a white uniform that accentuated the red pools of color on his cheeks. Will could hear his parents over the din as he entered the studio.

"Forget what the kid said, son," Dan Wilder instructed Leo, running a hand through his thick salt-and-pepper mane. "He's trying to upset you. Just . . . just ignore him."

"Shake it off, baby," Deborah Wilder added, giving Leo a little hug. "He's a bully and he is being very, VERY RUDE." She raised her voice at the end so that the offending party and his parents could hear.

"Every tournament, every practice he calls me four eyes," Leo protested, on the verge of tears. "I'm sick of it, Mom. I want to leave. I don't want to compete. Let's go home."

"You can . . . you could leave . . . I suppose." Dan removed his tortoiseshell glasses, which was a sure indication that he felt conflicted or under pressure. These were feelings he always sought to avoid. "Maybe it's best if we just leave. I . . . I could take us all out for some ice cream and—"

"ICE CREAM?" Deb Wilder exploded. "That bigmouthed bully attacks your son and you want to go out for dessert? If Leo walks out, Ricci wins. Oh no, Dan." Deborah deployed the booming anchor voice that her TV audience knew all too well. "No, that's what that bully boy wants. He wants you to walk out in tears. But you can beat him. That's why he's trash-talking you, Leo. He doesn't want to face you in the ring."

As Will got closer, a bear of a man cut him off, hastily moving through the crowd toward his mom and dad.

"Keep your voice down," Dan hissed to his wife, the sides of his square jaw pulsing. "If he wants to leave, why should we force him to—"

"I am not going to let him give in," Deborah said, pursing her full lips. "Ricci is a nasty little brat and he shouldn't be bullying our son."

"Okay, so Ricci's a *nasty little brat*," Dan argued, "but that is no reason for us—"

The bear of the man standing behind Dan shoved him hard. "You callin' my son a nasty brat, Wilder?"

"I . . . I . . . I . . . we were trying to defuse the altercation between your son . . . and mine," Dan stammered.

Deborah cut him off, facing the man with forearms like hairy tree trunks. "Your son is acting like a bully and he's not going to call my son names and get away with it. He should be disqualified from the tournament."

Ricci's father rubbed a fat finger across his nose, smiling. "Look, your kid needs to toughen up. He can't be scared of words. Ricci's just having fun." He poked Dan in the shoulder. "But you're an adult, Wilder. Don't be badmouthing my kid."

Behind the huge man, Ricci, a sloppy boy with ketchup

stains on his uniform, cut his bulging eyes at Leo. He repeatedly punched his fists in Leo's direction, never breaking eye contact.

A bell sounded and a paunchy man in a white karate uniform holding a clipboard came to the center of the studio floor. "Okay, we're going to start the first round of our tournament. The winners of tonight's regional match will compete in the state finals." He flipped a page on his clipboard. "First up is Leo Wilder and Ricci Severino."

Deborah used her sunglasses to push back her brown bangs. She lowered herself to Leo's level. He was still angry, his eyes wet with emotion behind the wire-frame glasses. "Go out there and face this bully. You won your division last year. Whether you win or lose right now is unimportant. I just don't want you to give up. Are you ready?"

Leo removed his wire frames and nodded. "I'm ready, Mom." He reknotted his black belt and turned to the floor. A small hand grabbed his arm before he could move. It was his younger sister, Marin.

She blew him a kiss. "Snap punch him in the face and butterfly kick his butt!" she yelled. Then throwing a punch that included a leg lift, she said, "Knock him to the mat."

Dan pulled Marin back into the throng. "Calm down, Attila the Hun. Let's watch the match, okay?"

Leo smiled and faced his opponent in the middle of the rubber floor with a bow.

"You look weird without your glasses, *Four Eyes*," Ricci whispered so the karate master could not hear.

Leo said nothing. But the color in his face turned a deep red. He looked to his mom with apprehension. She offered a sympathetic nod.

The boys ran at each other. Ricci's punches were too wide and Leo's first roundhouse kick missed the mark entirely. They now circled one another, half squatting, fists at the ready.

That's when the front door Will was lounging against pushed open. "I hope I'm not late, Willy." It was his mother's aunt Freda, a large woman in a blue muumuu with a towering twister of blond hair. She held a supersized smoothie in one hand and a crocheted purse, big as a feedbag, in the other. "The line at Smoothikins was crazy. Then they ran out of my gluten-free cupcakes—ugh! Where's your mama?"

Will pointed to the wall at the fringe of the fight mat.

"Deborah! Deborah!" Aunt Freda sang out, knocking aside startled parents and kids as she nudged her way to the front. "Had I known this many people were coming, I would have gotten here earlier and staked out a spot." She kissed Deborah on her cheek and settled into a place near the broom closet.

"You're going down, Squinty," Ricci said under his breath. The boy spun around and delivered a blow that sent Leo crashing into the far wall.

Will stood on tiptoes, trying to see if Leo was rising. A bruise appeared near Leo's trembling lower lip and his breathing was hard. Still he jumped up and tugged on the bottom of his uniform. His blue eyes locked on Ricci as he assumed a fighting stance.

"That's it, let's go, Leo," Deborah Wilder said, clapping.

"Another shot like that, Ricci, and you're disqualified," the judge warned.

"Kick him into next week," Marin bellowed before her father shushed her.

Will could tell Leo was angry. Whenever his brother got quiet, real quiet, Will knew it was time to run for cover. And now Leo, his fists pulled back at his sides, was still as a storm cloud before its first crack of thunder.

"Without your other set of eyes, your aim's not too hot," Ricci spat out from across the mat.

"That's enough, Ricci. Last chance!" the judge yelled. "Respect your opponent or you're out."

Leo spread his feet wide and ran at Ricci.

"Oooh, he's so fast," Aunt Freda said, sucking on the straw of her smoothie.

Leo sailed through the air, one leg straight out, the other cocked under him. While he was in mid-flight, Deborah's eyes narrowed. She could have sworn that Leo's face had gone as white as his uniform—stark white—a shimmering white. The flying kick caught Ricci in the shoulder. The kid fell into a clumsy spin and then tilted toward Aunt Freda.

Ricci's head collided with the middle of Aunt Freda's smoothie cup, the contents erupting in all directions. Pink goo plopped onto Aunt Freda's hair. The front of her blue dress looked like a flamingo murder scene. "Can you believe this? Look at me!" she screamed, oblivious to the passed-out boy at her feet. "Somebody's going to pay for this."

Leo, who had misjudged his landing, crashed into the broom closet. A bright illumination poured from the tight doorway.

Deborah and Dan, shielding their eyes from the light, rushed into the closet. Leo's hands and face held an iridescent glow.

"Mom, what's happening?" Leo asked, staring at his hands, tipped mops and pails all around him.

"I don't know, honey." Deborah couldn't believe her eyes. She touched his hands, which were room temperature. "Do you feel all right?"

"I feel fine." Leo smiled. "I got Ricci good. But what's wrong with my hands?"

Owing to the glare, it was hard for his parents to look at either Leo's hands or his face.

"Give me your . . . your sweater, Deb," Dan demanded, squinting. "We can't let anybody see him like this."

Marin stuck her head into the closet. Her little mouth dropped open. "Wowzy. Aunt Freda's all pinky and Leo's a lightbulb!" she happily exclaimed.

Dan laid his wife's sweater over Leo's head and wrapped an arm around the boy. "Get on the other side of him, Deb. Put your hands in your pockets, son."

They got Leo to his feet and led him out of the broom closet toward the front door.

On the studio mat, a smoothie-speckled Ricci tried to explain to his father how he had been knocked flat.

"Leo's face got bright like the sun. I couldn't look at him no more. And then he kicked me," Ricci said.

Before the big man could respond, there was a tap on his shoulder. He turned to find Aunt Freda, still decorated in smoothie juice, her face like a tight fist.

"I'm holding you responsible, Daddy." Her bloated hand flicked a glob of smoothie from her bangs. "This dress is an original," she said, shaking the splattered fabric, bits of fruit landing on Ricci. "Now where should I send the cleaning bill?"

The nervous karate master interrupted from the middle of the fight mat. "It looks like Leo Wilder is the winner of our first match. Congratulations, Leo." Applause greeted the sweater-draped victor as he and his parents blurred by.

"He's fine. Just a little overwhelmed by the excitement I guess," Deborah explained with a strained smile to the judge as they pushed Leo along.

Will automatically held the front door open. From his parents' expressions, he could tell something was very wrong. "What's going on?" he quietly asked his mom.

"Follow us to the car and don't ask questions," she snapped.

As the trio passed, Will saw light leaking through the weave of the fabric nearest Leo's face. If it wasn't for the legs beneath the sweater, his parents could have been smuggling a domed halogen lamp out of the place, he thought. Marin yanked Will by the arm, pulling him after the other Wilders.

Down the block, Leo could be heard asking, "If I won, why are we leaving? And why is it so bright under here?"

CHAPTER 3

MAX'S DREAM

Len Meriwether, after repeated attempts, parallel parked his dented maroon minivan along Main Street. Before exiting the vehicle, he stroked his little mustache in the rearview mirror. The thing looked like a tiny, worn broom sticking off his upper lip. After all the smoothing, the mustache was as unkempt as it had been before.

"Are you ready?" Len teasingly asked, rubbing the arm of his dumpling of a wife in the passenger seat.

Evelyn Meriwether's thick knees bounced with anticipation. "Let's do it, hon," she cried, clapping her hands together. She spun her head toward the back of the vehicle where her daughter Cami was listlessly staring out one window and her son Max, in his wheelchair, stared out the other. "Cami, darling, help Daddy with Maxie's ramp. If we don't get to the bandstand soon, we'll miss Mr. Sab's entrance. Ooooh, I can't believe he's here," she squealed. Wearing a white dress with beaded shoulders, she merrily jiggled out of her seat, struggling to hold on to several books, a camera, and a big white hat.

Cami had never seen her mother in such a state. For years, Evelyn Meriwether had listened to all manner of self-help audio books in the kitchen. Passing through day or night, Cami could hear one self-help guru after another advising her mom to "Find your inner peace," "Be your best self now," "Shed the weight you were meant to shed," "Tap your inner brilliance." But her mother's fascination with Pothinus Sab was something altogether different.

Over the last few months, Sab's slender face began appearing all over the Meriwether home. His bestsellers were in the bathroom, in the family van, on the coffee table in the living room, and stacked on Evelyn Meriwether's nightstand. "Doesn't he look just like a younger, more handsome, Omar Sharif?" her mother would croon anytime Cami even glanced at one of the books. Whoever Omar Sharif was, Cami could not imagine him being as creepy as Pothinus Sab. Nevertheless, when her mother saw the man himself on TV announcing the opening of a Karnak Center for Regeneration and Creative Therapy in Perilous Falls, the woman literally dropped a platter of chicken to the linoleum and shrieked with excitement. Evelyn was not just a fan; she was a self-professed *Pothinut*. In anticipation of the big event, she bought a new dress, ordered reserved VIP tickets near the bandstand, and made Len Meriwether promise to accompany her to the park. Now the big day had finally arrived.

Since Cami had a standing Saturday morning brunch with her friends, she had a good excuse to skip the Sab event. Cami volunteered to take Max with her. She knew he couldn't stand the sound of Sab's voice. Whenever he heard the dramatic Egyptian voice pouring out of the kitchen, he would start singing loudly or roll himself into another room.

Cami helped her father pull a metal ramp from the side of the van. Max's new motorized wheelchair allowed him to maneuver onto the sidewalk with just a flick of his left hand. "Have fun, Mom. I'm sorry, Dad," Max laughed, his head rolling along the black cushion that supported it. His Duchenne muscular dystrophy had taken a severe toll on his legs, his right arm, and his lungs, but his spirit was untouched.

"Let's go, funny man," Cami said, tapping her brother on the shoulder.

"Keep an eye on Maxie, and we'll see you at home after"— Evelyn's voice shot into the stratosphere—"Pothinus Sab!"

Len Meriwether shrugged apologetically to the kids, taking possession of his wife's books and camera. Evelyn positioned the wide-brimmed hat on her head and waved a plump hand in the air as she turned, practically dancing toward the park. Mr. Meriwether pursued her.

Watching them go, Cami slowly shook her head. "Let's

get into Burnt Offerings before she comes back or she'll drag us to see . . ." She eyed Max, signaling the inevitable. Together they sang with gusto: *"Pothinus Sab."* They laughed all the way to the restaurant.

Burnt Offerings was Cami and her friends' favorite breakfast spot. Owned by Simon Blabbingdale's cousin, there was always an open seat and an open tab for Simon and his friends. The bowed wooden floorboards of the restaurant groaned under the rolling weight of Max's wheelchair. He and Cami glided through a series of slightly tilted rooms, each with a fireplace big enough to dine in. The warm, low-beamed back room was dominated by a huge round table. Simon Blabbingdale sat at its center facing the doorway like a bored King Arthur awaiting the return of his knights. He read a thick paperback while beside him, Andrew Stout, a big kid with red hair, bent over a basket of muffins and a plateful of eggs. He was too busy eating to acknowledge Cami and Max's arrival.

"I'm glad you brought Max since we are down one of our regulars," said Simon in his typically nasal tone. He closed his copy of *The Grapes of Wrath* and folded his bony hands. "I cannot believe that Will is bailing on us again. For those taking note, this is the third week we've been stood up for one of his 'work sessions' at the museum. I'd like to know what kind of work he's doing exactly."

"Lay off him," Andrew said, his mouth full, swatting Simon with the back of his hand. "It's his family's business.

He's helping out and cleaning up and stuff. If you'd use your mouth to chew rather than talk, we'd all be in better shape. Will-man'll come when he can."

"It's great to see you both," Cami wryly observed, standing in the doorway. Pulling her long ponytail over her shoulder, she sat near Simon, Max rolling into the room behind her. "My mom and dad went to see that Pothinus Sab character. Crowds of people were headed to the park."

"Oh, the mayor is going to introduce him," Simon erupted. "She was telling my father all about it at the house this morning." Simon's dad was a judge and a very important figure in Perilous Falls. "She went on and on about how she invited Mr. Sab to come here and what a boost this will be for Perilous Falls. The mayor's still pretty upset about what happened earlier this summer." Simon leaned far over the table and whispered in a voice that could be heard well into the hall, "You know, with the croc monsters and everything."

"Like she battled them! What's her problem?" Andrew asked, sliding the muffin basket toward Max and Cami.

"Funny you should ask. Mayor Lynch actually mentioned Will and his aunt Lucille. She's convinced that his great-aunt is a menace to the town. She and my dad were arguing about it. The mayor claims to have evidence that Will's aunt and her friends caused all the trouble this summer. We did see some strange things."

Max stopped chewing his muffin and placed it on the small tray of the wheelchair. Concern washed over his face.

"I've seen strange things too. In my dreams." The boy stared at Simon.

"I hope you're not talking about ravens and blood." Simon began to giggle. "Remember after all the craziness a few months back? Max kept saying a black raven was coming and that there would be blood—"

"Just let him talk, Simon." Cami touched her brother on the arm encouragingly.

His eyes never left Simon. "I do still see the raven at night. It comes here. Its black feathers are in the streets. And it will bring blood—everywhere!"

"Where is the raven?" Simon asked.

"I don't know. But in my dream it flies through Perilous Falls. People pet it because it seems so nice. When they pet the raven, its feathers fall off and stick to them. Then everything gets dark. After that, all I see is blood. The raven brings blood and darkness.

"Lately, I've been seeing Will and his aunt in my dream. Will was chasing the raven. His aunt was very sad."

No one moved at the table. Andrew even stopped chewing. "Why was Will-man after the raven?"

"It took something. The raven took it and flew away."

"What did it take?" Cami asked.

"I'm not sure, but Will kept saying, 'Give it back, give it back.' He was confused. He couldn't see because it was so dark. Black feathers covered the whole town."

Simon lowered his rectangular glasses to the bottom of his nose. "I've never seen a raven in Perilous Falls ever, Max.

Is it one big raven or a flock of ravens that are supposed to descend upon us?"

"Can it, Simon." Andrew leaned back, his big arms dangling over the sides of the chair. "We should tell Will about this. If I was poppin' up in somebody's spooky dreams, I'd want to know."

Simon continued, undisturbed. "I only want to know if we are dealing with one raven or an invasion."

"One raven. I only see one," Max answered through gritted teeth.

Cami started flipping the end of her chestnut ponytail. She checked her brother's serious expression and turned back to her friends. "I agree with Andrew. Max told me about everything Will did with the relic this summer *before* it happened. And though I still don't understand some of it, like the Sinestrees—"

"*Sinestri*," Max corrected. "The monster voices in my dream said *Sinestri*."

"You heard them. I'll take your word." She flashed her newly brace-free smile at Max before resuming. "Even if we only mention it to him, Will needs to know about the new dream."

Simon tried to calm himself by casually buttering a biscuit. "Max was saying the same thing two months ago and nothing happened." The quivering hand holding the knife betrayed him.

"It's different now. I had the dream every night this week," Max said.

Andrew pushed away from the table and started to rise. "I say we go tell Will right away," he said.

"Of course you'd say that, lummox. Why do you want to worry him? I mean, you said it yourself—he's probably really busy." Simon's voice turned shrill. "Was there a lot of blood in your dream, Max? Did anyone get hurt?"

Max's eyes widened. "There was blood everywhere. Lots of people were screaming. Will was running," the boy said flatly.

"It's only a dream, right? It's not reality. It's a dream—a figment of Max's imagination. Could be nothing at all." Simon chuckled, vainly searching his friends' faces for support. Seeing none, he leapt from his chair, dropping the biscuit on the plate before him. "Okay, let's go tell Will."

In Jacob Wilder's office, Aunt Lucille strained to reach a pair of old transparent jars from a high shelf. The bottom of the jars were round and wide with twisted glass necks that spiraled upward. Dried red wax caps sealed the mouths of the jars. Aunt Lucille's blue eyes studied the pot-bellied glassware. They were completely empty. She held them behind her back and approached Will, who was seated at his great-grandfather's mahogany desk. He repeatedly spun around in the high-backed leather chair, his mind clearly on other things. "So Leo was in the middle of his match and he jumps at this kid and—"

"There'll be time to share all of that later. I need you to concentrate on your training now, Will." Lucille placed one of the jars on the edge of the desk. "What I am going to show you are the very same sight training jars that my father used to instruct my brother, Joseph—the same ones he used to train your . . ." She stopped herself, frowning. "All right, let's focus."

Will stopped spinning. "I have to tell you about what happened to Leo."

"Look into the jars as I show them to you," Aunt Lucille sharply ordered, disregarding Will's huffing. "My father always said we were never to tamper with any of these. Inside each jar is an object—objects most people cannot see. But for a *Seer*, for you, it should be fairly easy." She nudged the jar on the desk closer to Will, concealing the other behind her back.

"Aunt Lucille, Leo was in the middle of his match last night and he jumped—"

"What is in the jar? Just focus on the jar, dear."

"But he slammed into a broom closet and the whole thing lit up—"

"Unless there is a broom closet in the jar, I really don't care just now."

"His skin started to glow." Will was practically screaming. "Leo's face and his hands were lit up like an LED light."

Aunt Lucille blinked as if confused. She placed the jar behind her back onto the bookshelf. "Okay, you've got my attention. Explain without shouting. Leo's skin was aglow?"

"Like a lightbulb," Will said. "About twenty minutes after it happened, once we got home, his skin color went back to normal. What do you think happened to him?"

"He's a *Candor*." Aunt Lucille shook her head excitedly, causing her strawberry-blond spiral curls to shudder. She ran to a small table next to the fireplace behind Will. Her hand slid along the spines of a jumbled tower of books until she found a frayed beige volume.

"What's a *Candor*? And why are you so excited?" Will asked.

She slammed the book on the desk before Will, dust flying up. "All your questions will be answered, dear, I promise." She licked her fingers, flipping through the pages. "It's a very rare gift, like your ability to see the unseen. What did your father say when Leo brightened?"

Will scrunched up his face. "He threw Mom's sweater over Leo and got him out of the karate place. He didn't say much really. Except that Leo was probably overheated."

"Typical." She pursed her lips. "Ah, yes, here we are." Lucille pointed to a ragged page in the book covered with tight handwriting. She tilted it slightly so Will could read along. "These are my father's notes about supernatural phenomena he observed among the Brethren during his travels. Look at this."

While at Monte Cassino, during one of my first visits, I made the acquaintance of a Brother Lucido. Being intensely shy, he kept mostly to himself. He never came to meals with the community, preferring to eat alone in his cell. Then one night, I stepped out onto the hillside behind the monastery for some fresh air. The moon was so bright that evening, it gave the entire valley an uncommon clarity. Not that I needed the light for clarity. Over the hedges, I saw intense shadows swarming toward the monastery. They moved like large insects up the side of the bluff. My face must have registered the fear I felt at their approach. Brother Lucido had just stepped out of the back door when he observed my expression. "What disturbs you, Jacob?" he asked. I told him what I saw. "Do not fear. They are minor demons sent to disarm us," he said. "Return to your cell and do not be concerned." I started for the back door even as I saw the things close in on us from below.

Lucido placed two hands together and lowered his head. In that moment his face and hands burned with a white light. Opening his arms wide, a mighty radiance spilled in all directions. The horde of shadows instantly dispersed. Lucido later explained that he was a light-caster, a Candor. Minor demons thrive in darkness, he told me. His gift is different from my own rebutting illuminance in that my "ray" can be directed toward a specific target and has an effect on major demons. When a Candor ignites (that is the word he used over and over, "ignites"), he spreads light in all directions to scatter the fiends. Candors can be very effective against a simultaneous attack by minor demons. Lucido shared with me the methods through which he

learned to harness his gift. I will attempt on the following
pages to capture his reflections . . .

"Well, there you have it." Aunt Lucille tugged at the
sleeves of her silk jacket, as was her custom when she
was either excited or proud. "Though Leo's gift is not as
powerful as my *illuminance,* it can cover a wider area. Your
father must be beside himself. First you and your sight.
Then Marin and her healing abilities. Now Leo . . . There is
always a reason for these gifts, dear."

"It's a jeweled knife. A beautiful, jeweled knife." Will's
eyes were fixed on the glass jar at the end of the desk. "Was
it my great-grandfather's?"

"Was what your great-grandfather's?"

"The knife in the jar."

Aunt Lucille lowered her face next to the glass, her brows
knitted together "Is that what you see there, Will? A knife?"

"Yes." Will nodded in frustration.

"Would you like to inspect it?"

"Can I? Yes, I want to touch it. How do we get it out?"

"Look very closely first. Once it is removed, putting it
back could be difficult."

Will leaned over the jar, practically caressing the surface
with his hands. As he stared, a repulsed look overtook his
face. He jumped back, nearly dropping the jar on the desk.

"It's . . . it's a big claw or something. What happened to
the knife?"

Aunt Lucille grabbed the jar by its neck and pulled it away.

"There never was a knife in there. It was always a talon. The talon of a minor demon, according to my father. It assumed the shape of something desirable to you—something to pull you in. That's the way the *Sinestri* work. They adopt pleasing shapes to mask their reality—to deceive." She slid the jar back onto the top shelf of the bookcase.

"But it looked just like a knife." Will came around the desk to inspect the jar again.

Loud banging on the door stopped him where he stood.

"Lucille! Lucille!" the voice outside yelled. Will knew the voice as well as the sound of trouble in it. He followed his great-aunt to the door, his pith helmet in hand.

When Lucille pulled open the door, a figure was doubled over in the hall, winded from the climb. Wrinkled hands on his thighs, Tobias Shen bent at the waist, trying to recover his breath. His eyes were alive with excitement and worry.

Seeing Mr. Shen, Will remembered that it had been a week since he watered his "tree" down by the river. He had promised Mr. Shen, who was the groundskeeper at St. Thomas Church and a member of the Brethren, that each day he would water a walking stick he had planted early in the summer. It was sort of a discipline exercise for Will. One that he tried to make good on. Amazingly the stick or "tree" had sprouted blooms and even produced almonds from time to time.

"I know. I know, I forgot to water my tree," Will said pre-emptively. "I promise I'll do it right after my training today."

Shen straightened up, swatting at nothing in particular

with his left hand—it always made Will think of the catcher's mitt he once left in the weather for a whole summer.

"Water the tree when you can. It's very important. But I ran up"—Shen inhaled abruptly—"ran up because there is big, big, big trouble downstairs."

"Where?" Aunt Lucille asked.

"The Egyptian Gallery." Shen took Aunt Lucille by her arms, looking as if he could cry. "The Staff of Moses. It is gone."

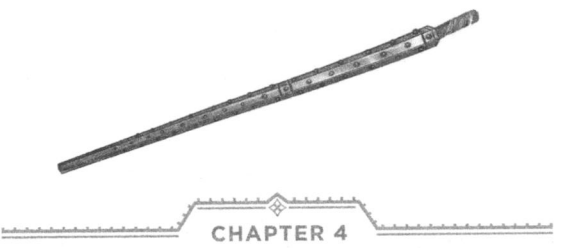

CHAPTER 4

POTHINUS SAB

In spite of the sticky heat, a dense crowd was packed near the Perilous Falls bandstand that day. Some brought their own chairs, while others stood in the hazy sun balancing children on their shoulders. Buses from Hinnom Valley, Sidon, and other nearby towns carried scores of self-proclaimed *Pothinuts* to see the life coach, motivational speaker, and bestselling author Pothinus Sab in person.

All eyes were on the delicate wrought-iron structure at the center of the park. City officials, including Dan Wilder, filed into the bandstand and took seats on folding chairs beside the main podium. The mayor had made it clear that she expected all city council members and Perilous Falls officials to be present at Sab's grand opening announcement. After all, it was Mayor Lynch who had invited Sab to open a Karnak Center for Regeneration and Creative Therapy in

Perilous Falls. After reading accounts of the amazing feats "the miracle worker" had accomplished in New York, London, Los Angeles, Paris, and Vancouver, she could not resist.

Through Sab's efforts, strife-ridden communities were "healed" and "regenerated." Illnesses were cured and the future had been accurately predicted. With the opening of each local Karnak Center, disagreements and even old rivalries ceased. Why couldn't a new facility have the same effect on Perilous Falls? Sab not only brought the promise of civic harmony, but to the mayor's mind, he could also be a boost to her reelection campaign. A popular mayor is a good bet in any election, but one responsible for bringing miracles to town could stay in office forever.

The air was electric as the spindly Mayor Ava Lynch climbed the steps of the bandstand. In her red suit that could have been a Canadian Mountie's uniform, the sixty-nine-year-old four-term mayor took the podium by force.

"My fellow citizens of Perilous Falls, a bright light has come to dwell among us," she bellowed in her most inspirational tone. "After learning of his marvelous work around the world—of which I know you are all familiar—I have invited the renowned motivational leader and spiritual coach Pothinus Sab to grace us with our own Karnak Center. And I'm pleased to announce: he has accepted the invitation!"

In the VIP section just in front of the bandstand, Evelyn Meriwether nearly injured her hands from clapping. So did most of the assembled. When the applause tsunami subsided, the mayor picked up where she had left off.

"Citizens, I'm as excited as you are. In fact, my belief in Mr. Sab and Karnak are so strong that I am donating a piece of my own personal property to be the site of the new center. The old Grimma Funeral Home on Dura Street will soon be transformed into the Perilous Falls Karnak Center for Regeneration and Creative Therapy." Despite the mayor's enthusiastic presentation, her helmet of black hair with the white traffic lane running up the center did not move in the least. "Would you please help me to welcome the wonder-worker, Egypt's own man of miracles, an honorary citizen of Perilous Falls, and my new friend, Pothinus Sab."

A surge of exhilaration brought the crowd to its feet. Women hooted and screamed. Dan Wilder, looking as if he could use a barf bag, uncomfortably checked the edges of the bandstand for a glimpse of the main attraction. After several minutes, the applause died down. People shifted and craned their necks for a sight of Sab. Silence fell over the park. Suddenly a voice at the back of the crowd yelped, "He's there. There he is with the baby."

Camera people ran to the back of the crowd to capture the first images of Pothinus Sab making his triumphal entry into Perilous Falls Park. Wearing a white collarless suit, he appeared to be cradling an infant in his arms. Walking several yards with the child, he planted a kiss on the baby's head and returned it to its weeping mother. Then extending his arms with great effort, he reached out to those on either side of the main aisle leading to the bandstand. Women pressed against the barricades, trembling at his touch. Multiple babies were dangled over the fence. Sab embraced a few of them and then, with a practiced expression of surprise, posed for the sea of phones held aloft.

"I just love his heart," a mother with a child on her hip said to Deborah Wilder, who had positioned herself in the press section. "Have you ever seen anyone care for people like Pothinus?"

"No, I can't say I've ever seen anyone quite like him," Deborah responded drily. She had to cover the event for her *Supernatural Secrets* television show. But her folded arms and skeptical expression ensured Deborah would not be mistaken for a *Pothinut.*

At long last, Sab bounded onto the bandstand stage. His black hair and goatee shimmered in the sunlight. Dark piercing eyes flashed as he raised his palms over the crowd. It instantly stilled. Touching his slender fingers together, he half bowed toward the standing city officials. "Madam Mayor, I am overwhelmed by your welcome and your generosity." He solemnly turned to the audience once more. "I have come from a faraway land to bring you renewal and hope." At once parched and stinging, his voice had traces of the desert wind in it. "As I move through Perilous Falls, I have seen such unhappiness here. Such profound sadness." He seemed almost pained.

Some members of the audience exchanged confused looks. Sab dramatically clutched the golden amulet hanging from the chain at his throat, closing his eyes. With his free hand, he labored to push away some invisible obstacle.

"I can feeeel your struggle. In these trying times, it is hard to avoid anger. And you have much to be angry about, don't you? Well, here's a surprise: Don't hold it back! This is the problem—we withhold the anger that needs to be free. Beyond that anger is the joy and the regeneration that you desire. But first you must releeease your anger. Get it out! Who is going to start?" Sab pulled the microphone off the stand and with the rhythm of a jaguar, slunk to the right side of the bandstand. He leaned over the iron railing, reveling in the crowd's reaction. "What angers you most? What is irritating you, my friends?" He stretched the microphone over the heads of the audience.

"I'm sick of politicians who stop listening once we elect them!" one woman screamed. Loud applause greeted her words. Mayor Lynch and some of the city council forced smiles and adjusted their seats.

"I haven't worked in five months," a middle-aged man bawled. "Worked my whole life and I can't find a job. Is that fair?" Loud grunts of empathy echoed throughout the park.

"I hate my neighbors. Their miserable dog drops mountains of poop on my lawn—twice a day—which I have to clean up."

"My teacher is an idiot."

"I have a boss who lies, cheats, and cares about one thing—feeding his big gut."

"My husband never listens to me!"

"I have the most ungrateful children. They got everything and now they don't even call."

Grievance after bile-filled grievance belched up from the crowd. Pothinus Sab sauntered across the bandstand, encouraging the mob to continue its "honesty." He seemed energized by each new complaint. "My friends, this is what the Karnak Center is all about: facing reality and discovering new paths forward together," he jubilantly told the audience.

Dan Wilder studied the faces on the lawn. Every one of them held a spiteful expression. He could not believe how in a matter of moments, the audience had transformed from delight to fury. They hung on Sab's every word, but there was not a smile to be seen. Escalating moans of vengeance and rage hovered in the air.

Like a conductor hearing a familiar score, Pothinus Sab was utterly unaffected by the gripes and threats surrounding him.

"How refreshing it is to hear your truth, my children," he said, raising an open palm at the podium. He paused, scanning the crowd. "Shall I tell you what I see in your town's future? Would you like that?" A roar rose up from the people in the park. "Bring the sacred vessel forward," Sab commanded.

A tiny, shriveled man in white linen robes wobbled up the bandstand stairs. He carried a brass pot covered by a metal plate. A little statue that could have been a golden hippo stood atop the plate. It was identical to the amulet at Sab's throat.

"Many thanks, Sarsour." Pothinus Sab removed the plate from the pot. He stared deeply into the hole. His hands shot up to his temples. "Ooooh, such things I see." The audience leaned forward. High overhead, clouds smudged out the blue sky.

"Misery upon misery is coming to Perilous Falls. Bloody . . . fiery . . . ugly things. I shall not share more—I cannot." He left Sarsour and the pot, stepping off the bandstand. Some in the crowd begged him to continue, every eye trained on Sab alone. "You will be shaken, my children. But I want you to know, and I am very serious, Pothinus will not abandon you in your trials. No matter what comes in the days ahead, the Karnak Center will be open to all of you—if you want it to be. Is that what you wish?"

Thunderous applause broke out in the park.

"It is good that I have come now. In moments of crisis we need protection, no? The Karnak Center and our practices will be a safe haven in the midst of your woes. But trust is required of you. I have often found—and I have seen it in every corner of Perilous Falls—that attachments to the worn-out, tired beliefs of yesterday enslave us. These old, brittle notions block our acceptance of new thoughts, new beliefs, better ways—isn't that true?"

Cries of "Yes," "It is," and "We love you, Pothinus" could be heard. Sab humbly bowed his head, speaking into the microphone as if praying. "We shall not allow the past to hold us back. We shall not be bound by ancient edicts. No! Together we shall find a new way, a new approach—true regeneration for each of us here in Perilous Falls." The crowd embraced him with their applause.

Mayor Lynch led the standing ovation behind Sab. All the council members rose in jubilation, except for Dan Wilder. Something in the distance mesmerized him. When he tried to stand, jarred by whatever he saw in the crowd, he stumbled. His face a mask of worry, Dan walked off the back of the bandstand without a word. He found Deborah in the press section and took her by the arm.

"What are you doing?" she yelled to be heard. "I need to see this."

"There is nothing more to see. We have to leave now." He ran the back of his hand across his wet forehead. "I've seen enough."

He forcefully pulled Deborah away from the crowd. Given Dan's agitation, she opted to go with him.

Behind them, over the loudspeaker, they could hear Pothinus Sab's conclusion. "I invite you and your families to the official opening of the Karnak Center next week. For all those who join us, I will have something very special: a tried and true protection from harm. Would you like that? With this protection, we will discover true regeneration! Will you trust me? Will you? WILL YOU?"

Evelyn Meriwether's eyes spilled tears of joy. "Oh yes. Yes. Yes!" She reached a hand over the barricade to Sab, who was only a few feet away. Len Meriwether stood behind her sullenly chewing a piece of gum, his hands clutched behind his back.

Evelyn turned to her husband. "I want to bring Maxie to the Karnak Center next week," she told him in a rush.

"Pothinus will know how to get rid of Maxie's nightmares. I just know it."

"Can he cure nightmares too?" Len looked as if he had just eaten a bad oyster. "I didn't hear him say anything about nightmares, Evelyn."

"Oh, shush," she said, swatting his arm and resuming her loud applause.

In the Egyptian Gallery of Peniel, most of the Brethren stood in a semicircle, Abbot Athanasius at the center. Will stared at the empty display case in the middle of the room, his mouth agape. Tuthy the mummy was still beneath glass. But in the display beside it, the staff was gone—gold covering and all.

"How could it have simply disappeared?" Abbot Athanasius intoned, rubbing his forearms as if he had a chill. His haunted blue eyes fell on each face before him. "There was no forced entry. The locks are still intact and the alarm did not sound."

"It had to be one of us—someone in the house," said Baldwin, who pushed a younger brother aside to pass to the center of the room. "If I may, Abbot?"

Athanasius nodded.

Baldwin laced his stubby fingers together across his firm midsection, striding before the empty glass case. His great beak of a nose appeared to be pointing at the bare pillow under glass. "Bartimaeus, when I walked through the gallery last night, you and Will were here. Was the staff in its case when you left the room?"

"Sure it was." Bartimaeus seemed guarded. "Will was scrubbin' the cases and—You saw the staff, didn't ya, Will?"

"Yes, sir. When I cleaned the glass, it was there. It was locked up." Will pointed to the locks on the edge of the rectangular display.

Baldwin lifted his head as if trying to look down at the boy with another pair of eyes situated in his nostrils. "And what time did you leave, William?"

"Around five-thirty. I had to go to my brother's karate meet and—"

"The doors were secure when you left? Surely the alarm was engaged." Baldwin ignored Will, his thick head turning suddenly. "Correct, Bartimaeus?"

Bart worked his bottom lip, staring at the floor. "So I um . . . I told Will . . ."

"You told Will what? Spit it out, Bartimaeus," Baldwin barked.

Will wanted to say something, but the air was so tense and Baldwin so aggressive that he thought it best to keep quiet.

"I went to see the abbot and Lucille about . . . another matter—"

Baldwin cut him off. "So the boy remained here alone

with the staff. Hmmm." He shot the abbot a look, then tapped the top of the display. "William. You were cleaning the cases?"

"Yes, sir."

"But how could you have touched the cases with the alarms engaged?"

"See, that's what I was trying to tell ya," Bartimaeus interjected, leaning forward on his crutches. "I turned the alarms off so Will could do his cleaning, but he put them back on when he was done. He had the code."

Baldwin raised a threatening finger at Will. "Is that true? Did you reset the alarms?"

Will's hazel eyes were like saucers. He started rocking back and forth. "I might have forgotten."

"You might have forgotten? Hahahaha." Baldwin's deep laughter mocked the boy. "A priceless treasure of antiquity is missing and he 'might have forgotten' to put the alarm on. Isn't that convenient?"

"I was in a hurry. I didn't want to be late for my brother's match. It just slipped my mind," Will tried to explain.

"Vicar," Valens said, sliding beside Will, his chin down near his chest. "I'm certain he didn't do it intentionally and Will did follow the abbot's instructions. The cases are awfully clean." He winked at Will.

"Cleaning cases does not require cleaning them out." Baldwin smacked the edge of the empty glass box with his palms. "Where is the staff, William?"

"I don't know."

"You were the last person to see it and you forgot to engage the alarm. Once more: Where is the staff?"

"He didn't take it, Baldwin," Aunt Lucille said loudly. She stepped in front of Will. "He may have been careless, but he is not a thief. What reason would he have for taking the staff?"

"Since when does he need a reason?" Ugo Pagani asked. The chubby brother tightened the rope at his abundant waist. "He snatched the relic of St. Thomas from the Undercroft. Maybe his fingers were getting a little itchy again," he deadpanned in pure Brooklynese, leaning against a wall of the gallery.

Will blushed and looked to Aunt Lucille.

"I am feeling a lectle eechy myself." It was the combustible Spanish brother, Pedro Montaigu. He was muscular and compact with dark green eyes. Hands flailing, he hurried into the next gallery like a squirrel with its tail on fire. "I have had enough of theese. Interrogate the others. I was at the chapter meeting last night, Veecar. As were many others. I have not so much as seen the staff in months." He waggled a finger at Bartimaeus and Will. "They are to blame. All theese is cutting into my training session—if you will excuse." He stalked out without another word.

"I was at the chapter meeting, too, and I've got herbs to cut and lunch to start," Ugo said, following Pedro's lead. He shuffled in the direction of the sarcophagus-lined adjoining gallery. "If you're looking for the staff burglar, my money would be on the kid. He's the only one besides Bart who

knows the alarm code. Gotta be him or Bart. Sorry, guys."
He shrugged and headed to the next gallery.

A quarrel broke out with some brothers arguing for Will's
guilt, others warning of a rush to judgment.

"Brothers, peace. Be still!" Athanasius roared. He pinched
at his bearded chin as if some calming agent were hidden
there. "Baldwin and I will consider all the evidence, and we
may speak with each of you further. We don't know when
the staff was stolen. It might have been after the chapter
meeting. It could have happened anytime between five-
thirty last night and this morning when Valens discovered
it missing. This is no time for disunity, Brothers."

Tobias Shen barged into the room, a grin on his face.
"I was locking up the doors and shooing the public from
Bethel Hall. Look who I found prowling about." He stepped
aside to reveal Cami, Andrew, Simon, and Max Meriwether,
who brought up the rear in his wheelchair.

"Are we interrupting something?" Andrew asked in a
small voice, eyeing the angry faces all around.

"Your timing's actually pretty good," Will said.

Simon took in the new faces and walked over to Will, a
rigid smile in place. "Who are these strange men?" he whispered.

"My strange friends here at the museum—nothing like
you guys."

"We need to tell you something—privately," Cami said,
taking Will by the arm. "Max has been having intense
dreams. You're in them."

"Don't even tell me that." Will exhaled.

The Brethren wandered into other galleries and paired off down the main hallway. Only Bartimaeus, Aunt Lucille, Tobias Shen, Baldwin, and the abbot remained.

Bart's crutches carried him between Abbot Athanasius and Lucille. Clearly preoccupied, he stared off into the distance. "That staff is still here. I can feel its presence. Somebody—one of the Brethren—has hidden it. But it's not gone. Not yet anyway."

"Baldwin, conduct a thorough search and report back to me," the abbot ordered. "Search every room of Peniel."

"Does William Wilder have a room here?" Baldwin asked seriously. After checking Aunt Lucille's icy expression, he decided to leave without another word.

In a razor edged whisper, Aunt Lucille confided to Athanasius, Tobias, and Bart, "Should the staff fall into the wrong hands, none of us can predict the potential harm or the consequences." Her attention drifted to Will and his friends across the room. "We simply have to find it."

Huddled in the corner of the Egyptian Gallery, the kids briefed Will on Max's dream: the raven, the blood, the feathers, all of it.

"Where have you seen ravens in Perilous Falls?" Will kept asking his friends. "What is this raven? Is it a real raven?"

Max shook his head against the leather pillow of his wheelchair. "I don't know, but it takes something you want. You keep yelling, 'Give it back. Give it back.' Then you chase after it. Your aunt was very sad, crying and very sad."

"My aunt Lucille?!" Will tapped the brim of his great-grandfather's pith helmet against his kneecaps. "Does the raven take a staff in your dream?"

"A staff?" Cami asked, her eyes turning to the display behind her. Seeing it was empty, she refocused on Will. "Where's the staff?"

"Beats me. It's gone. They just found out this morning."

"Who'd want an old stick?" Andrew asked, scratching at his neck.

Simon ripped the glasses from his nose, gawking at the vacant case. "The Staff of Moses is gone?!" he blurted way too loudly.

Will's head whirled. Max had accurately foreseen the black raven's feathers fluttering in the halls of Peniel and now "something" had been taken. Before the "blood" and "darkness" made an appearance, Will had to try to stop it. But how? He wasn't sure which of the Brethren could be trusted. And where was this raven? Could it be one of the seven rising demons mentioned in the prophecy? Will was so confused, he wasn't sure who he could share any of this with.

It was time for action. He flipped the pith helmet onto his head. "Meet me in front of Peniel. We've got to make a plan."

"Can I at least look at the mummy first?" Simon pleaded.

Will rolled his eyes and kept walking. He offered a pre-occupied wave to Aunt Lucille and the other adults and exited the Egyptian Gallery. One by one, without so much as a goodbye, his friends silently followed Will in a straight line, as if on their way to a bank heist.

The abbot noted the peculiar departure. He, Aunt Lucille, Tobias, and Bart had been closely monitoring the kids' conversation from a distance. "Tobias," he said as Max rolled out of sight.

"Yes, Abbot."

"Trail Will and those young people. He shouldn't have told them about the robbery. Observe what they do over the next few days."

"They're only kids, Athanasius," Lucille said.

"Kids haven't time for staffs or ravens or blood," Athanasius said in a hush. "Those that do must be watched." He locked eyes with Lucille. "And protected."

CHAPTER 5

A Plan and a Plague

Rushing into the sunlit courtyard outside Peniel, Will's four friends raced to catch him.

"Could you slow up a minute? What's the rush, Will-man?" Andrew sputtered, grabbing Will by the back of his shirt.

"Keep moving," Will said, tucking the back of his shirt into his pants. He peered around the edge of Bethel Hall. "Let's go to Twenty-Five Numbers."

Will and his four friends slipped past the wrought-iron gates surrounding Peniel and crossed the street into Azal Alley.

"William, why all the cloak-and-dagger?" Cami asked at his back.

"We need to talk where we won't be heard. Bad stuff is happening. I'll explain inside."

A neon sign blinked 25 NUMBERS ARCADE. Kids were streaming in and out of the blacked-out glass door.

"Why are we going in here?" Simon complained. "I won't be able to hear myself think."

"That could be a nice change of pace for you," Will said, holding the door open. "Thank me later."

An enormous room of glowing, dinging, gyrating games and attractions hypnotized the kids plugging quarters into them. Will and his friends maneuvered past the machines, sliding into a bright yellow booth in a corner. Max rolled his wheelchair sideways along the table so he could listen. Will leaned in, as did his friends.

"As you've seen, the Staff of Moses is gone," Will said, his eyes ablaze.

A big knowing smile split Simon's face. "Where are you hiding it? Is it at your house? Is it in your bag?"

"No, it is not in my bag. I didn't take it. The Brethren—the guys at the museum—think I took it, but I didn't. Honest."

Cami sat back against the slick cushion and gave Will a sidelong glance that could have frozen a small body of water.

"I'm telling you, Cami, I don't have it," Will said, removing his battered helmet.

She bent over the table, placing her elbows on the Formica. "If you don't have it, then you must know where it is. Otherwise, you wouldn't have dragged us to the loudest spot in Perilous Falls."

"I don't know where it is," Will cried. "But we do need to find it."

"*We* need to find it?" Andrew crossed his muscled arms. "This doesn't involve an Undercroft or any riverboat captains, does it?"

"Quiet, moron," Simon told Andrew. Bouncing in his seat, he asked Will, "What do you need us to do?"

"When I heard Max's dream, things started clicking." Will toyed with the pelican medallion on the front of his pith helmet. "Whatever this raven is, it must have taken the staff. I mean, that can't just be a coincidence, right, Max? And if the raven brings blood and darkness to Perilous Falls, shouldn't we try to stop it—him—whatever it is?"

"Yes," Max said. "Will has to try to stop the raven. We can help. But Will has to try to stop it."

Cami drummed her hands on the tabletop. "Hold on a second, Hardy Boys. Who do the guys in the black robes at the museum think took the staff? They don't have any leads?"

"They believe it's somebody on the inside. The locks on the display case were unbroken and then I forgot to put the alarm on—"

"You forgot?" Simon blurted out, practically crawling halfway over the tabletop. "How do you forget a thing like that? So the robbery is kind of your fault."

Cami slowly flipped the end of her ponytail with her index finger. "Why do you assume the raven has the staff, Will?"

In his mind's eye, Will flashed back to the black shiny

feathers he had seen choking the hallway in front of the Egyptian Gallery the day before.

"Just a hunch, I guess." Will shrugged. "You know, instinct."

"Why do I feel like you're not telling us something?" Cami always could see right through him.

"I don't know. Maybe you're just not trusting enough."

"I was trusting enough to bring my brother out here to share his dream with you. But let's forget that for a second." Cami's expressive hands were slicing the air now. "How do we find this raven when we don't even know what it is?" She turned her green eyes to everyone around the table. "Anybody? Where would a raven be?"

Andrew blankly stared at her. "Ravens? Ravens? Except for a couple of peacocks, the zoo doesn't have any birds, so that's no good," he said.

"Keep thinking," Will said. "If we can find the raven, we can find the staff. Max, it's a big black bird in your dream, right?"

"Yep," Max said.

"We should go to Bobbit's Bestiary," Simon offered. "Mr. Bobbit'll know where we can find ravens. He sells all these exotic birds and things. He sold us a macaw when I was a kid. My mother took it when she left." There was a sudden faraway look in his eyes and the table fell quiet.

Will squeezed Simon's arm for a second; then he broke the silence. "Bobbit's works for me, pal. Let's go."

Simon shook his head at Will. "Sorry, speedy. Mr. Bobbit is closed on weekends. He won't open again until Monday."

"Okay, then, first thing Monday morning, we meet at Bobbit's place," Will said. Everyone but Max nodded in agreement. "Sounds like a plan."

Andrew lightly elbowed Will. "I get why you want to find the raven with the creepy dream and all. But why are you so excited about this Moses stick? Unless the raven hits somebody with it, how much trouble can an old museum piece cause?"

"Plenty," Will said, slipping his helmet on. "If the wrong person gets hold of that staff, you'll be begging for the return of those croc monsters."

Returning to Rapids Lane, Will found Marin in the shade, playing on the front lawn of their home. The little girl knelt with her back to him. *She's probably playing with her dolls or digging up the garden again,* he thought.

"Hey, Marin," he casually said, heading for the front door.

"Hiya," she muttered without turning around.

Curiosity getting the best of him, Will peeked over Marin's shoulder. She was arranging what he thought at first were small stuffed animals. Until he took a closer look.

"Why are you touching those things?" he asked. "Leave them alone."

"Shhhh," Marin said, meeting his eye. "I'm going to help them."

"Marin, they're dead." Lined up in front of her, on the edge of the garden, were two lifeless birds and a deceased squirrel. "They carry disease, you know. Go inside and wash your hands."

Leo dropped from the thick oak branch overhead, giving Will a start. "Since we came out, I've been telling her not to touch those things. She doesn't listen—just doesn't listen." Leo brushed his hands on his pants leg and confided to Will, "We need to talk about my light trick."

Will squarely faced Leo. "You shouldn't talk about it, especially outside."

"You've got to admit it's a little cool that we all have our own things," Leo said, nodding.

"What things?"

"You know . . . Marin has her screaming and healing powers. You see demons. And now I light up. Do you think we're supposed to work together?"

"It's not called 'lighting up,'" Will whispered, pulling Leo closer by his sleeve. "It's called *igniting*. And people who spread light are *Candors*."

"How do you know?" Leo whispered back.

"Aunt Lucille showed me a book that our great-grandfather wrote. He knew some *Candors*."

"He did? So what can candoring do?"

Will put an arm around his brother. "Ask Aunt Lucille, she'll tell you everything. But stop talking about it—and don't try to *ignite*. You could hurt yourself. When you use these special gifts, Leo, sometimes it draws the attention of bad . . . beings and—"

"YEEEAH!" Marin screamed. A small pigeon, very much alive, flew out of her hands and fluttered up to a tree branch above them.

Leo and Will watched slack-jawed as she picked up the second dead bird. "What are you doing?!" Will asked her, checking that no one was watching from across the street. "Put the bird down, Marin."

But it was too late for that. Marin cupped the limp young pigeon in her small hands and when she opened them, the bird flew down the street.

"See? I helped them," Marin said with a crooked smile.

"Get inside and don't touch the squirrel," Will said, taking both his brother and sister by the arms. "Mom!" he yelled, opening the front door. "We're having a little problem out here with the kids."

That night, Dan knelt beside the tub in his upstairs bathroom to run water for Marin's bath. He turned on the spigot and leaned back, trying to watch a baseball game on TV through the open door of his bedroom.

"Marin. It's almost bath time, honey," Dan yelled downstairs. "Deborah, can you make sure she bathes? I don't want to miss the end of this game." Moments later, it happened.

At her palatial home on Gabbatha Place, Mayor Ava Lynch tied her hair back, preparing to wash away the makeup she had caked on that morning. She twisted the two stainless steel handles on either side of the duckbill faucet. Cupping the water from the basin, she splashed it onto her angular face. In the huge light-rimmed mirror behind the sink, she took note of each crevice, each line, the sagging skin above her eyes, and how the years had marked her. As she dipped her hands once more into the basin, it happened.

Evelyn Meriwether had just put Max's classical music on in the den, which always relaxed him after dinner. Returning to the kitchen, she was confronted by a sink full of dirty dishes. Cami followed her in.

"Let me help you, Mom," Cami said, grabbing a towel from a drawer. "I'll dry if you wash."

"How could anyone refuse an offer like that?" Evelyn said with a giggle. She ran water over the dishes and pressed a button on the countertop CD player. The haunting voice of Pothinus Sab filled the kitchen.

"*I often ask employers: Why do you give your workers so many breaks? Why do you take people away from their work?*" the gritty voice echoed from the speaker. "*We need our burdens. Welcome your burdens! Embrace your burdens! For there you shall find true regeneration.*"

"That's us, Cami," Evelyn said, soaping up the dishes. "Who'd have thought we'd find true regeneration at the kitchen sink?"

"Uh-huh. Whatever you say, Mom," Cami sighed, toweling off the wet dish. She reached for the next dripping plate, then it happened.

Lucille Wilder may have been the first one in town to witness the phenomena. From the window of her baby-blue wedding cake of a house perched along the Perilous River, Lucille absently glanced out the window, down to the dock where her boat, the *Stella Maris,* was moored. Under the floodlight at the end of the dock, the river seemed to be flowing in the wrong direction. It usually ran north from the Perilous Falls. Not this night. Lucille opened the door to the front porch and sprinted down to the dock for a closer look. The water left scarlet stains as it licked the rocks along the river's edge, startling her. She stared hard at the water, trying to make sense of it. The color of bleeding beets, the river flowed backward beneath her pier. Could she be imagining this? Lucille's head pounded. She froze for a moment, gawking at the red cascade. Her hand instinctively went to her nose. The river carried the stink of death. Collecting herself, she spun on her heels, sprinted behind her home and up the winding path toward Peniel.

"What in the—" Dan Wilder shouted when he saw the thick red liquid spreading through the water in the tub. He crab-crawled into the corner of the bathroom at the sight. Then he lunged for the spigot to stop the red intrusion. Squeals could be heard from the floor below, which sent Dan racing to the staircase.

Downstairs he found his wife and Will in the middle of a board game at the dining room table. Will had just leapt to his feet. Deborah stared at the glass in her hand, panting, as if it contained some alien life-form.

"Dan, look at this." Deborah's eyes were fixed on her glass. "This was water. A minute ago it was clean water. I drank it." The contents were now bloodred and smelled like something from a backed-up toilet.

"Put it down on the table, Deb," Dan advised.

"What's going on?" Will asked. Deep in his stomach, he felt a pinching sensation. Max's dream was coming true. Blood. The raven had brought blood.

"You should see the tub upstairs," Dan said, pacing in a

jittery circle. He nervously ran a hand along his cheek, the one marked by three slight scars. "There's red . . . water . . . coming out of the faucet."

"I understand rusty pipes or dirt darkening the water," Deborah said, trying to compose herself, still staring at the red goo in the water glass on the table. "But what the heck is that? I just drank it. Will saw . . . It was water, right?"

"Yes, ma'am. It was water," Will said. He pushed past his brother and sister, who stood in the dining room doorway, looking perplexed.

"I've got to go upstairs. I'll be right back." Will climbed the stairs and ran into his bedroom.

"Let me call city hall. Probably a broken water main or . . . a . . . a," Dan stammered. "I'm sure it'll be fixed soon." He stumbled toward the kitchen.

"A broken water main does not explain what is in my glass, Dan." Deborah grabbed the scarlet glass and paraded it into the kitchen. "Look at this! I wasn't filling this up when the color changed. It turned red on the table! Explain this!" She held the glass near Dan, who frantically punched numbers into the kitchen phone.

Upstairs, Will did his own frantic tapping on his cell phone. It rang and rang until Cami finally picked up.

"Will, there is blood in our kitchen sink," Cami said, the sounds of commotion and shrieking in the background. "My parents are totally freaking out. Mother wants Dad to take us all to see Pothinus Sab."

"I know. Except for the Sab thing, similar situation

here," Will said, on the edge of losing it. "My mother's glass of water turned all red. Could it be blood? Do you think it's blood?"

"It's not egg dye. Did you smell it?"

"I tried not to."

"It's blood, William. You should see our dishes."

Will's cell phone bleeped repeatedly, letting him know that he had another call. It was Simon. Will connected everyone in a three-way conversation.

"My father was in the shower. Will, he looks like he cut himself shaving—if he shaved HIS WHOLE BODY!" Simon shrieked. "Boy was he angry. He came into my room in a robe. His skin was completely red. I said, 'Were you trying to make that pasta sauce again?' That's when he flipped. He's stained from head to—"

"Simon, hold up a minute," Cami insisted. "You know what this means, guys? Max's dream was totally right. He wasn't even surprised when it happened. We've got the blood, so where is the raven?"

No one had anything to offer until Will jumped in.

"The raven must have the staff. The display case at Peniel had this whole explanation of the miracles Moses performed with it. Do you all know what the first one was? He turned the river water to blood."

"Wait, wait," Simon said. "So you're saying the plagues of the Old Testament are hitting our town because somebody stole the staff?"

"I am," Will said flatly.

Simon hesitated and then spewed, "My dad thinks red clay got into the water supply or something."

"Parents are supposed to try and calm you down. That's their job. But the truth is sometimes scarier," Will said, almost to himself. He could feel his heart racing and wished he could crawl under his sheets and wake later to find that this was all some nightmare.

"We've got to figure out where this raven is," Cami said, "and why it's doing all this."

"I agree." Will was resolute. "Has Max said anything else about the darkness? You know, 'the raven brings darkness' stuff?"

"Not a word," Cami said.

"Well, we can't let the 'darkness' come. . . . Simon, you're Mr. Sunday School. Figure out what else Moses's staff can do and let's all meet Monday morning at Bobbit's like we planned. I'll remind Andrew."

At that moment, a pounding on the front door pulled Will's attention away. He quickly got off the phone and stood at the banister overlooking the foyer.

When Dan Wilder opened the front door, Heinrich Crinshaw, the mustached chairman of the city council and his next door neighbor, walked into the house uninvited. He seemed to be in the middle of a conversation that had started long before he arrived.

"The mayor is in a lather, Dan. Whole town's up in arms," Crinshaw said, the circles under his eyes darker than usual, the bags beneath them fuller. "Mayor just called. She was washing her face, splashed the blo—the red liquid all over. Screaming, just screaming on the phone." His beady eyes darted side to side. "The water commissioner is already down at the river investigating. The mayor has called a special session of the city council, Monday morning. We'll need you there."

Dan, sensing Crinshaw's nervousness, placed a hand on his shoulder.

"I'm fine, Dan. Fine," he said in a trembling whisper. "You don't think it's really blood, do you?"

Aunt Lucille jammed her rusted key into the heavy front door of Peniel. She intentionally smashed her palm into the dragon's face carved onto the door, the one being speared by a knight. She proceeded to the marbled bathroom off Bethel Hall and threw the faucet on. Crystal-clear water flowed out.

As she exited, a wooden stick caught her across the stomach.

"Where do you think you're goin'?" a threatening voice warned.

Lucille took hold of the wood. "Bart, unless you've got an armed posse with you, you'd better lower that thing before you get hurt." The crutch blocking her path descended. The hall suddenly flooded with light.

"Scared the daylights out of me, Lucille. What are you

doin' here? So I was heading down to bed and PEEYONG—
there you went flying by in the dark. I thought, 'I don't
know who this is, but they're not snatching anything else
out of this museum.'" Bartimaeus laughed a little and situated his crutch under his right arm.

"You've had no water problems here?" Lucille asked.

"Water problems? Uh-uh. I just grabbed a glass before
I came up." He laid a hand on his belly. "Least I hope we're
not having any water problems. So what's the story?"

The appearance of Valens squinting from the hallway in
a blue robe like an awakened youngster on Christmas Eve
stopped their conversation.

"Bart? I saw the light and thought I should check on
you," he said. "Oh, Lucille. Getting rather late for a visit."

"Some odd things are happening around town," she said.

"The water you mean? It's terrible, isn't it?"

"How did you know about the water?" Lucille crossed her
arms.

"What are you two talking about?" Bart asked.

"The water is running red in Perilous Falls," said Valens.
"I heard screams outside the bedroom window, so I turned
the radio on in my room. It's quite terrible. Though it must
be affecting only a few areas. We're fine here. Brushed my
teeth only moments ago. Look." He smiled, revealing his
pearly whites.

"I don't like this," Bartimaeus said, walking toward the
door marked PRIVATE. "Someone or something is caus-

ing this." He stopped his advance and turned back to his friends. "Lucille, you know the score. This is big-time."

"They're using the staff," Lucille said gravely.

"I don't understand," Valens said. "Who's using the staff?"

"The *Sinestri* control the Staff of Moses. It's begun. We need to inform the abbot."

"Where ya think I'm headin'?" Bartimaeus said, hobbling through the private door.

"What's begun?" Valens asked Lucille, drawing the robe over his chest.

"The plagues—terrible trials for the people of Perilous Falls and all of us."

"But we're safe here at Peniel, aren't we?" Valens asked with a weak smile. "Surely we're safe here."

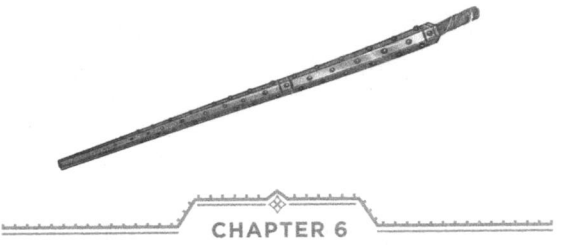

CHAPTER 6

BOBBIT'S BESTIARY

Sunday was odd, even by Perilous Falls standards. Every-one seemed to be on the streets. Residents mobbed groceries and convenience stores, quickly buying up all the bottled water in town. Phones at city hall rang off the hook with outraged citizens demanding "the clean water we pay our taxes for."

Local TV broadcasts examined the "red-stained water" infecting the town. Even Deborah Wilder was called in to file a story for WPF Channel 4, the local station that pro-duced her *Supernatural Secrets* series.

Deborah discovered that there were places in town where the water still ran clear. She reported that three sites—St. Thomas Church near the Falls, Peniel, and the new Karnak Center on Dura Street—all somehow had clean water.

By Sunday afternoon, lines of bottle-toting residents had

formed at the three locations. The line at Peniel was particularly long, snaking in front of the wrought-iron external
gate clear down High Street. Tobias Shen and Brother Godfrey manned the hose attached to the side of Bethel Hall,
filling the bottles of all comers.

"*Je vous en prie*—ah, forgive me. You are most welcome,"
said Godfrey, passing an overflowing bottle to a woman. He
was a stooped, kindly brother in khakis and a polo shirt,
and his speech had a delicate French air. "It is our pleasure.
May it bring you blessings." He nodded his head, which he
did at the start and conclusion of any meeting.

An old Hispanic man stepped forward next. "This place
must have its own well," he said, relinquishing his bottle
to Tobias Shen. "Can't be river water running up here. Just
look at the rapids." They all turned, glancing over the treetops to the red raging waters of the Perilous River below.

"Stay away from the river if you can," Tobias warned the
man. "There is danger, so, so much danger there." He glared
at the water as if never wanting to see it again.

Lucille Wilder had similar feelings. Early that morning,
after church, she had taken the *Stella Maris* out along the
stinking river to collect water samples. With rubber gloves,
she dipped vials into the current at the end of her dock,
near the falls, and downstream, close to Dismal Shoals. She
immediately conveyed the samples to Ugo Pagani, Peniel's
resident herbalist, cook, and chemist.

Lucille followed Ugo to his lab, a bright room in the
rectangular tower at the back end of Peniel. He negotiated

between the large black marble tables covered with Bunsen burners, glass tubing, scales, and brightly colored vials.

"Pee-yew," Ugo said, opening one of the samples. "Smells like your cat just barfed up some old Fancy Feast. The aroma in your neighborhood must be something special, Lucille." He guffawed to himself while separating the samples onto slides and into beakers.

"I don't have a cat—and I didn't come for your jokes. Just tell me what we're dealing with, Ugo dear."

"This could take a while." He poured a few drops of the red water into a container of blue fluid. "Your perfume'll be ready for bottling in a few hours, madam." He half bowed, releasing a raucous laugh.

Aunt Lucille gave him the fish eye, turning her back to Ugo's boiling and beaker shaking.

She occupied herself at a corner table before a slim medieval window. Opening an old volume from her father's office, a large Bible, she turned to the book of Exodus. There she studied the plagues God sent to the Egyptians via Moses and his staff.

Before she was finished making her notes, Ugo Pagani spoke in his sweetest New York tone. "Okay, we're closin' up the reading library. I have results." He wore a leather apron over his black habit. Ugo ripped a pair of goggles from his puffy face.

"Go on, don't keep me in suspense," Lucille said, shutting the Bible.

"The suspense is half the fun." Ugo held a printout in his

gloved hands. His black bushy eyebrows lowered. "This is surprising . . . that river stinks BAAAD! Ha-ha-ha." Lucille looked away and pulled at the cuffs of her silk jacket, trying to ignore his attempts at humor.

"Okay, okay. Here's the goods: It's blood. Mammal blood. I can't say if it's human or animal yet. But it's not dye."

"Any guess as to what would cause the entire river to fill with blood?"

"Your reading material probably offers better guesses than I can provide," Ugo said.

Baldwin walked in unannounced. He seemed to trace an invisible line around the entirety of the lab with his hawk nose before he ever addressed Lucille or Ugo.

"Well," Baldwin said, staring at the red bubbling beakers on the tables behind Ugo, "at least we know what we're dealing with."

"But we don't know where that staff is," Lucille said, rising. "Have you got any leads?"

"Yes, I do. Bartimaeus, your great-nephew, or possibly you, Lucille." Baldwin watched her closely.

"Me? Oh, Baldwin. I haven't touched that staff in over a year. I have access to *everything* in the collection . . . Me? If I'm a primary suspect, you'd better restart your investigation."

"You have a key to the display locks. You know the alarm codes. It's a possibility."

Aunt Lucille was having none of it. "You also have a key to those locks. The same one Valens borrowed to clean the mummy. Did he return it to you when he finished his work that night?"

"He did," Baldwin said defensively. "He placed it on the hook in my office before he went to the chapter meeting. I questioned him at length."

"Aah." Lucille walked in wide, defiant steps to Baldwin, stopping only a few inches away from him. "So there would have been time for you to use the key, take the staff, and mingle with the community after the meeting. You didn't make it to chapter that evening, did you?"

"How did you—I was securing the house. I am the vicar of this community." His temper simmered beneath every word.

Lucille brightened, her eyes suddenly merry. "Do you see how empty charges sting when they aren't backed up by very much, dear? I'm glad we had time to chat. Now I have to go figure out how to save this town." She waved a hand in the air. "Thanks for your help, Ugo."

Both men watched her go.

Ugo lifted one of his red vials to the light overhead, shaking it. "You didn't pinch the staff, did you, Vicar? Make a little supernatural Kool-Aid on the side?"

Baldwin was in no mood for jokes. "Clean up this mess and stop your foolishness, Ugo. This is deadly, serious business."

"It's stinky business too." Ugo chuckled, returning to his beakers. "Something smells about all of this."

Before meeting his friends on Monday morning, Will leapt on his red scooter and sped to the yard at St. Thomas Church. It was out of his way, but he had to make good on his promise to Mr. Shen. He filled an empty gallon container with the clear water that flowed from the faucet on the back side of the church. He then carried it to the leafy walking stick he had planted along the riverside months before.

While dousing the "little tree," he caught sight of the river below. The dark red current of Sunday was no more. The water was now tinged a deep pink, like flat champagne, and it flowed over the falls and downstream as it always had.

Maybe the worst is over? Maybe the staff didn't cause the red color at all? Could have been some sick animals in the river or something.

Just considering other explanations lightened Will's mood. He purposely tried to push from his memory the red substance that appeared in his mother's glass at the dining room table.

Scooting down Main Street toward Bobbit's Bestiary, Will comforted himself with a series of possibilities.

If the river water wasn't really blood, then Max's dream might be wrong. The missing staff might be just a coincidence. And the staff isn't actually mine. It's not like it belongs to me. This has nothing to do with me! The old jaunty smirk returned to his face. *So who cares if this raven took it? Whatever the raven is, maybe it's none of my business? The last thing I need to do is go poking around and find myself face to face with another demon*—

He slammed on the brakes at the corner of High Street and Phosphorus Way. What he saw not only erased his smirk, but turned Will's mouth to a perfect O. Fluttering down the street, collecting on the corner around the edges of Bobbit's Bestiary, were long, shimmery, black feathers. Hundreds and hundreds of feathers hovered just off the ground.

"Great," Will said to himself, a sickening sensation rushing through his gut. "This was not part of the plan."

"Will! Will!" a high-pitched nasal voice rang out from behind him.

Will searched for the source of the voice, but he saw no one.

"Pssst. Over here. At nine o'clock."

To his left, Will spotted a thin hand shaking back and forth from behind a bush.

"Simon?" Will asked.

"Shhhh . . ." Standing indignantly, Simon wore a black trench coat, a black brimmed hat, prescription sunglasses, and shorts. With his exposed pink legs, he looked like a flamingo awaiting a downpour—which did not seem to bother him one bit. "Quiet or you'll blow my cover. Come over here."

Will put the kickstand down on his scooter and joined Simon on the other side of the shrubbery.

"Sit down," Simon insisted. Will reluctantly did so.

Simon pulled a paperback Bible from his coat pocket. "I've been doing a lot of research," he said, "and I found all the plagues of Egypt in the Old Testament. Pharaoh wouldn't let the Israelites leave Egypt to worship God. So God sent ten plagues. Ten! Here's the list, and it is not pretty." Checking over his shoulder, he cautiously passed Will a folded, handwritten piece of paper. It read:

The Plagues

✔ 1) **The Nile turned to BLOOD!** Moses and Aaron "lifted up *the staff* and struck the water of the river, and all the water in the river was turned to blood."

2) **Frogs!** "Aaron stretched out his hand over the waters of Egypt; and the frogs came up and covered the land of Egypt."

3) **Gnats.** "The dust of the earth" was struck by the rod and gnats appeared on "man and beast."

4) **Swarms of flies.** "There came great swarms of flies into the house of Pharaoh" and in "all the land of Egypt." We should buy fly swatters now.

5) **Plague kills livestock.** All the cattle of the Egyptians died. Load up on hamburgers while we can.

6) **Boils.** Moses and Aaron took ashes from a kiln and threw them in the air before Pharaoh. This dust "became boils breaking out in sores on man and beast."

7) **Hail, thunder, and fire!** "Moses stretched forth his rod toward heaven: and the Lord sent thunder and hail, and fire ran down

to the earth." People and animals in the field died. Only the Israelite lands were spared.

8) **Locusts.** Moses lifted the rod, causing locusts to cover "the face of the whole land." They ate all the plants and all the fruit on the trees.

9) **Darkness.** Moses lifted his hands to heaven and there "was thick darkness in all the land of Egypt for three days."

10) **Death strikes the Egyptians.** There was crying throughout the land. Remember Max's dream. Really scary.

Will folded the paper back up and slipped it into his pocket. "Maybe the red water was just a . . . you know, the only thing that'll happen. We can't get all worked up because the staff was stolen." A glance across the street at the pile of floating feathers surrounding Bobbit's Bestiary convinced Will that he was lying to himself.

"Guys?" It was Cami, raising her voice as she and Andrew approached. "Will? Simon?"

Will popped up from behind the bush. "We're here *strategizing.*" Will's eyes were fixed on the feathers at the corner. "Maybe we don't need to talk to Mr. Bobbit after all. Have you seen the river? It's much, much lighter than it was yesterday."

Andrew dropped his chin to his chest. "I hope Will-man's not chickening out on us."

"We don't have anything else to go on, William," Cami said. "It can't hurt to ask Mr. Bobbit if he knows anything about ravens." As she spoke, a thin hunchbacked old man exited Bobbit's, carrying a broom. He swept the mat in front of the doorway.

Will could not stop watching him. The old man's broom passed right through the dark feathers piled at least six inches thick before the door.

"Okay. Let's all go in together," Will said in a rush. "We'll quiz Mr. Bobbit and leave."

The gang immediately crossed the street.

If it wasn't for the decomposing zombie with the broom blocking the door, they could have entered the store directly.

"What you young'uns want?" the old man asked, sweeping, never lifting his eyes to them.

"Umm, we would like to look at some of the animals," Cami said. "I'm thinking of buying a bird."

The old man's gray eyes met Cami's. "Birds are messy." He had a nose like a hanging squash and a jutting chin. "There are plenty of birds outside in need of feeding."

Will went to speak, but his face contorted. AH-CHOO! AH-CHOO!

"I see the dust is causin' your friend trouble," the old man said, yanking at the waist of his much-too-large beige pants, laughing to himself.

AH-CHOO! Will tried to control the sneezes, but he couldn't.

Simon stepped to the front. "We'd like to talk to Mr. Bobbit. My family has bought birds from him in the past."

"I haven't been here that long." The old man pointed his

broom handle at Simon's knobby knees. "Where are your pants, son?"

"I'm wearing shorts," Simon huffed.

"Hard to see 'em with that coat. Big boy like you should be in long pants."

Simon was about to say something when a tinkling bell sounded and the glass door behind the old man opened.

"Can I help you?" asked a sweaty man with a pear-shaped face, sticking his head around the open door. His nose seemed to be stuffed up. "Don't mind, Crocket. He's new and can be short at times. Come in, come in." He hastily brought the four friends inside the cavernous store. It was lit by gas lamps and had cages hanging from the ceiling and others set into the walls.

"I'm Timothy Bobbit." He wiped his nose hard with a handkerchief and wobbled behind the counter that ran the length of the shop. As he convulsed into a coughing fit, Will thought he looked tired, as if his light had gone out. Bobbit patted the countertop with his palms. "I am in a bit of a hurry. How can I help you all?"

"We wanted some information about birds," Will started, fighting back a sneeze.

Bobbit was jittery and obviously wished the kids were anywhere but in his store.

"As you can see, young man, we have hundreds of birds. I am really pressed for time." He pulled a cage covered by a white cloth from the rear shelf, placing it on the counter. "What kind of bird did you have in mind?"

"Ravens. We were thinking ravens," Simon interjected. "Do you sell ravens or know of any really big ravens?"

Bobbit adjusted the white covering on the large cage so the webbed pink feet inside could not be seen. "No, we don't sell ravens. But I could order one."

"Are there any here in town that you know of?" Will asked. "A raven that might steal things?"

Bobbit fluttered an impatient hand in the air. "They all steal things. They're scavengers. The *Corvus corax* are a very intelligent breed. There is a small habitat across the river that I've heard about but . . . why do you want to know about ravens?"

Whatever was in the covered cage expelled a loud hiss. It made Will jump.

"We're just interested in them—summer project. Raveny kind of thing," Will explained with a forced giggle.

Bobbit wiped his wet brow with the handkerchief, checking his wristwatch. "I wish I had more time." He coughed violently and added, "But I have an important delivery to make. A very important delivery."

Deep in the store, birds in their cages rustled and cooed. Timothy Bobbit picked up a shapeless tweed sports coat from the back of a chair and slipped it on. He buttoned it over his potbelly and wide-striped tie.

"You all may look around for a few minutes if you wish. But please touch nothing. There are some very rare breeds of animals and . . . Well, don't touch them." He stuck a finger through the big brass ring on the top of the covered birdcage and lifted it from the counter, carrying it in his arms. Whatever was in the cage poked at the fabric from inside. Its explosive honking even caused Bobbit to turn his head away. Andrew opened the front door for him.

"Thank you, thank you," Bobbit panted. "Crocket, these young people may look around for a bit," he told the old man now sweeping the sidewalk in front of the store. "Don't let them touch anything." Then turning to the kids in the doorway, he said, "If I come across any ravens, I'll be sure to let you all know. Goodbye, now. Goodbye."

Bobbit jogged awkwardly up the street, both arms around the covered cage.

"We should follow him," Cami whispered to the others as they stepped out of the store, watching Bobbit cross the street.

"I think she's right." Andrew nudged Will as he walked past him outside. "What's he in such a hurry to deliver?"

"And who is he making the delivery *to*? That's what I'd like to know," Simon said.

Will was the only one still standing in the open doorway. The gentle chirp of the birds and growls behind him made him look back into the store. Down the center aisle bordered by wooden cages, he spotted a woman with frizzy hair. She reached up to one of the pens in the rear of the store. "We don't sell ravens. If I come across any ravens, I'll be sure to let you know. We don't sell ravens . . . ," she repeated to herself.

He turned back to his friends outside.

"You all follow Bobbit. I'm going to poke around here," he whispered so the old man couldn't hear. "We can meet up later."

His friends wanted to argue with Will, but they needed to chase after Bobbit if they didn't want to lose him. Crocket started hosing down the sidewalk, oblivious to Andrew, Cami, and Simon leaving.

Across the street, Tobias Shen tracked the young trio. He had been observing them from behind a large oak tree for the past twenty minutes. As they followed Bobbit down High Street, Mr. Shen shadowed them, darting behind bushes and greenery while never losing his quarry.

Inside Bobbit's Bestiary, Will turned his attention toward the woman in the back of the store.

"Excuse me," he said cautiously.

"Oh, hellooo," the woman said in a singsong voice. She continued to reach into the cages, never looking Will's way. "You can come back here. I don't bite, and these fellows hardly bite at all."

CHAPTER 7

MISS ANN HYE

Mayor Ava Lynch impatiently tapped her fingernail on the surface of the city council dais. She was obviously bored by the long report Harve Bleakly, the Perilous Falls water commissioner, read to the council that morning. Under normal circumstances, she had little use for Bleakly, but listening to his attempts to downplay the contaminated water infuriated the mayor. She pulled a mirror from her shiny black leather purse and checked her face. She needed more powder. Faint rust stains on her chin were bleeding through the makeup she had applied earlier. She repeatedly blotted extra powder onto her chin and then . . .

CRACK. She snapped the mirror case shut into the microphone before her.

Harve Bleakly stopped midsentence. Everyone turned toward the mayor.

"Harve, honey, we are all deeply impressed by your con-scientious work and your efforts to explain away the trau-matic events of this weekend," the mayor said in a voice dripping with poisoned honey. "However, I, for one, have a little problem with your explanations."

"Mayor Lynch, we haven't concluded our tests and . . . uh . . . there's no need for alarm since the red water has dissipated—"

"Ah-ah-ah. Don't patronize me, sugar. You may not be able to see it, because I went through great pains this morn-ing, but like so many of our citizens, my skin has been dyed RED." She dropped her voice into an intimidating whisper. "I don't enjoy having stained skin, Harve. So just tell me: what changed our water's color?" She clawed the outer edge of the mahogany dais, as if she could leap over it and knock Harve Bleakly to the ground.

"One of the tests indicated the presence of blood, but it could also be red silt." Bleakly fiddled with his aviator glasses. "Some on my team think it might be a global warm-ing event . . . or something."

The mayor fell back into her leather chair and rolled her eyes to the ceiling, eliciting laughter from other members of the city council.

Heinrich Crinshaw turned his microphone on. Stroking his thin mustache, he read flatly from an open folder. "Mr. Bleakly, your report says the river's current was running backward on Saturday. Where did the red water originate downriver? Was there a source?"

Harve walked forward with a photo. "We've isolated it to a spot up here, north of town. It's an area called Dismal Shoals on some of the older maps."

Mayor Lynch bolted up. "Dismal Shoals! That's where all those gator things sprang up earlier this summer. We've got pictures of them just swarming out of Dismal Shoals. Now, this is interesting."

Dan Wilder on the other end of the dais kept his head down, flipping through documents. He could feel the heat rising up his back, forcing moisture onto his forehead. In that moment, he recalled the pictures Mayor Lynch had given him months earlier showing Aunt Lucille, Tobias Shen, Bartimaeus, and Will boarding the *Stella Maris* at Dismal Shoals. The police reports claimed that horrible, gatorlike creatures had crawled out of the ruins of a temple there. Dan sensed what was coming.

The mayor, now fully engaged, her eyes like pinpoints, barked into the microphone, "I'd like to move that we expand our special investigation into the strange events at the river to include this water-coloring incident. There could be a connection between this and those gator things. Someone or something is to blame for this trouble. Mr. Chairman, I'd like to call a vote."

Only Dan Wilder voted against the motion. It passed by a wide majority: 5 to 1.

Harve Bleakly promised to report any further findings to the council. Chairman Crenshaw was about to convene the meeting when Mayor Lynch waved a long, red-stained hand in his direction.

"If I might urge one more little vote, Mr. Chairman?" The mayor gently smoothed a hand over the great black-and-white shell atop her head. "After witnessing the anguish of our citizens during this water incident, I believe we need a consultant—someone who can help calm the tensions in our fair city. He might also help us understand some of these peculiar occurrences."

"Who did you have in mind, Ms. Mayor?" Crinshaw asked mechanically.

"Well, it should be someone with experience and a spiritual perspective—not religious, but spiritual," the mayor said.

"Not that sideshow charlatan," Dan Wilder muttered under his breath into the open mic.

"Excuse me, Dan?" The mayor's tone was accusatory.

"I didn't mean to . . . I just hope we aren't considering Pothinus Sab for this consultant position."

"That is an excellent suggestion, Dan." The mayor smiled, shimmying forward in her chair. "I like that. Shall we vote on Pothinus Sab, Mr. Chairman?"

"No, I wasn't suggesting him." Dan frenetically shook his head, as if watching some horrible accident in slow motion that he had no way of stopping. "I think he's a fraud. What is his expertise?"

Heinrich Crinshaw pounded his gavel on the dais as if Dan were not talking. "Very well. Let's call a vote on

Councilman Wilder's excellent motion that Pothinus Sab be named consultant to the city. All in favor?" Crinshaw began to calmly count the raised hands at the table.

"I object, Mr. Chairman. Heinrich!" Dan tossed his hands in the air. "I did not offer Sab as a consultant."

Crinshaw scribbled the vote in his ledger. "The ayes have it and the motion passes," he announced with no emotion. "Dan, were you abstaining from the vote? Or did you oppose the measure?"

"When was there time for a vote?" Dan bleated. "I was trying to have a discussion about Sab's expertise."

Crinshaw hit the gavel again. "Very well. We are adjourned." Crinshaw and the other city council members started to push away from the dais. The mayor walked over to Dan, who was furiously shoving papers into his briefcase.

"This is a complete farce, Ava," Dan complained.

"Don't be so sore, Danny," the mayor said with mock pity. "Your suggestion was the highlight of the day. Sab will greatly help our investigation. You just wait and see."

A cacophony of chirps and squeaks, caws and honks surrounded Will as he approached the thin woman at the back of Bobbit's Bestiary. He grimaced, wanting to cover his ears from the racket. *This is like an Evil Enchanted Tiki Room,* Will thought.

The woman at the back of the store could not be more

serene. She wore a layered off-white dress that had the haphazard appearance of a pile of laundry. In the bend of her pale, thin arm she cradled a bowl filled with what appeared to be green oatmeal. With a delicate spoon, she scooped up the green paste and lifted it to the hungry beaks straining through the bars on all sides.

"You came at feeding time. Aren't you lucky," the woman said in a high, airy, musical voice. The moment Will made eye contact, she broke her glance, turning away shyly. "We get so few visitors. Mr. Bobbit doesn't like me to . . . I don't often get to speak with the customers. But you seem nice. Different."

She shook her hair—a nest of dark hay—over the side of her face, concealing it from view. It made Will want to lean in even closer.

"Are those ducks you're feeding? They're big," he said.

"Oh, you're silly." She laughed lightly, continuing to feed the caged fowl. They angrily snapped at the end of her spoon with their black-tipped pink bills. "They're not ducks. You're Egyptian geese, aren't you? Tell him what you are." Their honking and hissing escalated.

To Will they looked like oversized ducks that had crossed several lanes of traffic—and kissed a few bumpers. The geese had mismatched patches of gray, rust, and black on their coats. Brown stains ringed their yellow eyes, and rust circled their necks like nasty strangle marks.

"They're not going to win any beauty pageants, are they?" Will pushed his pith helmet back, smiling.

"I think they're lovely," the woman snapped, turning her back to him. She attended to the cages at the back wall. "If you only see the outside, you miss a great deal. External beauty is not everything."

"I was making a joke. I wasn't saying . . ." Will struggled to recover. "You're really good with them. I can tell they like you, ma'am."

"We spend a lot of time together, the birds and me. I care for them deeply." The geese hissed in their cages, beating their brown wings madly against the thin bars. The woman glanced at Will for a moment, lighting on his helmet with her small black eyes. "It's rude to wear a hat indoors." She hid her face once more under her wiry black overgrowth.

Will removed his helmet, examining the cages to his left. In one of the lower pens, near his waist, he spotted a huge black bird. "Is that a raven?"

"You shouldn't be looking in there." The woman spun around and dropped a canvas curtain, covering the lower set of cages. "Mr. Bobbit wouldn't like it if I—You won't tell him, will you? I didn't show it to you. You found it yourself. You're not going to tell on me, are you?" Her black pupils pulsed with fear as she hugged the metal bowl to her chest.

"No, I promise not to tell him," Will said soothingly. "But I need some information, miss. I think you can help me."

"What sort of information?"

"My name's Will. I'm looking for a raven. Mr. Bobbit said he didn't sell ravens, that he didn't even know where to find them." He pointed to the covered cages. "But isn't that a raven, miss? Miss?"

"Miss Ann. I'm Ann Hye. Pleased to meet you," she sang, her tiny eyes darting. "I shouldn't say what's in the cage. I have to feed the geese now."

She returned to the big cages at the rear.

"But isn't this a raven, Miss Ann?" Will lifted the canvas curtain to reveal a black bird, cowering in the back of its cage.

Ann Hye tried to resume the feeding. She finally stabbed the spoon into the green goo in her bowl, her eyes to the floor. "It is a raven," she said quietly. "He lies. Mr. Bobbit lies."

Outside, Crocket pressed his face against the front window, staring hard at Will.

"Miss Ann, you have my word. I won't mention anything to Mr. Bobbit. I don't even know him." Will delicately approached the woman. "Did he say anything about a staff?"

Ann Hye gasped, drawing a small hand over her mouth. She nodded incessantly. "He's been talking about that museum, the one up the street. He said there was a staff there. He's been talking about it a lot." Ann drew close to Will. The caged wildlife stilled. "He hates the old woman, the one who runs the place, but he does have a friend at the museum. He knows one of them . . ."

"Who does he know?" Will's head ached. He could feel his anger rising. "And why does he hate the old . . . Lucille, Lucille Wilder?"

"I don't know. I don't know names. I just heard him on the phone a few times with Mr. Sab . . . Pothinus Sab. He's one of our biggest clients."

"Sab? What's Sab buying? Is he buying ravens?"

The geese hissed and honked suddenly. "They're getting hungry. They like my special recipe. It's grains and grasses and greens." She pulled a clean spoon from her pocket and scooped it into her bowl. "Here." She rammed the green mixture into Will's mouth. He spit it out into his hand.

"Don't be rude. Eat it. It's good for you. All natural. It'll fatten you up." She trilled a laugh and flitted back to the demanding geese.

"Please, ma'am, you've got to answer me. Is Sab buying the ravens?" Will pressed.

"No, silly. He buys geese. He likes them plump and healthy." She pet a goose on the head with the back of her twiglike finger.

Will put his helmet back on. The bitter taste of the goose feed felt like acid in his mouth. "Miss Ann, will you tell me if Mr. Bobbit says anything else about the staff or if you learn anything about who's buying the ravens?"

Ann Hye nodded without looking his way. "I'll watch him for you. Though you mustn't tell him we talked. You mustn't tell him I told you about the staff or showed you the raven. Mr. Bobbit would be very angry with me."

"I promise," Will said, wiping his hand on a tissue he spotted behind the counter. He headed for the front door. "So long," he said with a quick wave.

Mr. Bobbit lied to me about the ravens. What else is he lying about?

Pulling at the front door handle, he thought about Bobbit's hatred for his aunt Lucille and grew furious. He flung the door wide.

"Hey, boy!" Crocket warned as he rolled up a hose. "Careful with the door. You best stay away from here, understand? There's nothing in that store for you—'specially when Mr. Bobbit's not here."

Will nodded curtly and stomped away without another word.

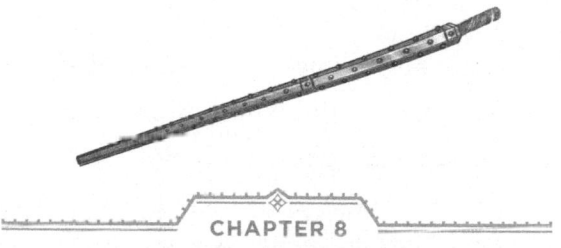

CHAPTER 8

INTO THE DARKNESS

Mr. Bobbit waddled down Dura Street, clutching the huge covered birdcage. He passed the old de Plancy Cemetery, with Cami, Simon, and Andrew trailing him from afar. They were close enough to hear the honks of the bird beneath the white wrapping every so often.

"Bet you anything he's headed to the Karnak Center," Cami said, putting an arm out to stop the guys from running ahead. "Everywhere I turn it's Pothinus Sab. My mother is really into this guy."

Simon pulled off his sunglasses, trading them for his indoor pair, which were in the pocket of his black coat. "The Karnak Center? That's the old Grimma Funeral Home. It's abandoned, isn't it?"

"Not anymore," Cami said. "Mayor Lynch donated it to Sab to open a new center here. My mother told us all about it, and she'd know." She motioned for her friends to join her behind some weed-choked headstones in the cemetery, where they could secretly watch Bobbit.

The Karnak Center's beige stone exterior was protected by a row of ram statues, lined up like angry guard dogs on either side of the main door. A shallow rectangular pool stretched from the steps of the central doorway to the street. But Mr. Bobbit didn't enter through the main door.

Instead, the fleshy man wound his way through the cemetery and climbed a narrow stairway on the side of the building. At the top of the landing, he coughed into a handkerchief until his face turned red. He then rapped on the metal door. Within moments it opened, permitting Bobbit and his birdcage to vanish into the interior darkness.

Fifty yards away, the kids crouched in the shadow of a big stone angel holding a sword over a dragon. Andrew leaned around the dragon's head. "We better follow him. I sure ain't staying out here."

"Then let's go in the front door. We'll tell them we're visitors," said Simon. "This is a public center, isn't it?"

"I'm not sure we should go in," Cami warned. "Maybe we should see what Bobbit does."

"No way," Andrew said, starting to move for the Karnak Center. "We need to find out what those guys are up to in there. They're up to something."

Outnumbered, Cami threw her hands into the air and joined the boys in their march to the front door.

Simon shied away from the row of menacing rams staring at him as he passed. "Real inviting, isn't it?" he said, snorting.

"Be quiet and move," Andrew said, blowing past him and scaling the front stairs. Andrew reached for the doorknob.

"Take it easy, moron," Simon whispered. "Shouldn't we knock first?"

"Oh sure. Let's send a letter announcing our arrival time," Andrew mumbled. "Do you want to see what's going on in there or not?"

Cami slipped between the boys. "Stop fighting. If we're going in, just open the door. Better yet, let me."

Stepping into the expansive front room, they felt a heaviness in the air. Their bodies stiffened.

Firelight shone on the crimson walls. A shallow rectangular pool like the one outside took up most of the floor space. It was flanked by rows of fat sandstone columns on the left and right. At the back of the room, two massive stone pharaohs stood on either side of a pair of bronze doors that stood fifteen feet high. Engraved onto them was the image of an Egyptian figure that had two tablets coming from the top of his head.

Cami wrinkled her brow. "Are those corncobs on his head?"

"Maybe they're feathers drawn by a primitive," Simon suggested.

Andrew scratched his head, considering the image. "Looks like the dude's got a double cone head to me."

Before the conversation could continue, voices down the hall intruded.

"My dear, dear friend, I said two fresh geese *daily*. Two," the accented voice asserted. "You'll recall I specifically asked for *two*. Yes? Where is the other?"

"Well, the ones at the store are on the small side. But I could . . ." It was Bobbit, and he sounded nervous.

"No matter. I know you will bring more, won't you? It is most important that we have two fresh, plump geese each morning."

Cami pulled the guys close to her. "That's Pothinus Sab. I'd know his voice anywhere. Come to my house and you can hear it round the clock." She motioned for the boys to follow her so she could hear more clearly. They moved deeper into the room, next to the pool.

"You can count on us, Mr. Sab," Bobbit said, interrupted by coughs. "I'll have my stock associate bring another goose over right away. I am still feeling terrible—my stomach aches and this cough . . . You said that I would be improved by now. But this—" Jagged coughs gagged his speech.

"Your condition puzzles me. I have just the thing for you. Sarsour, fetch us one of the new tonics I made up this morning," Sab crowed. "Mr. Bobbit, you will feel right as rain after only two doses of this tonic. For all the goodness you offer us, let us offer some goodness to you."

The tiny man, Sarsour, looking like a red raisin in white, tottered out into the main room and passed between the pool and the polished doors. To avoid detection, Cami,

Andrew, and Simon backed into the shadows of two hulking columns. Perhaps they backed up a bit too far.

"Wonder what's wrong with Bobbit?" Cami asked.

"I'm more interested in what Sab is doing with the geese," said Simon.

"Do you feel that?" Andrew said.

"Shhh," Cami hissed. "I'm trying to listen."

"The floor is shaking," Andrew whispered.

"I can feel it t—" Simon didn't finish the word before the floor gave way beneath them. All three friends slipped through the newly revealed hole with great force, tumbling into darkness.

Lucille Wilder removed a chain from her neck and the dangling ancient key it held captive. She laid them on a small table against a whitewashed wall. The chain looped through an ornate gold cross with jagged teeth along the bottom— the key to her father's office.

Lucille stood at one end of the second-floor ballroom in her home. She retied the cloth belt at the waist of her stylish Asian-inspired workout uniform.

Her blue eyes made contact with a series of trapezes, ropes, and hoops dangling high above the shiny planked floor. At the far end of the room, a menacing black mannequin with cannonlike arms stood at attention. A red laser shot from its head, scanning the room for activity. Lucille took a deep breath, pressed the small remote control button in her hand, dropped it, and ran as if her life depended on it.

She leapt onto a nearby trampoline and flew up to the trapeze. The laser on the mannequin found her. It immediately spit a red ball in her direction. She dodged it by throwing her legs up over the top of the trapeze and bending her body backward. The trapeze swung high and when it nearly reached the ceiling, Lucille somersaulted in midair, close to the ropes on the other side of the room. The laser dot made contact with her head. *PLOOP.* Out shot another red ball from the mannequin.

With one hand, Lucille clutched the rope not far from her laser-eyed opponent. She straightened her body like a rod and began spinning as if on a mad carousel. The laser couldn't get a fix on a location, so the black thing shot ball after ball in her general direction. But it was too late. Before any of the balls could strike her, Lucille kicked the mannequin over, pulled a high-powered water gun from the wall, and sprayed the beaten enemy until a pool had formed around it.

"Not bad for an old dame," she laughed, striking her thigh.

"Not bad at all." It was Will who had been watching from a half-open door.

"How long have you been there, dear?"

"Long enough to see you kick that thing's butt." Will approached her, eyes fixed on the weapon still in her hand. "What's that?"

"Something Brother Philip whipped up for me. It's a holy water dispenser—with a bit of a kick." She handed it to Will.

It looked like a machine gun except for the oblong metal tank above the trigger that held the liquid ammunition.

"So when do I get to train in here?" Will asked.

"This is your lucky day." She took back the weapon, hanging it on the wall. "Speed and agility are necessary to outmaneuver these demons. You've mastered the somersault, but more is needed. Physical training must always accompany our mental and spiritual preparation."

"Why are you still training so hard?" Will asked.

"Because until you're ready, I have to protect you, Will." She took his helmet off and mussed his hair. "As long as I'm around, you'll be just fine, kid. Now let's get you up on the ropes."

Will was troubled and Aunt Lucille could see it. After some questioning, he came clean about his visit to the pet store, Bobbit's lies, and the raven he saw in the cage. He even told her that Bobbit hated her.

"Why would you even go there, Will? And since I don't know the man at all, how could he possibly hate me?" Lucille wondered.

"Well, he does. His assistant at the shop told me everything." Will began to untie the laces of his red sneakers. "Something about this whole thing scares me. The missing staff, Max's dream, Bobbit's lies . . . I think I should look at the prophecy again. To at least see if the book opens." The Book of Prophecy only opened when touched by the "chosen one," and only if the time was ripe for the next message to be revealed.

Aunt Lucille turned to the huge windows covering one wall of the ballroom. She stared out at Peniel, high atop the jagged cliff behind her house. "You should consult the book again. Perhaps tomorrow, dear. There's no time now. I've invited your parents over to discuss training your brother and sister. Leo can't just be *igniting* all over town—"

"I'm confused, Aunt Lucille." Will was on his feet. "I have this sick feeling that something bad is happening and maybe if I read the prophecy . . ."

"Are you seeing things again? Shadows?"

"Not really shadows . . ." He focused on his sneakers. "Feathers. Black raven feathers."

"Bartimaeus told me about the feathers. Anything else?"

"No, but if I could see the *prophecy*—"

"You must be careful with the Book of Prophecy, Will," Aunt Lucille scolded him. "Once you open it, there is no going back. It doesn't merely reveal things. At times it initiates them. Better to let events unfold. Watch what happens and then once we have confirmation that things are amiss—"

"Things are *amiss*? How much more *amiss* do they have to get?" He pulled out the list of plagues Simon had given him earlier. He raised them to Aunt Lucille's face. "This is what's coming, Aunt Lucille. It's already started."

"I know. Oh, and that *was* blood in the river by the way." She coolly scanned the lines on the paper. Something she read caused a knowing smile to wash over her, and she snatched the paper from Will. "Your list is a little overblown. The staff only controls six of these plagues. I've been doing my own research." Lucille picked up a pen from the small table where her key lay. Will's eyes widened when he spotted the office key, which he instantly recognized.

Lucille dramatically struck lines through Simon's plague list. "That's better." She handed it back to Will. "Moses and his staff were only responsible for the blood, the frogs, the gnats, the hailing fire, the locusts, and the three days of darkness."

Will was puzzled "Oh, that makes me feel a lot better."

"I wasn't trying to make you feel better. We need to find that staff fast. But at least you don't have to worry about swarms of flies, the livestock dying, or boils. See, things are looking up. Speaking of up . . ." She jumped, grabbing the trapeze and hoisting her legs over the bar. "I want you to get up here, hang upside down, and swing to those two ropes there." She dismounted, landing firmly on both feet.

"Sure thing, but I've got to send a quick text message before we start." Will fished his cell phone from his backpack in the corner and punched a text out to Cami:

At my aunt Lucille's. Where are u guys? Where did Mr. Bobbit go? Let's talk later.

As Will reached for the trapeze, Aunt Lucille's doorbell gonged. "That'll be your mother and father. We can do more of this later. Can you pick up my sparring partner there?" Aunt Lucille pointed to the capsized mannequin and flew out of the ballroom. "Coming, coming . . . ," she said as she reached the staircase.

Will picked up the dummy, slipped on his red high-tops, and walked over to the small table in the corner. He stared at the cross-shaped key, wreathed by his great-aunt's gold chain. Puckering his lips, he considered the conversation he and Aunt Lucille had just had. *You must be careful with the Book of Prophecy. Once you open it, there is no going back.* He started to leave. Then struck by a second thought, he turned back to the table. Will swiped the key and chain, threw them into his backpack, and raced downstairs to join the rest of the Wilders.

Cami rubbed her lower back, which had landed on something sharp in the dark basement of the Karnak Center.

"Are you okay? My arm is killing me," Simon complained as he withdrew it from beneath Andrew's torso.

"I'll survive," Cami said, "but something jabbed me in the back."

"Simon, turn on your watch light," Andrew commanded.

A weak green glow lit up the area where the kids had landed beneath the now-closed trapdoor. Andrew grabbed Simon's wrist, directing the watch's beam over the floor. Dull brown objects like pickup sticks were scattered around them. Cami lifted one off the floor.

"They're bones. Why are bones down here?" Cami asked. Indeed, the broken little bones were in sticky piles on all sides.

A spooked Simon scrambled away from the bone piles, taking their only light source with him.

"As long as you're running, find a light switch and be quiet," Andrew told Simon.

Simon ran the green beam over the walls until he came upon a rusted push button switch. When he pressed it, two uncovered lightbulbs flashed to life in the middle of the room.

They were in a dank basement. A few tiny blacked-out windows near the ceiling and an opening to a hallway were the only visible entryways to the room. To the right of the hallway opening, three brown-streaked porcelain tables with attached sinks stood side by side. Rows of rickety wooden shelves jutted out from the wall behind the kids. On them were hundreds of triangular glass bottles, filled with colored liquid, which instantly captured Simon's attention.

"What is this stuff?" Simon asked, picking up one of the bottles. He brought it to the light and read the stenciled label. "'REGENERATIVE TONIC. EXCLUSIVELY PRODUCED AT THE KARNAK CENTER FOR REGENERATION AND CREATIVE THERAPY. NEW YORK, LONDON, VANCOUVER, MILAN.'" He returned the tonic to the shelf, peering at the bottles. "Weird stuff. Wonder what it's made of. There are no ingredients on the label."

"I wouldn't do any taste tests if I were you," Cami advised. She was on her knees, studying a mound of bones on the floor. She smelled the pile before her, which made her eyes sting. "These are fresh. There's blood and meat on these bones." She began to search the corners of the room, looking for who or what might have just finished snacking. "Guys, I don't like this. Do you see anything that could have eaten recently?"

"I wish *I* hadn't eaten recently," Andrew said, making a disgusted face. He was more concerned with a machine bolted to a metal table in the corner. There were gold metal shavings sprinkled around the table. A handle protruded from the machine's side. Andrew gave the handle a shove. A panel on the top of the device sprang open, revealing a flat metallic surface pitted with irregular holes.

"This thing's like a waffle iron, but I don't think it makes waffles," Andrew said. The holes were oval shaped—molds for something. Andrew accidentally kicked a dented bucket next to the table, causing a clatter.

He bent over, tilting the bucket to the light. Inside were hundreds of gold animal figures. He pulled a couple out. "They're little hippos," he said. "But look at the face. It's got the snout of a dinosaur or something." He threw one in the bucket and pocketed the other.

"Now you're a figurine connoisseur, moron?" Simon started walking toward Andrew. "Let me see one of those things."

"Shhh." Cami jumped to her feet, a finger over her mouth. "Listen!"

The boys stopped moving.

"I don't hear nothin'," Andrew said.

Then a growl, low and beastly, broke the silence. Simon grabbed Andrew's arm. Cami clutched Simon. It was some kind of animal, but which kind?

All three friends started searching the dark corners of the room.

Down the hallway, beside the porcelain tables, a key turned in the lock.

"Turn off the lights," Cami told Simon. "Get behind the shelves."

Simon punched the light switch off. In the darkness, he stumbled to join Andrew and Cami behind the shelf farthest away from the hall.

Within seconds, light flooded the room. Sarsour, Pothinus Sab's assistant, waddled into the basement, rolling his long linen sleeves away from his shriveled hands. He toddled between the shelves of tonic, muttering unintelligible things to himself. His gaze swept over the bottles. A clink of glass several rows away made him stop.

The little man walked out to the center of the basement.

"Ammit? Is you?" he asked in a choked, sandpapery voice. Sarsour tentatively edged his way toward the last shelf in the corner. "Ammit?"

He drew a hooked knife from his belt and jumped into the space between the wall and the last shelf.

Sarsour caught sight of Cami, Andrew, and Simon pressed into the corner. "What you children doing here?" he angrily screeched, advancing on them.

"We . . . we fell, sir. We were just visiting. Walked in the front door and fell," Simon tried to explain.

"It okay." He slowly advanced on the cornered trio, a half smile on his shriveled face. Raising the cruelly curved knife high above his head, he rasped, "You will not be here long."

CHAPTER 9

CROAKERS

"What you do here?" Sarsour demanded, inching closer. His face looked as if it had been burned and had yet to heal. "Tell me. Tell me."

"It's all a misunderstanding," Cami said. "We heard about Mr. Sab and wanted to see the Karnak Center."

"I don't believe you," Sarsour cawed.

Andrew palmed a pair of tonics off the shelf behind him, which he seriously considered chucking at Sarsour's wrinkled red face.

"You two get on wall!" the tiny man yelled, pointing the knife at the boys. "Girl, come with me. Come now."

The kids nervously eyed each other.

"Girl, you come now. Now!" Sarsour threateningly poked the knife in Cami's direction.

Andrew started to move. "It's okay," Cami told him,

blocking Andrew's advance with her arm. "Stay there. I'll be fine." Biting her lower lip, she stepped toward the knife-wielder.

Before Cami could take a full step, two rigid hands struck Sarsour at the base of his neck. The little man let out a choked gasp. Before he fell to the floor, the knife was plucked from his tiny hands. Standing behind Sarsour, now holding the little man's blade, was Mr. Shen.

"This is the second time I have found you where you should not be," Shen said with a warm smile. "Let's go. This place of death is not for the young."

"How did you find us here? Where did you come from?" Simon asked, suddenly emboldened.

"So many questions, Mr. Blabbingdale. I've been following you all morning. There is a storage room off that hall in the back. It has a very unsecure window." Shen eyed the bottles of tonic and then the piles of bones littering the floor. "It is time to leave," he said with some urgency. "Go, go, go. Down the hall. You all should accompany me to Peniel—to the museum."

Shen made sure the kids were well on their way. Before following them, he slowly turned his head, peering into the shadowy recesses of the basement. The bone piles troubled him. He clutched the knife defensively, as if expecting something to jump out at him. A brass bowl covered with a curious metal plate, topped by a gold animal figure, aroused his curiosity. He used the knife to pry open the lid. Inside were the bloody entrails of some poor creature, knotted up like deflated snakes. He quickly glanced over his shoulder, certain that something lurked in the gloom.

But rather than explore further, he decided it was more important to protect Will's friends. He laid the knife atop one of the porcelain mortuary tables and slipped down the hall.

"Deborah, if the children could perfect their gifts without assistance, I wouldn't even bring it up." Aunt Lucille had pulled Will's mother onto the sprawling front porch of her home to make her case. The rest of the family, including Dan, lunched in the kitchen. Flint-colored clouds moved in over the river.

"They need training. You don't want poor Leo illuminating like a streetlamp every time he gets upset. He has to learn to control it, dear. Otherwise it could get unseemly." Aunt Lucille stood very close to Deborah, her hands folded.

Deborah pushed strands of her hair behind her ears. Lines of worry showed on her forehead. "Dan won't go for this. He doesn't even know about Will's training. If we start shuttling Leo and Marin in and out of Peniel, he'll figure it out, Lucille."

"We don't have an option here. We can't let their extraordinary gifts wither."

"The kids are young. There'll be time to train them."

"There may not be." Aunt Lucille's blue eyes bore into Deborah. "The *Darkness* is increasing. That blood in the river was just the beginning. Leo and Marin have special gifts; they deserve a fighting chance to make full use of them. We may *need* them."

"I don't want my children recruited into some secret battle, Lucille."

"Neither do I. Though, if that is their destiny . . ." She laid a hand on Deborah's arm. "Ours is not to question the gift or to determine its final purpose but to protect and perfect it. Help me do that for your children."

Deborah slightly shook her head, looking back into the front door of the house. "I don't know how smart this is."

"If we don't train them now, they could hurt themselves and possibly others. Is that what you want?" The question hung in the air like a slap in the face.

Aunt Lucille's glance drifted down to the river. In memory, she saw herself at thirteen, alone in tears behind the house, torched trees and a burning fence surrounding her. She'd been returning home from a friend's house when something invisible slashed at her from the darkness. In the blind tussle to defend herself, she'd accidentally touched her fingers and thumbs together, forming a perfect triangle. A red-and-white ray exploded from her fingers in every direction. The sudden surge of power drained her energy, and she lost consciousness. Minutes later, she awoke to her mother screaming from the second-floor window of the house. "Sarah Lucille. What have you done? What have you done?" she shouted. One of the huge oaks had been cut away from what was now a blackened stump. The top of a picket fence framing her mother's vegetable garden smoldered. Little Lucille stared in shock at her glowing hands and wept.

"Okay, fine," Deborah said softly. "You can train the kids. But Dan can't know. We'll do it right after school and only for an hour. No more than an hour."

Aunt Lucille instantly wrapped Deborah in her arms. "Thank you, Deb. This is the right decision."

"What is the right decision?" Dan stepped out on the porch. He eyed his aunt warily.

Before Lucille could respond, Deborah cut in. "I'm going to do a piece on a new exhibit at the museum. . . ."

"It's a wonderful collection of Mary Magdalene relics. . . ." Aunt Lucille followed Deborah's lead. "We have her actual skull from the Basilica of St. Maximin in France, her tooth from the Met, and a splendid reliquary of her foot from a Roman church. We had the relic itself here for years. . . ."

Dan looked at his wife as if he could read her thoughts. "You told her about Leo, didn't you?"

"Told me what about Leo?" Lucille deadpanned.

"I know exactly what you're thinking. You've got to train Leo because some dark force is rising." Dan leaned against the porch banister, his back to the river. "You don't give up, do you?"

"Surrender was never my strong suit," Aunt Lucille said, returning Dan's stare. "*You* were trained, dear. It didn't pan out, but we tried. . . ."

Deborah draped an arm around her husband's neck. "Let's go inside," she said.

"I don't want to go inside." Dan straightened up. "Aunt Lucille, do not fill the children's heads with your . . . exaggerations. There will be no training. It's empty fantasy."

"The Bottom Dwellers were fantasies? That bloody river was fantasy?" Aunt Lucille's voice got shrill. "The *Sinestri are* rising, Dan. You can close your eyes all you want. I know they are coming."

Drawn by the raised voices, Will, Leo, and Marin wandered out through one of the huge floor-to-ceiling windows that opened onto the porch.

"The water commissioner testified today that it could have been silt that colored the river. Red silt!" Dan thundered.

"These demons are *real*—as you well remember. Bartimaeus still has the scars from shielding you, Dan. The beast slashed him horribly. Whether you acknowledge it or not, Son, grave evil and wondrous miracles surround us."

Will spoke up. "A demon attacked you, Dad? When did that happen?"

Dan seethed, his temples pulsing. He glared at his aunt. "Aunt Lucille is making up stories, kids. She's good at that, making up stories—"

SPLUT . . . SPLUT . . . SPLUT . . . SPLUT . . . SPLUT . . .

Dull splatting noises, like buckets of pudding hitting the wood siding, could be heard all over the house.

Aunt Lucille's eyes got big as saucers. They swept over the baby-blue floorboards of the porch, where the sound seemed most intense. She rushed over to the open window, pushing the kids back in the house.

"Everybody inside," she demanded sharply, lowering the window in front of them.

"What is this . . . a . . . a . . . game? What are you playing at now?" Dan trailed Aunt Lucille as she slammed the shutters on the other windows. "Answer me!"

"Deborah, take your husband inside," Lucille commanded.

SPLUT . . . SPLUT . . . SPLUT . . .

"What is that?" Deborah asked.

"You'll want to be inside, Deb. Trust me," Lucille told her. "Go on."

Deborah relented, but not Dan.

"Once in a while, you should consider a natural explanation for the things that happen. This endless demon talk is scaring the children," Dan chided Lucille.

She defiantly folded her arms, leaning into Dan's face. "The children will be fine. It's the scared adults I'm worried about, dear." She slowly turned to face the river. Dan frowned, turning his head toward the water as well. He did a double take.

SPLUT . . . SPLUT . . . CROOOOAK . . . SPLUT . . . SPLUT . . . CROOOOAK

Out of the river, a slow-motion wave of blackness rolled toward them. As it advanced, Dan realized it was not the tide but thousands of slick black frogs hopping over each other toward the house.

"Oh no . . . Why are they . . . coming?" Dan stammered.

"Go inside, Dan, and close the door behind you," Lucille instructed in a steady voice. "Protect the children. The frogs are surrounding the house. Pray they don't get inside." The low croaking and the sounds of slimy bodies slamming into the floorboards beneath her feet intensified. "Go ahead—try to convince me this plague has nothing to do with the Staff of Moses."

Dan didn't answer her. He scooted inside the house, shutting the door behind him.

Lucille rolled back her sleeves, pressed her forefingers and thumbs together to form a triangle, and inhaled deeply, closing her eyes. She abruptly extended her two arms, sending a blinding ray of light toward the riverbank. The beam cut into the bouncing wall of frogs, dissolving every one it touched to a green and red mist.

Elsewhere in Perilous Falls, the black croakers were flopping out of drains and fountains. Any source of water vomited hundreds of sleek ebony frogs.

Children in the Perilous Falls Park squealed when they saw the creatures advancing on the green grass. They raced to the top of play sets, trying to escape the croaking horror closing in on all sides. Helpless parents bounded up slides and embraced their children on plastic bridges to keep them from falling into the roiling black chaos below.

At city hall, screeching brakes and the sound of what she initially thought were cicadas outside caused Mayor Lynch to glance out her corner window. On Main Street, she saw five cars and a bus crash into one another as if they'd hit an ice patch.

"What in the . . . ," Lynch muttered to herself, reaching for her desk phone. Her index finger poked the keypad. "Heinrich, get Animal Control up here and peek out your window. It looks like somebody covered downtown in asphalt. The grass, the street, everything is covered in . . . frogs! Black frogs! I'm calling Pothinus Sab. This is madness. . . ." She slammed the phone onto its cradle and dialed Sab.

Pothinus Sab couldn't hear the ringing. He was on the packed front steps of the Karnak Center welcoming people onto the property.

"Come, my children, come." He wore a glossy white collarless suit that made him look like a Middle Eastern angel. His arms opened wide. "Isn't it good that the Karnak Center is here for you? Isn't it?"

Hundreds of people from the neighborhood who had congregated on the front and side lawn of the Karnak Center applauded. Many stared in amazement at the wrathful frogs that hopped right up to the curb of Dura Street and occupied the de Plancy Cemetery, but stopped at the border of the Karnak land.

One heavyset man and his friend stomped over the undulating black street to find safe harbor on the pristine grass of Karnak. The big man's boat shoes and the bottom of his overalls were stained with red-and-black goo. "Answer me something, Mr. Sab?" the man asked. "How come those frogs are all over my yard, all over town, but not up on your property?"

Sab descended the stairs of the Center and approached the fellow, placing two hands on his thick shoulders. "It is the positive energy holding them back. It is the regenerative forces we curate and extend from here that protects. What is your name, my friend?"

The hefty man pulled the toothpick from the side of his mouth. "Mikey, sir. This here's my friend Harry." He indicated an ashen, lanky man in a faded seersucker suit at his side.

"I am glad you are here." Sab laid a thin hand on Harry's shoulder as well. "Tomorrow I want you to come back. The protection of the Karnak Center can be yours every day. I want you never to lose the safety you are feeling now. Will you return tomorrow?"

Harry stared at him warily, but Mikey, caught in the moment, nodded. "I will come back, sir. We will."

"Good. I expect all of you back here tomorrow for the grand opening. It will be a life-changing event for us all. Tell your friends." Sab turned to the crowd, touching the faces of children and embracing the elderly as he walked toward the front door. "Isn't it sad that the local government, the politicians, the religious leaders, everyone seems powerless to help you in this moment? But Pothinus told you trials were coming. Did I not? Let us hope these horrible frogs will disperse. But in the meanwhile, take your ease. You will be safe here at Karnak. We have some refreshments for you. Stay as long as you like."

Sab snapped his fingers at Sarsour, who on his command carried a tray of drinks through the crowd. The people applauded and peppered the air with cries of gratitude.

Harry Johnson turned to his friend. "Mikey, unless that bearded fella's going to teach us to fly, how in the blazes are we going to get home?" He poked a finger at the croaking mass just three feet away that seemed to be held back by some invisible wall.

Between the slats of the front window, Will peered at Aunt Lucille on the porch of her home as she continued to cut down the frogs at an astounding pace. In the wake of her ray's passing, a smoky mist lingered at the river's edge. But as soon as it cleared, another battalion of frogs leapt forward.

Leo and Marin sat tensely with their parents on a curvy Victorian sofa. The *SPLUT, SPLUT, SPLUT* noises came from all sides of the living room. Leo raised his voice to say, "I have a question: Can I get a jar from the kitchen to catch a few frogs? Remember, when Wally the Turtle died, you told me I could get another pet. I want a frog."

Deborah rubbed his knee. "Let's pick pets another day. I don't think these frogs are ready to be domesticated."

"But, Mommy, I've never seen frogs like those ones," Marin said, her eyes huge. "If Leo gets a boy, can I have a girl frog?"

"It's my idea, Marin," Leo protested, his full lips turning down. "She cannot have a frog, Mom!"

An exhausted Aunt Lucille burst into the room, slamming the door behind her. Her face was moist. "There are too many of them. This is not an isolated event. The frogs are pouring out all along the river." Lucille bolted suddenly to a cabinet in the corner of the living room. She pulled out two round silver containers that looked like fancy ice buckets.

Will joined her in the corner. "I need to see the Book of Prophecy now!"

"Can we put down the frog invasion first?"

Will stamped his foot and sighed. "What is that?" he asked, eyeing the silver containers.

"Exorcized salt. It's blessed. I have to spread it outside to keep these croaking devils away from the house."

"Aunt Lucille," Leo called out, eyeing the silver containers, "can I use one of them to catch a frog?"

"Not now, dear. You wouldn't want to catch one of these stinky things," she said, giving him a peck on the head.

Will's cell phone buzzed. It was a text from Cami:

We're safe at the museum. Mr. Shen rescued us from Karnak Center. Lots to tell you about Bobbit!!! Where r u?

Will texted her back:

**Stay put. Don't leave museum. Frogs every-
where down here. I'll be there as soon as I can.**

He had barely hit SEND when the back door of the living room flew open, startling everybody.

Abbot Athanasius bounded in as if escaping a battle-field. He shut the door with the back of his shoulder, nearly crashing into Will. "William, I'm glad you're here."

At his side, he clutched a souped-up water gun, identical to the one in Lucille's ballroom. He greeted the rest of the Wilder family and then conferred with Lucille.

"I barely made it across your yard. Thank goodness for Philip's pressure washer here." He patted the side of the gun and laid it on the end table. "Nasty little things, those croakers. Unless we intervene, what's next, Lucille?"

"Gnats I'd expect," she said nonchalantly, pushing the pair of silver containers on him.

"But why? Why would the *Sinestri* want to use Moses's staff to torture a whole populace?" Athanasius's eyes searched the air. "These plagues are part of their plan. I just can't imagine what that plan is."

"We'll get to the bottom of this, Abbot," Lucille said, pushing back her sleeves again. "But first I need to sur-round the house with this salt—if you could help me? I'll clear a path with my illuminating beam. You spill the salt behind me."

Across the room, Dan Wilder was transfixed by his cell phone. "I have to go to city hall. You all . . . stay . . . stay here." He kissed Deborah and hugged the children. "Willy Stout and one of his officers are picking me up in an SUV. He says it's a mess out there. Accidents and . . . frogs. Don't drive, Deb."

There was a pounding on the back door. Through the glass, Dan could see Sheriff Stout carrying a bloodied shovel.

"Darned things came out of nowhere," the sheriff said, sticking his head in the door. "How y'all doin? Come on, Dan, I'll get ahead a' you and scoop 'em out of the way so we can make it to the vehicle. Hope you're not wearing your good shoes." He pinched the brim of his hat as a goodbye and started shoveling a path through the yard. Dan followed him out.

Through the window, Will watched the two men wade slowly into the sea of black frogs. As they progressed, the wriggling black creatures closed ranks behind them.

"It seems rather fantastical, doesn't it?" Abbot Athanasius quietly asked Will, standing behind him.

"It's crazy. I need to go see my friends and—"

"That would be unwise. You have to remain close to Peniel and you should restrict your conversations to your family and the Brethren only."

"One of the Brethren took the staff." Will grimaced. "One of them caused all of this."

Athanasius inhaled, tugging at his beard with two fingers. "We will discover who took the staff in time, William. This is about your safety. There are no frogs at Peniel; there was no blood in the water there. It is hallowed ground. The *Sinestri*'s power can only move through human agents at Peniel. The Brethren have—"

"The Brethren can't be trusted," Will spat out. "If you all know what's happening, why can't you stop it?" Will stared at Athanasius for a long moment. "Some of the Brethren think Mr. Bart and I took the staff. I need to figure out what's going on and clear our names."

Aunt Lucille walked over, sensing the tension. "Will, have a rest while the abbot and I spread this salt. We'll have a nice discussion together when we finish." The abbot picked up the silver containers and without another word moved to the front door. Lucille trailed him out onto the porch.

In moments, Will could see the glow of Aunt Lucille's red ray between the slats blocking the front window. The children and Deb ran over to peek through the cracks of the closed shutters.

Will knew he had only minutes. He slipped his pith helmet on and picked up the abbot's high-powered water gun. "It's now or never," he said to himself.

Silently, he opened the back door, hooked his finger around the gun's trigger, and stepped into the croaking swamp of frogs blocking the high cliffs of Peniel.

CHAPTER 10

THE SECOND PROPHECY

Mayor Lynch barged into Judge Solomon Blabbingdale's chambers at city hall, ignoring the clerks and a secretary in the outer office.

The judge sat at the rear of his oak-lined room, a cell phone to his ear. He held a finger up to the mayor as she entered. "Ava, with all this excitement, I'm trying to locate my son, Simon," he said in his clinical manner. In a few moments, he hung up with annoyance. "He isn't answering. He told me he was meeting with some friends." The judge placed the phone back in the drawer and looked at the mayor through his tiny gold spectacles. "Have a chair, Ava."

"I come on official business, urgent business."

"So it appears." He wobbled his head a bit. "Am I supposed to guess?"

"There is another animal outbreak in town and as a

matter of public safety we have to use our powers to stop it," the mayor said calmly.

"I don't sign restraining orders on animals—rather hard to enforce. What do you need, Ava?"

She dropped the folder she had been carrying like a concealed weapon onto the desktop. "Everything's there, the photographs, weeks' and weeks' worth of data . . . I need an arrest warrant. It's already written, there at the back. It just needs your signature, sugar." Mayor Lynch sat in the stiff chair facing the judge's desk. She crossed her legs and assumed the air of someone awaiting the final polish at the nail salon.

Judge Blabbingdale released a light whistle as he flipped through the folder. He pulled his spectacles down to the edge of his nose and slid the folder back to her. "Ava. There is not enough here to justify an arrest. This is all circumstantial. Is she a threat to the community?"

"Yes, I believe she is."

"Pictures in a boat near a gator infestation, or whatever it was, are not evidence—"

"Lucille Wilder is responsible for all of it. That is the finding of our investigative committee. I'm not making this up. Her own nephew is a committee member."

"Dan is?" The judge pulled the folder back and scanned the papers. "It's not enough, Ava. I can't authorize her detention." He opened his palms toward her. "I'm sorry."

"Then I'll need to have a hearing to question *everyone* even remotely associated with Lucille Wilder." She rifled through the folder until she found the picture she sought. "Have you seen this picture, Judge?" She slapped it on the desktop. "Now, why is your little Simon in the company of Lucille and these suspected figures? Everywhere Tobias Shen or Bartimaeus Johnson or Dan's boy shows up, trouble follows. And there's little Simon Blabbingdale right in the thick of it." She yanked two more photos out, poking a nail at the images. "Isn't that your son there? And *there*?"

"Oh, Ava, stop it."

"Sign the warrant. She needs to be questioned in court. Lucille Wilder is the link to all these odd events. She's controlling these outbreaks. First the gator things, then blood in the river, now a frog infestation. For the sake of this town, we have to stop her."

The judge sneered at the documents and photos littering his desk and let out a little whistle.

Water spewed from Will's gun, dousing the frogs blocking his way. The instant the blessed water hit them, the frogs emitted weird constricted burps and dissolved into a mist. Will raced through Aunt Lucille's backyard, clearing a path as he proceeded—never letting go of the trigger.

Anticipating the spray, the frogs started to frantically leap atop one another.

Will made it through the clearing, past the massive oak trees to the edge of the winding, rocky path that led up to

Peniel. The steep trail seemed to be made of black liquid, roiling and bubbling as the slick frogs jostled about. Pressing forward, Will continued his relentless spray. Except for the nasty sulfur smell when the frogs dissolved, he was sort of enjoying himself. It was kind of like a video game with reeking special effects.

As he neared the top of the rocky hill, he pumped the trigger. Only spurts of water emerged from the gun's nozzle. The holy water reservoir was drained. To ward off the insane hoppers, he desperately ran the butt of the gun along the ground. After he hit one frog, it tumbled like an off-kilter golf ball landing on its back. A high-pitched growling sound flew from its gaping mouth. Looking closely into the open jaws, Will spotted a row of serrated, yellow teeth. "Glad I didn't see that earlier," he said to himself, swatting the amphibian to the side without delay.

As he neared Peniel, he noticed something. The frogs had moved away from him even without being hit by the holy water. There was a clear circular zone at his feet through which the frogs did not advance. As he inched forward, the frogs continued to back off, preserving the unobstructed circle around him. *This is weird.*

Afraid to press his luck, Will dashed into the front gates of Peniel, where not one fanged frog breached the property. It was a marvel and a relief. He pushed through the heavy front door and sought out his friends.

He could hear them in Bethel Hall, beyond the outer library, with Bartimaeus and Mr. Shen. He thought it best to stow the gun in the library before going farther.

"Will-man, what took you so long?" Andrew asked, shoving Will gently as he came into Bethel Hall.

"There were—*are*—a lot of frogs outside."

"Frogs?" Mr. Shen asked, leaning his head back. "What do you mean, Mr. Wilder?"

"They came up out of the river. Millions of them. Black, slimy things—and they have teeth."

Bartimaeus laughed bitterly. "How'd I know when he said frogs, he wasn't talkin' about Kermit?" he told Shen. "So gnats and fiery hail and all the rest'll be coming soon. Hmmm. We gotta do somethin' for the people, Tobias. Somethin' to shield 'em."

"You four, stay indoors," Shen said, pointing at the quartet. "No frog hunting, Mr. Wilder."

He motioned to Bartimaeus to follow him down the main hallway. But just as he went to move, the diminutive Brother Philip, a man with parted black hair and intense eyes, came stomping his way. Valens chased after him. Like a Jack Russell terrier on two legs, Philip barked down the hallway, "Where is the abbot or Lucille?"

"Neither of them is here," Shen said. "There is an amphibian explosion outside. I imagine that is occupying them at the moment."

"There're going to be some explosions inside too," Brother Philip said in his usual conspiratorial voice. He had a peculiar way of positioning himself at an angle from whomever he was addressing. Then he would side-speak at them. It gave whatever Philip said the air of a state secret. Just what one would expect from a former CIA technical intelligence officer. "Valens and I just found something in Baldwin's office that I think you all should see."

"It's all very sad," Valens said, looking forlorn. "But at least now we know . . ."

"Does it have somethin' to do with the missing staff?" Bartimaeus asked.

"Yes, it does," Philip said, cautiously eyeing the kids.

"We shall take things as we find them," Shen said, grimacing. He started off down the hall, followed by Philip and Valens.

"We've got frogs outside and snakes inside," Bartimaeus said to himself. He turned to Will and his friends. "Stay indoors, you hear?"

They all nodded.

"Mr. Bart, I need to use the restroom. Can you open the door for me?" Will stood before the door marked PRIVATE.

Bartimaeus rifled through his pockets, found his key ring, and released the lock. "So when you're through, pull the door shut. It'll lock behind you."

"Sure thing," Will said.

Bartimaeus hobbled after Tobias and the others. As soon as he was out of sight, Will held the door open for his friends. "Come on. Come on," he urged them.

"Where are you taking us?" Cami asked as she passed into the small stoned foyer. "I assume we are not going to the bathroom."

"My great-grandfather's office is upstairs. There's something I need to do."

On the way up the tight spiral stone staircase, Simon shared everything they had seen at the Karnak Center earlier. "The Sab guy demanded two fresh geese a day from Mr. Bobbit. Why does he need two fresh geese? And there were bones all over the floor of the basement," Simon said.

"Then this creepy little guy that looked like a raisin was going to stab us," Andrew added. "If your friend Mr. Shen hadn't come along, we would have been the next bones on the floor." Everyone quieted when they reached the top of the staircase and saw the imposing ancient mahogany door. Two metal bands ran side to side with a great black hole at the center.

Will dug his great-aunt's key out of his backpack.

"Where'd you get that?" Cami asked, suspiciously regarding the gold cross key in his hand.

"From my aunt Lucille." Will held the key with both hands just as he had seen Aunt Lucille do each time they ventured up to Jacob Wilder's office. He plunged his hands into the black hole in the middle of the door. All around it were carved figures in anguish. Will twisted his wrists to the right, then to the left. Two metal panels shot out from the sides, trapping his wrists inside.

"This doesn't look good," Simon said, nervously eyeing the ceiling and the ground. "Is the floor going to crumble or something? Should you be doing that?"

A repetition of clunking noises reverberated in the hall.

"It's just the door opening. Don't worry. I've seen my aunt do this lots of times."

Just then, the panels holding his wrists slid back and the door opened automatically.

"What did I tell you?" Will said, walking into the generous office.

"Are we supposed to be in here?" Cami asked, taking in the rounded room and the weird artifacts stacked about. There were piles of books everywhere and shelves loaded with swords, a skull, and odd-shaped jars. Near the entryway sat a sarcophagus overflowing with coins, goblets, and even jewelry.

"Was your great-grandfather a pirate or something?" Andrew asked, ogling the loot.

"No, he was not a pirate. He was a collector, a protector of historic items. Items with special powers." Will walked behind the tank of a mahogany desk at the rear of the room and turned toward the fireplace on the back wall. "Guys, I need you to turn around. I've got to do something here."

They did as they were told and all three friends faced the entryway. Though Simon had to make a comment as he turned. "If water starts filling this place, or anything peculiar happens, I want you to know that I am leaving, Will. I mean it."

Will already had his hands on the heads of the two stone angels carved into the fireplace. He spun them simultaneously. A panel above the mantel slid to the side and a weathered, olive-colored book emerged. He returned the angel heads to their original positions and invited his friends to come behind the desk.

"Andrew, can you pick the book up and place it on the desktop?" Will asked.

"Are you going to do a magic trick or something?" Andrew responded.

"No, I'm not doing a magic trick. I just can't touch it yet."

Cami's eyes narrowed. "Why can't you touch it?"

"You'll see in a minute," Will said.

Andrew lifted the huge book from the mantel. Seven hinged locks, each a unique sculpted claw or hand, wrapped around the outer edge of the book. Every lock but one marked a different page in the great volume. Andrew carefully laid it on the desk.

Will's friends gathered around to stare at the book. Aged copper curlicues surrounded a leather panel at the center of the cover. The strange gold calligraphy on the panel read:

The Prophecy of Abbot Anthony the Wise

The Lord came to me upon the waters and said:
Take thee a great book and write upon it as I instruct thee.
My spirit trembled, for the visions He placed in my head
    frightened me.

Still, I write in obedience:

In those days, when the people have grown hard of heart

and belief has dwindled;

when wickedness has become commonplace; and the Brethren

 have broken their unity;

then shall I raise up a young one to lead them.

He shall be the firstborn of the root of Wilder.

He shall have the sight of the angels

and perceive darkness from light.

Behold, when his time is ripe, he shall come riding on a colt,

 the foal of a donkey, and his blood shall spill.

This shall be the sign that the battle is near

and all must prepare.

For in those days the beasts shall rise from the pit

to test my people . . .

"A donkey. You rode a donkey at your brother's birthday party. And your hand was bleeding." Simon backed away a bit. "Who are you leading, Will? Who are the beasts?"

"Calm down, Simon. I'll explain everything later. Have you seen what is happening outside? Look out the window."

Simon turned to the arched slit of a window behind him. Thousands and thousands of frogs swarmed over the land outside Peniel's gates.

"Do you want that to continue? Do you want to see worse?" Will told him. "I have to read the new prophecy to see what's coming and what I'm supposed to do." Will threw his pith helmet onto the desktop and extended his hands toward the ancient book.

"Is there some key to open it?" Cami whispered.

"Just my hands. When the time is right, the next prophecy opens for me." Will drew a deep breath, rubbed his palms together, and grabbed the sides of the book. It quivered at his touch. The first lock, which resembled a reptilian forearm and claw, snapped open. Then the second lock, a carved hairy arm with talons, unhinged as well.

The three friends startled at the suddenness of the book's action.

"Oh no, oh no," Simon kept saying, jigging as if he needed to make a bathroom run.

"It's okay, Simon. It's time." Will gawked at the book as it slowly spread open to the second prophecy. Andrew and Cami did not so much as breathe. Simon panted in the corner, nervously eyeing the exposed prophecy. "It's just a book; it's just a book; it's just a book," he whispered to himself.

Will leaned over the volume and read the slanted calligraphy:

The Lord came upon the waters again and spoke:
Woe to my rebellious children who carry out a plan not mine own;
They make a pact with the Darkness
and seek shelter in the shadow of Egypt.
They embrace the idols of the Sinestri and wallow in their anger.

The day of their calamity is at hand.

When the Staff of Moses is taken by force, the Darkness shall stir
    once more.

For then the second of the SEVEN beasts shall rise.

This one hides itself,

feeding off the wrath of the people and the fatted geese.

This raven wolf of death shall use Moses's staff to unleash
    plagues upon the people.

But it is my chosen one it seeks to destroy.

For at the conclusion of the three days of darkness,

the last plague will bring death to the firstborn of the house of
    Wilder.

To save himself and the people,

my chosen one must wield a staff even more powerful than the
    rod of Moses:

the STAFF OF AARON.

Both staffs must be retrieved and safeguarded or all will be lost.

To preserve his vision and commit no evil,

my chosen one must forsake all anger.

I shall give him authority over the unclean spirit,

but he must take nothing to confront the beast except Aaron's
    staff.

Silence and trust shall be his strength,

and assure his victory over AMON.

A great rush of air suddenly whipped through the room. From the sarcophagus near the door, coins and gold cups tinkled onto the floor. The stone casket seemed to be coughing up everything within it.

"I knew it. I knew something peculiar would happen. We shouldn't be here," Simon squeaked.

Will grabbed a rusted sword from the shelf along the wall. He nervously pointed it toward the sarcophagus. A pair of hands thrust up through the coins still in the stone box. The kids screamed in terror as the hands clutched the outer walls of the coffin.

Cami threw her arms around the hysterical Simon.

"You've got super vision. Is that a rising beast?" Andrew asked, a lump in his throat. "Is that a rising BEAST?"

"I'm not sure," Will murmured.

CHAPTER 11

THE AMULET OF AMMIT

Brother Philip and Valens led Tobias and Bartimaeus down several frescoed hallways. They passed through the shadowy outer herb garden and into the remains of a thirteenth-century monastery, reconstructed on Peniel's grounds.

Philip whispered sideways to Tobias as they marched down the stone hallway. "I went to Baldwin's office to ask him for the keys to the mechanical shed. Valens had been helping me in the workshop, so he came along too. I needed some gears for a project I'm working on. We walk in. The vicar's gone. I figured we'd borrow the key to the shed and leave him a note."

"I fetched the key from the cabinet on the wall," Valens said, wide-eyed. "Philip began writing his note at the desk and that's when he kicked it with his foot."

"Kicked what?" Shen asked.

Philip threw open the door to Baldwin's tight, neat office. There were schedules on the wall and shelves of old volumes arranged by size. A pair of bronze boxing gloves on the middle shelf acted as a bookend. Only a fountain pen and some writing papers populated the vicar's desk. Brother Philip pulled back the chair as if exposing a murder weapon.

"See for yourselves," he whispered accusingly.

Shen squatted down. Jammed between the wall and the desk, something glinted in the dark. He pulled at the gold, jewel-encrusted object, freeing it from its hiding place.

"That's the covering of Moses's staff. Don't this beat all?" Bartimaeus said. "And the vicar was trying to pin the robbery on Will and me. So where's the sapphire staff?"

"Baldwin probably knows where it is," Philip piped up. "I'm only glad Valens found it with me or people might have thought I had planted it."

Tobias Shen stared at the golden covering, his eyebrows rising. "We should inform the abbot, and for the time being, let us tell Baldwin nothing."

"Whatever you say, Tobias," Philip droned. "But you have to admit, it doesn't look good for the vicar. Come on, Valens, I need those gears."

Valens nodded apologetically and left with Philip.

"If we can't find that staff, we've got to help defuse its power." Bartimaeus scratched at his forehead. "There must be somethin' we can do to protect this town."

Tobias rapped the edge of Bart's crutches with the jeweled sleeve. "I have an idea." His broad smile caused creases to erupt all over his face. "We shall take matters into our own hands. We must move quick, quick. Get the key to the garage, but don't leave a note, Bart."

"If he wants a note, the vicar'll have to get a pen pal," Bartimaeus said, reaching into the key cabinet.

Whatever crawled up from the sarcophagus in Jacob Wilder's office did not slow its advance. Will ordered his friends to stay behind the desk. He drew closer to the stone coffin while more coins and golden trinkets tumbled to the floor.

Will held the rusty sword over his head and waited for the thing to emerge from the casket of coins and jewels. Cami and Simon huddled in the corner. Andrew stood beside Will, his fists at the ready in case his help was needed.

Then all at once, with a spray of coins, Aunt Lucille popped up in the sarcophagus.

"I had forgotten how much junk my father piled into this thing," she said, breathing hard. "I thought it would be quicker to come this way rather than fight my way through the frogs. Though maybe I was wrong." She started to laugh, running her hands through her strawberry-blond locks. Her mood instantly darkened when she saw Will's friends. "Oh, Will, what have you done? Your friends shouldn't be part of this. Do you realize the danger you've placed them in?"

"Danger? What kind of danger?" Simon asked, shell-shocked. "Wait. How did you get here?"

"That's a bit involved." Aunt Lucille stood up in the coffin and shook some coins from her silken sleeves. She spied the open Book of Prophecy on the desktop and shot daggers at Will. "Well, everyone has read it, I suppose," she complained. "Time for me to have a go." She excused herself and walked behind the desk, reading the words she had protected for more than forty years.

After scanning the calligraphy, she asked, "So where is Amon? Have you seen the demon, Will?"

"No, ma'am. All I know is Max told us that a raven was coming. Amon must be the raven," Will said.

Simon wandered over to the empty sarcophagus and tapped the floor of the stone casket with his foot. "Miss Lucille, how did you get in here? Is there a trick door?"

"Something like that," she said, turning back to Will. "We must locate the staff, dear. We can't risk the demon unleashing any more plagues. Each one puts you in more peril."

Will's legs turned to jelly at her words. He started to lose his balance.

Aunt Lucille caught him by the shoulders. "No fear now . . . I won't let anything happen to you, Will."

"I know you won't," he said, only half convinced. "It's just . . . the prophecy says that the last plague brings death to the firstborn of the house of Wilder—that's me! The demon 'seeks to destroy' ME!"

"It seeks to destroy us all. We'll find the staff before anything happens," Aunt Lucille said stoically. "We've got to." Will and his friends told Lucille everything they had observed at Bobbit's Bestiary and the Karnak Center: the delivery of the geese, how Sarsour tried to kill them, and about the bones and potions in the basement.

"Do you all think Pothinus Sab knows who or what is eating the fattened geese?" Aunt Lucille asked.

"He could be eating the geese himself. Maybe he's Amon?" Cami wondered.

"Let's not repeat that name too much," Aunt Lucille whispered, shaking a finger at Cami. "Amon is a demon—a very ancient, powerful demon. It feeds off hatred and anger. It will whip up resentment wherever it can. The prophecy says that the people 'embrace the idols of the *Sinestri'*—but what idols? Have you seen people with idols?"

"*Sinestri*? My brother had a dream about that," Cami said, inching toward Aunt Lucille. "What is a *Sinestri*?"

"They're a league of major demons. The enemy. I don't mean to scare you children, and I wish you knew nothing of this. But you're so far in that there is no turning back now. Will's great-grandfather battled these beasts and *we* continue to battle them today."

Simon's eyes were the size of Ping-Pong balls. Andrew frowned, his hands in his pockets, as if the thoughts racing through his head actually hurt. Cami furiously stroked the end of her ponytail, trying to process all she was hearing.

Aunt Lucille opened her arms to the kids in an obvious

attempt to calm them. "Now look, it's not as bad as you're imagining. Demons are not all powerful. They can be defeated." She placed her hands on her hips and looked each one of them in the eye. "As I think about it . . . maybe you all are meant to be in this battle. Each of you could aid Will and collect information. You could be our eyes and ears in town. Who would suspect a group of kids? But I must swear each of you to secrecy. The more people you share this with, even your families, the more danger you place us all in. You're *collaborators* now. Can you keep the prophecy and Will's role in it a secret?"

All three agreed. Andrew suddenly jumped, a light in his eyes. "Could this be an idol?" he asked Aunt Lucille. From his pocket he produced the small golden figurine he had pinched from the Karnak Center's basement.

Aunt Lucille gingerly plucked the thing from Andrew's palm with her two fingers. She turned it in the faint light leaking through the window and groaned. "It's Ammit. See the crocodile head, the front legs of the lion, and the rear of a hippo? Ammit is an Egyptian mythological creature—a rather nasty one."

"Wait, that crazy peewee at the Karnak Center said 'Ammit' when he came into the basement. Remember?" Simon said. "He was calling for Ammit."

Cami and Andrew nodded in fearful affirmation.

"That's very odd," Aunt Lucille said, thoughtfully looking off in the distance. "Here's what I know. At the final judgment, ancient Egyptians believed that the heart of the dead were weighed on a great scale—a feather on one side, the heart on the other. If the heart was heavy with sin, it tipped the scale, and Ammit consumed it. The creature was known as the Devourer of the Dead. I can't imagine why anyone would want an amulet of such a horrible creature. Where did you get this?"

"From the basement of the Karnak Center—there were hundreds of them," Andrew said.

She went to return it to him, but Andrew raised his hands, unwilling to touch the amulet again. "You can have it," he said.

"The Karnak Center's grand opening is tomorrow. Pothinus Sab is promising to protect people," Cami said. "My mother is a huge fan of his. She's even taking my brother there for some kind of therapy."

Aunt Lucille snapped her fingers. "You all should tag along with Cami and her family. Afterward, come back and tell me everything you see. As risky as it is, you should go as well, Will. You'll see *things* your friends might miss." She raised her eyebrows for emphasis.

"I need to find the Staff of Moses and Aaron's rod," Will said.

"Sab could be your link to finding them. Figure out who is feeding on anger and the fattened geese and you'll find the Staff of Moses," Aunt Lucille said. "By the way, where is my key?" She raised an open palm to Will.

He sheepishly dug in his pocket and handed it over. "I had to read the prophecy."

"I understand, dear," she said bitingly, turning from him. Lucille asked Cami to step aside since she was standing in front of a black metal door built into the stone wall. Lucille slipped her key into the door's lock. "You kids should go to the other side of the room, over by the sarcophagus." Once they were in place, she turned the key and pried open the arched metal door.

Will squinted in anguish at what he saw inside. Swirling black shadows hovered over the assorted objects piled high within. A huge gilded mirror was turned on its side. What appeared to be a sculpture of a withered gray hand sat upright on a marble table. Aunt Lucille placed the amulet of Ammit next to the hand, closed the safe door, and engaged the lock.

"You may want to question that Mr. Bobbit," Aunt Lucille advised, slipping the chain holding the key around her neck. "Surely he knows who's eating his fowl."

Will sidled up to Aunt Lucille. "What is that? Is it a safe?"

"It's a thing you should never open," she whispered. "My father stored dark artifacts there—anything he thought too dangerous to leave lying about." She glimpsed fear in Will's face. "You saw something inside?"

"Shadows. Lots of them," he said gravely.

Lucille reached into the small front drawer of her father's desk. "I want you to wear something for me." She held up a simple silver ring with a circular glass bubble where a stone should have been. Inside, something solid and brown clung to the glass.

"What is it?" Will asked, slipping it on his finger.

"It belonged to my father. That's the blood of St. Januarius in there. The Italians call him San Gennaro. He was a fourth-century martyr. As you can see, the blood is dry, hard as a rock." She pointed to the oval glass brooch on her lapel and whispered, "My brooch also contains Januarius's blood. When either of us is in danger, the blood will liquefy in both the ring and the brooch. It's a good way to keep tabs on each other. Keep that ring on your hand when you go to the Karnak Center."

Simon, overhearing the tail end of their conversation, announced to the room, "Well, it looks like another fun-filled field trip to the Karnak Center for us."

Andrew was preoccupied by what he saw out the window. "Uh, how are we going to get past these frogs?" he asked.

"Miss Lucille, can we take your sarcophagus home?" Simon inquired.

"It's not public transportation, Simon."

"But you traveled here in it, right?"

"What a clever boy you are. Such an imagination," Aunt Lucille said, closing up the Book of Prophecy.

Will had his eyes on the Veil of the Virgin, the silk relic under glass he had seen his aunt carry up from the vault. Staring at it on the side shelf, he had a thought: *If this demon Amon feeds on anger, and this relic can dissolve anger . . . it might not be a bad idea to keep it close.*

"You all should spend the night here at Peniel," Aunt

Lucille said. "There are some guest rooms on the east side. We'll let your parents know you're here—and safe."

"Come on, guys, let's go downstairs," Will told his crew, zipping up his slightly heavier backpack and leading them to the door.

By Tuesday morning, the frogs had mysteriously dispersed as quickly as they had arrived. There were still frogs on the lawns and grassy areas of Perilous Falls, but nothing like the tsunami of croakers that clogged the streets the previous afternoon and evening.

News reports warned people to "avoid contact" with the remaining amphibians. On the morning shows, citizens complained about the painful bites the frogs had left on their legs and arms. Clusters of ugly red boils marked the site of the bite marks.

The emergency room of Chorazin General Hospital was packed with people awaiting care. But no physician had ever seen boils quite like these, nor were the normal salves and medicines providing any relief.

To avoid the emergency room lines, Deborah Wilder managed to secure the last early morning appointment with Dr. Bede, the family pediatrician. With only two empty seats in the waiting room, Leo and Marin shared a chair, which led to constant bickering over who was taking up more space.

The night before, Leo, his mom, dad, and sister were camped out in Aunt Lucille's living room. At three a.m., a crescendo of croaking outside the house awakened Leo. Worried that the frogs were getting closer, he ventured out onto Aunt Lucille's porch. The frogs remained behind the salt perimeter his great-aunt had spread around the house that afternoon, but they now seemed angrier and certainly louder than before. Leo walked down the steps of the front porch right up to the salt line for a closer look.

Just to see what they would do, he kicked at the frogs beyond the barrier. One hopped onto his pants leg. When he went to swat it off, the creature sunk its teeth into Leo's forearm. Screaming in pain, he fell backward.

In a panic, he yanked at the frog's body, trying to loosen its grip. A stinging warmth spread through his forearm. Leo jiggled the arm back and forth, hoping the thing would release him, but its jaws held fast. Then just as he was about to scream again, his face burned with a white heat. The glow spread down his arms, ejecting the frog, which flew into the swarm beyond the salt line. Leo's chest rose tremulously, sending a broad spray of light outward in all directions. Every frog touched by the light flipped backward, sailing over the grass all the way down to the river.

His mother appeared on the porch, staring in disbelief. She helplessly watched Leo's body convulsing with fear as a steady ripple of light illuminated the great sloping lawn. "LEO! LEO!" she cried, wrapping him in her arms. His shaking ceased and so did the intense light show.

Deborah still embraced Leo in Dr. Bede's waiting room. His right arm was splattered with blisters. "They itch, Mom. Can't I scratch them?" he asked, puffing out his lower lip, making the question seem even more pitiful.

"No, you can't. Dr. Bede will know what to do."

A bored Marin cartwheeled down the aisle, trying to occupy herself.

"If I can't scratch my bumps, can you at least get Marin to stop her flip-flopping?"

Deborah told Marin to stop. The little girl sullenly walked in between the three rows of waiting patients, running her hand along the arms of the chairs as she passed. She hummed a little song to herself.

"Can I at least pat my arm? It's really itchy," Leo complained. He leaned into his mother's ear. "If I light up, I'd bet the itching would stop."

"Don't you dare," his mother warned. "If you do that, I'll—" She meant to continue, but a woman leaping to her feet and shrieking near the check-in desk stopped her.

The woman had short, spiky hair and rubbed the back of her hand as if trying to release a genie trapped inside. "It's gone. Oh my—the bumps! They're completely gone." She got very quiet, pointing at Marin, who continued to make laps around the room, tapping the waiting patients as she passed. "That little girl touched me and I saw the bumps go away."

"Me too, honey," an old woman with a face like melted rubber said, tears in her eyes. She stared at Marin. "Sweetie, what did you do to us?"

Marin guiltily put her hands behind her back.

People all over the room began to clap and hug the girl.

"Look at my knees," a man in shorts said a few seats down from Deborah and Leo. "Not only did she heal the sores, but they also bend so easily now. You've got a miracle worker there, lady."

Deborah froze, trying to think what to do.

"I'm sorry, Mama," Marin squeaked out, surrounded by the patients.

"It's okay," Deborah said, not meaning it. "Let's go, guys." She took Leo and Marin by the hands and headed for the door.

As they vacated the office, Leo could be heard down the hall saying, "Hello! My arm is still itchy. Can I at least hold MARIN'S hand? If I've got to be her brother, I may as well get something out of it."

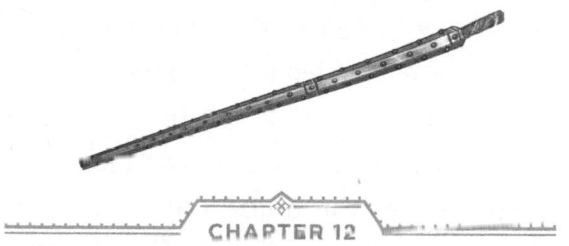

CHAPTER 12

KARNAK'S GRAND OPENING

The long truck marked CITY OF PERILOUS FALLS rumbled down Falls Road. It stopped at the first corner in front of a small wooden house with shingles like gingerbread and petunias blooming under all the front windows.

Tobias Shen leapt from the truck wearing a gray city worker's uniform. He pulled a short-brimmed cap over his head and approached the front door of the house. The owner spied him, suspiciously, through the locked screen door. She was a beefy woman in frayed slippers, holding a full cup of coffee in her hand.

"What do you want?" she asked with all the warmth of a jackhammer.

"Good morning, ma'am. We're spraying the neighborhood for pests," Shen said. "We wanted to inform you before we started. Have a very, very wonderful day." He gave her a half bow and walked back to the truck, dodging the occasional frog plopping across the walkway.

Behind the screen, the woman never moved. She just stared at Shen like a troubled bloodhound.

Shen yanked a hose from the side of the truck and began spraying liquid all over the woman's front lawn.

"Hurry up and get the house too," Bartimaeus yelled through the open window of the truck's cab. "We got hundreds more to go."

The homeowner stuck her head through the parted screen door, her face pinched and stern. "Hey, you. Never mind doing that," she hollered at Tobias. "I don't need the treatment and I think it's hurting the frogs. Whatever you're spraying is making 'em shrivel up. Let 'em be. They're kind of cute."

"Madam, they have teeth and a venomous bite." Tobias continued spraying the lawn and sidewalk. "These frogs have attacked many, many people. I have a job to do."

The woman put her coffee cup down on the walkway and lumbered toward Shen. She picked up the hose and bent it, stopping the spray.

"Ma'am, I insist that you let me continue. Your safety is at stake."

"From where I'm standing, *your* safety is at stake." She tugged the hose hard.

Bartimaeus stepped from the cab of the truck and got on his crutches. "Lady, what are you thinkin'? Put the hose down. That's a city hose; it's not your property. Unhand the hose."

But she wouldn't. "I don't want this man killing my frogs. They're beautiful little creatures."

Shen held the nozzle tightly and tried to direct the trickling water toward the remaining frogs. But he was only partially successful.

Bartimaeus stared up at the sky, apparently searching for patience. "Lady, I'm sorry to say this, but you don't know what ya dealing with here. Do ya want one of these frogs to bite you? These are pests, ma'am—and they need to be eliminated."

"I like 'em and I've never seen a species like this," the woman said. "They could be endangered."

"We're endangered, lady. These frogs dine on *people*. They eat flesh—that's you and me. Now I suggest ya get inside your house before one of these little suckers starts treating your leg like a Happy Meal."

"I'm a grown woman. I don't need a city worker telling me to go in my own home," the woman raged. "Do you see that name on the mailbox? Says 'Bruckburger.' I'm Alveda Bruckburger and I'll go where I want on my property."

"Ms. Bruckburger, if you won't go inside and let us finish this treatment"—Shen got very quiet—"there may be no house to go into."

She released the hose, panic on her face. "Are you threatening me? What are you two going to do to my house?"

Bartimaeus rolled his eyes. "Lady, we're not doing nothin' to your house. We're trying to help."

She jogged to the front door faster than expected. "I'm calling the police. I don't want another drop of your pest control on my lawn or on my home. Do you understand me? Do you understand ME?"

Tobias and Bartimaeus looked at one another. "You win, ma'am," Bartimaeus said, turning off the pump at the truck. "If ya don't want the treatment, have it your way. We'll come and check on ya in a few days in case you reconsider."

Shen shook his head disappointedly. "You may regret not having this protection, madam."

"Just get your hose and your poison off my property." She slammed the screen and then bolted her door.

"So that went well," Bart said, adjusting his cap.

"No more asking permission. At the next place, we'll spread the holy water over the grass, spray the house, and talk to no one," Shen whispered, rolling up the canvas hose.

"Sounds like a plan to me. Let's drive a few blocks out and work our way back here, in case the cops come," Bartimaeus said. He stowed his crutches and lifted himself into the cab of the truck. "No telling when the next plague'll strike—and this whole town better be wet and ready when it does."

Shen stashed the hose and joined Bartimaeus in the truck. In moments they peeled out and were spinning around the corner.

Most of Perilous Falls and even people from surrounding towns had jammed into Dura Street that morning to hear Pothinus Sab. For more than an hour, they had stood in alleys, climbed nearby trees, and even sat atop cars to hear Sab officially open the Karnak Center. But most of the crowd had come for one reason: the "protection" Sab had promised to all those who attended the event.

Will and his friends approached as mobs of people pressed toward the Karnak Center's entryway. Far in the distance, they could see Sab standing on the top step of the sandstone building.

"Yes, yes—press in, my children. This is the reward I have been speaking of—your protection. On this monumental day, I will give each of you an amulet—at least one per household," Sab said, dangling a gold necklace with the Ammit figure over their heads. "But like all good things in life, they are limited, so you will have to compete with your neighbors to get them. The strong will make it to the front. The others, well . . . we will help you all in time. Keep pressing forward. That's it. Our inner greatness is often discovered through a challenge. Isn't that true?" He laughed, depositing the necklaces into straining hands.

"Something is wrong with this guy," Simon said to Will, the crowd around them turning rowdy. There was shouting and yelps near the Karnak Center. People began to throw aside those blocking their path to Sab.

"Your enthusiasm is wonderful. Are we ready to get rid of all the things holding you down? This is the first step. An ancient symbol of rebirth and regeneration," Sab barked into a handheld microphone. "Come, take your protection. Claim it! True regeneration requires struggle."

Shoving and arguments overtook the crowd. Will's attention was riveted to the Karnak grounds.

"Guys, do you notice anything about this place?" Will asked Simon and Andrew.

The boys looked around. "Ticked-off people standing in the sun?" Andrew said, shrugging.

"You don't see a dark shadow over the building and everybody here?"

"Should we be seeing a shadow?" asked Andrew.

Will puckered his lips, sliding them to the side. "Let's go find Cami and her family." He pulled both his friends with him. They ran along the edge of the crowd as fights broke out everywhere.

"How dark is the shadow, Will? What does it mean?" Simon asked, suspiciously checking the people around him. "Is it the 'shadow of Egypt'?"

"It's really dark, almost black. It's everywhere." Catching sight of Cami and her family in the alley next to the Karnak Center, Will motioned to the boys to keep up with him. Unlike the front lawn, only a few people were in the alley, including the Meriwethers, who were decked out in their Sunday best. Mr. Meriwether and Max wore ties and jackets; Cami and Mrs. Meriwether were in flowered dresses.

"Don't even ask," Cami said apologetically, running a hand over the loud floral pattern she wore. "This is my mother's idea."

"You look nice," Will said, bobbing his head. He continued nodding, unsure of what to say next.

"Thanks," she said, pushing her hair behind her ears and breaking eye contact. Both she and Will blushed a little.

Out front, over the screaming throng, they could hear Pothinus Sab wrapping up the opening ceremony.

"My dear children, there are no more amulets today. Can you believe more than three thousand have been given away? Three thousand!" There was applause between the shouts and shrieks. "More will be made in the days to come, and when you return to Karnak for one of our regeneration and creativity sessions, we will gift you with your own amulet at that time. OOOH! Look what I have found in my pocket. Twenty amulets I had completely forgotten about. These are the last of the lot. Here."

Sab gleefully laughed, tossing ten amulets into the crowd on the left, then ten more to the jostling mob on the right.

"Get all your hostility out. Get all your anger out. This is how we pave the path to peace. Don't let someone else take your protection. It's yours. Fight for it!" Sab said indignantly. "I only ask one thing: that you all return to Karnak. Will you do that? Will you do that for me?" He smiled, extending his arms wide in a selfless gesture while the sounds of punches and applause filled the street.

"Cami, come over here and stand by us," Mrs. Meriwether

insisted, fluffing her hair in the alley. "The woman who called me said we had an appointment with Poth—Mr. Sab—right after the ceremony. And it sounds like it's over."

Cami did as she was told. Will, Andrew, and Simon stood behind the Meriwethers outside the battered side door.

"They're not coming in with us, are they, Cami?" Mrs. Meriwether asked, looking at the boys.

"I think they'd like to meet him. Big fans," Cami whispered to her mother.

The metal door jerked open before they could continue. Sarsour, wrinkled and red-faced, eyed each of them from inside the doorway. When he saw Cami, he grunted, frowning at the girl.

"We have an appointment with Mr. Sab," Evelyn Meriwether said.

"You were in basement," Sarsour belched, pointing at Cami accusingly. "You. You too." He pointed at Simon and Andrew.

"Where are your manners, Sarsour?" A voice like sandpaper scraping a smooth surface sounded in the darkness. Sab lowered Sarsour's stubby pointing finger and pushed him back inside. "Come in, my friends. You must be Eeeevelyn." He took Mrs. Meriwether's plump hand and kissed it, his wide black eyes never leaving her face.

"Oh, Mr. Sab. I am so excited. I could just burst."

"No need for that, Eeeevelyn. Just imagine the mess." With a flourish of his gold and black silken robe, he extended an arm toward the hall behind him. "Come. Where the mother goes, the family must follow, yes? Isn't that true?" Sab flashed a fake smile accompanied by a half bow as each of the Meriwethers passed. He regarded the boys with the same benevolence, until he caught sight of Will. Sab suddenly lost his false expression, his eyes narrowing in concern.

"You are not a member of this family. Are you?" Sab asked with a trace of worry.

"No, I'm a friend. I'm Will."

"Will . . . Wilder?" Sab uttered in a low tone, closing the door. Will nodded. Sab reassumed his smile and like a great cat slipped down the hall. He headed off after the Meriwethers. "Step into my consulting parlor—it's just here."

Sab threw open a door, revealing a square room with a gold painted wooden chair, like a throne, at the center. A group of low backless stools completed the circle of chairs. The sandstone walls held framed papyrus prints of Egyptian gods with enlarged heads. The largest print hung behind the gold chair. It looked exactly like the image on the bronze door in the main hall of Karnak: a kingly figure wearing a double plumed crown sitting impassively on a throne.

"Who is that?" Cami asked, ogling the papyrus.

"Ah. You have an eye for power," Sab said, indicating the stools where he wished them to sit. "That is a great and powerful Egyptian god. He is the hidden one, the god of creativity and regeneration—a reminder of what we can all be. Sit, please. Sit."

They followed his directions. Max guided his wheelchair next to Will, as far away from Sab as possible.

"Does the god have a name?" Cami pressed.

"His name is Amon," Sab said solemnly. "Just saying his name is like a prayer, isn't it? Why don't you all repeat it with me? It is a wonderful way to start our session. Amon. Amon . . ."

The only person who echoed Sab was Mrs. Meriwether. The kids were too shocked by the mention of the demon's name to speak. And Max had such a dislike for Sab that he would have refused to do anything the man asked on principle.

Sab's black eyes fell on Cami and each of her friends, finally resting on Will. "Not cooperating? No matter, there are many paths to regeneration." Sab grinned, sitting on the golden throne, his hands on his knees.

"He even looks like the Amon picture," Andrew whispered to Will. "Look at the way he is sitting."

Simon's legs began to tremble. "Do you think he's the demon?" he squeaked.

"Shhhh," Will begged, trying to remain calm. His nose was feeling a little itchy, but everyone in the room could see Sab. He was obviously a human being. Maybe he was possessed by the demon Amon? Will couldn't be sure.

"My assistant tells me that your son—Max, isn't it?— was experiencing some worrisome dreams," Sab addressed Evelyn Meriwether as if no one else were in the room. "I am certain I can help him. There is an ancient tonic that has been known to relieve people of dark dreams and promote a lasting sleep." He slunk from the chair to a wooden chest decorated with hieroglyphics in the corner of the room.

"I am sure you would welcome a nice, long sleep, wouldn't you?" Sab asked Max over his shoulder, pulling something from the wooden chest.

"Not really. I sleep fine," Max said hastily.

Evelyn Meriwether turned, bristling. "That's enough," she told Max.

Sab placed a flask of red juice on the seat of the throne. "Max will have to drink a few of these a week. They are most pleasant. Some of our other clients have experienced remarkable recoveries in only a few short days," Sab said, all smiles.

Mr. Meriwether's little mustache shifted side to side. "Is this some kind of medicine? Should we check with our family doctor before he takes it?"

Evelyn Meriwether grimaced at her husband for daring to question Pothinus Sab.

"These are all natural treatments, sir," Sab said, as if speaking to a confused child. "Rather like vitamins or liquid minerals."

Will stared at the tonic. It had a faint dark purple glow around it.

Sab uncorked the bottle. "Drink half of it now, the rest at bedtime. It has a most refreshing taste."

He would have gone on, but a clamor in the hall and the sound of a ravaged voice yelling caused Sab to pause. He placed the tonic back on the throne.

"I need to see Sab," the raspy voice yelled in the hallway. "Yes, I ate one goose. So what? I thought it would give me strength. I'm much worse. Look at me! I've been taking the tonic for days now and—" A nasty coughing jag stopped the speech.

Sarsour appeared at the door. "Bobbit is here. He ate one of the geese."

A flash of anger shot across Sab's face, which he masked quickly. "You will excuse me for a moment, my children." He half bowed and raced into the hall. Sarsour stuck his fat tongue out at Andrew, who watched him with suspicion.

Mrs. Meriwether picked up the decanter of tonic. "Maxie, you don't want any more of those dreams, do you? Drink this. Come on now."

Will leapt up for a closer look at the glass in her hand. He moved his face very close to the glass. "Mrs. Meriwether, what do you see there in the bottle? What color is it?"

"It's pink. Are you color blind, Will? The tonic is pink," Mrs. Meriwether said huffily.

"It's not pink, Mother. It's green. Can't you see it's green?" Cami asked.

Mr. Meriwether was sure it was blue. Simon thought it was purple. Max said, "I don't care what color it is. I'm not drinking it."

Andrew was at the door, intently watching the scene in the hall.

"At first I thought it was red," Will said, still gazing inside the bottle. "Now I realize it's clear. There's a tooth swimming in the bottom of the bottle. You all probably can't see it, but you have to take my word for it. This tonic is not what it appears to be." Will moved toward the doorway, where Andrew was beckoning him.

"Don't let Max drink that stuff," Will quietly told Cami.

Mr. and Mrs. Meriwether began to bicker in suppressed voices about whether Max should swallow the tonic immediately or at all.

"You've got to hear this, Will-man," Andrew said at the doorway. "Bobbit cooked up one of the Egyptian geese he was supposed to deliver to Sab. He sure looks fat to me—could be your man."

Max rolled his wheelchair to the door, cutting Will off. His eyes were brimming with emotion. "My dream last night was pretty bad. Your aunt was crying a lot. She couldn't reach you." Max labored to continue, his face trembling against the headrest of his wheelchair. "The raven was slashing at you. It was a big raven with sharp teeth and a staff. It had the staff."

"You're like my own personal coming attractions, Max. Let's talk later and don't drink the tonic, okay?"

Max said, "I won't. If his tonic is anything like his CDs, drinking motor oil would be more fun. No thanks."

Will patted Max on his arm, then joined Andrew at the open door. Simon came up behind him.

Out in the hall, Sab tried to restrain his voice, though he was clearly upset. "It makes no difference to me how. I expect two fattened geese here tonight, Mr. Bobbit. Do you understand me?"

Bobbit looked as if he were going to fall over at any moment. His coloring was pasty and his eyes unfocused. "I don't know if I have another plump one. They're all on the skinny side now. Why do you need them?"

"Sarsour, you will accompany Mr. Bobbit to his shop. Find two *appropriate* geese or bring a substitute if necessary." Sab turned to Bobbit and said in a biting whisper, "Perhaps there is some other cherished pet at your store, another rare breed that you have been saving for a special occasion? Is there such a creature? IS THERE?"

"I don't know." Bobbit fearfully took a few steps back. "I'll find something. Mr. Sab, before I go, may I have a different tonic? That last one made my stomach burn," Bobbit pitifully complained. "It's like needles inside my belly."

"Fetch him my special brew, Sarsour. Then go to the shop at once."

Bobbit tried to ask more questions, but Sab was already on his way back to the consulting parlor. He practically ran into Will, Andrew, and Simon.

"Why are you in the hall?" Sab asked, glaring at them.

"Bathroom." Will had to think fast. "We need to use the bathroom and didn't want to roam around looking."

Sab scowled and only brightened once he saw Cami's parents arguing inside the room. "The facilities are at the end of this corridor. Come back quickly. This is no place for unchaperoned boys to be wandering." Sab swept past them into the consulting parlor.

Will ran in the exact opposite direction Sab had indicated. His friends followed him into the darkened hall.

"Isn't that funny? I had to use the bathroom too," Simon snorted. "Great bladders must think alike."

"We're not going to the bathroom," Will said. "I want to check out that big room on the other side of the pool. The one behind the bronze doors we saw on the way in."

"Why do you tell everybody you have to go to the bathroom when you don't have to go to the bathroom? You need to come up with some new excuses," Simon said. "The last time we went near those bronze doors, we fell into the basement. Tell him, moron."

Andrew playfully raised a fist toward Simon. "There are some trapdoors around the columns in there. I don't like this place."

At the end of the hallway, the boys walked between two oversized columns to the rectangular pool. Their nostrils were assaulted by the smell of incense and chlorine. To the right were the huge bronze doors bearing the image of Amon. Will walked right up to the doors and clutched the handles to pull them open. He stopped when he noticed a clay seal on the seam between the doors. "We'd better not break that thing or Sab'll know we went in. There's got to be another entryway." Will dashed past the column on the right into an alcove. There he found a square bronze door that looked like a miniature version of the door on the front of the Karnak Center.

"I wonder if this is the shrunken Egyptian god entrance," Will joked.

"Or maybe it's Sarsour's hobbit hole," Andrew said, laughing.

Will pressed the door open as he reached into his backpack.

"Are you sure we should go in, Will?" Simon said. "Won't Sab be looking for us?"

Will pulled a flashlight from his backpack, flicking it on. "I need to see what's inside. It'll be fine. Short stuff is gone and the *Prance* of Egypt is in the other room. What could possibly go wrong?"

Andrew and Simon locked eyes for a second and from their shared expression, the silent, collective answer was: "Everything."

CHAPTER 13

THE WALLS HAVE EARS

"There's got to be a light in here somewhere," Simon said, feeling along the stone wall of the small chamber.

"I doubt it," Will said, directing the flashlight's beam across the room. The first thing he saw were the white feathers scattered over the floor. "Do you all see those?"

"The feathers?" Andrew asked. "Sure, I see the feathers."

"Well, that completes your eye test," Simon said, teasing Andrew. "Now let's see how you do on comprehension and reasoning." He snorted to himself, still patting his hands on the wall behind Will and Andrew. An even bigger hand found the back of Simon's head, swatting it with force.

Will turned away from his friends and yanked on a huge metal door on the left side of the room.

"This must lead to the main chamber, the one that was locked by the pool." He studied the door with his flashlight.

The locks were all engaged and accessible only from the inside. Will kicked the door in disgust.

Casting his flashlight beam across the rest of the room, he discovered a black marble table with a number of blood-stained knives upon it. There were baskets loaded with fruit beneath the table. A jumbled pile of brass birdcages, like the one Mr. Bobbit had carried into the Karnak Center, teetered atop one another in the corner. A wooden table inscribed with Egyptian lettering held folded white linen garments, a faceless stone head, and three vials of yellowed oils.

"What do you think they use this place for?" Andrew asked.

"Well, it's not the rec room," Will worriedly answered. "They probably take the feathers off the geese here and prepare them—for cooking, maybe?"

"It's a prep room for some kind of ritual." Simon rattled away, moving along the wall. "I've been reading about how in Ancient Egypt, the priests offered food and drinks to their gods several times a day. They would even dress the statue of the god up in new clothes."

"Why did they do that?" Will asked.

"They believed food nourished the spirit of the god or the dead in the afterlife. The clothes were a sign of devotion."

"And they did this even for 'the great god, Amon'?"

"Even the great god—" A tiny squishing noise erupted

near Simon. His voice cracked as he said, "Will, shine your light this way."

Will spun the beam around to illuminate a shaky Simon, his hand touching something on the wall. "What is that?" Will asked, drawing closer.

"They're ears! They're all fleshy," said Simon, recoiling.

One side of a tablet hanging from the wall depicted Ancient Egyptians raising their hands in prayer. On the other side, where Simon's hand had been, six lifelike blue ears jutted from the panel.

"Are those things real?" Andrew exploded.

"They feel real," Simon said, staring at the ears. "In Ancient Egypt, this is how the gods heard the pleas of their people."

Each time someone spoke, the blue ears quivered slightly.

"Shhhh." Will placed a finger to his lips. "Be quiet. It's listening. The demon must be able to hear us."

As Simon stepped, something crunched beneath his foot. He jumped back.

Will lowered his light to the floor. Stacks of broken red wax and wooden figures lay along the wall. Pins protruded from the sides of a few of them. Heads were separated from many of the figurines. What disturbed Will was that all the figures looked exactly alike and they all wore pith helmets.

"That's really weird," Andrew said, placing a hand on Will's arm.

"They're little Will Wilder action figures," Simon blurted, bending down.

"Don't touch." Will pulled a Ziploc bag and a pocketknife from his backpack. He speared one of the figures. It had broken arms and pins sticking from its head. He felt a touch of nausea as he dropped it into the bag. *Why would they do this to a doll that looks like me?* He motioned the boys toward the entryway.

"Sab has got to be the demon," he whispered. "He knew me when I walked in the door. He's cutting up statues of me, eating geese like crazy. . . . The only problem is, everybody can see Sab. Demons can't be seen by most people. None of this makes sense." He shoved the Ziploc bag into his backpack. "I'm going to take this to my aunt Lucille. But first I've got to drop by Mr. Bobbit's place. I want to make sure he doesn't have the staff and that he's not snacking on too many geese."

"We'll come with you," Andrew said.

"No. You all stay with Cami. Make sure Max doesn't drink that poison Sab is offering. I'll catch you guys later." Will ducked under the little doorway and headed out the front.

Andrew and Simon returned to Pothinus Sab's consultation parlor. When they arrived in the room, Sab was standing next to his golden chair, smiling ear to ear. He occasionally closed his eyes as if savoring sweet music. But only the shrill voices of Mr. and Mrs. Meriwether yelling at one another could be heard.

"He is fine, Evelyn. He doesn't need any medicine," Mr. Meriwether fumed. "The answer is no."

"I am his mother. Maxie will sleep better without those horrible dreams," Mrs. Meriwether shot back. "He'll drink some right away, Mr. Sab. Won't you, baby?"

"I said no," Mr. Meriwether roared. Cami got between her parents and attempted to convince her mother that it was time to leave.

Sab slipped over to Max. "Are your dreams very bad, young man? Tell me, what do you see in your dreams?"

"None of your business." Max shut his eyes defiantly. Andrew and Simon stepped beside Max's wheelchair to support him.

Sab's mouth turned down. He laced his fingers suddenly as if trying to control his anxious hands. "Withheld secrets can cause terrible harm," Sab whispered to Max. He turned to the other Meriwethers. "Miss Evelyn, I have a notion," Sab intoned for the whole room. "Max and I were just enjoying a little talk. There is another way to administer the tonic. It is a tried-and-true method—very effective."

The Meriwethers' argument stopped for a moment. Sab glided over to the wooden cabinet. Returning to the center of the room, like a magician, he presented a blue lacquered box, studded with scarab amulets.

"What is that, Mr. Sab?" Mrs. Meriwether asked.

Sab's large black eyes made contact with everyone assembled. "Miss Evelyn, I rarely offer such a special therapy. But for your dear boy, this could be just the thing."

He moved his mouth close to Evelyn's ear and lowered his voice. "I could give Max a shot—a natural shot of the tonic. He would experience no pain and the effects would be instantaneous."

Mrs. Meriwether seemed wary. "How would you do that?"

He opened the decorated box. Inside squirmed a long, oval-shaped black insect with hooked pincers. Mrs. Meriwether jumped at first, but Sab caressed her hand. "It's an earwig. Quite harmless little fellow, really. It will absorb some of the tonic; then I'll offer it to Max for a look. One tiny pinch and his nightmares will be no more. Does that sound satisfactory? It won't even leave a mark."

Mr. Meriwether cleared his throat loudly. "What are you two talking about?"

His wife was lost in thought. "Be quiet, Len," she said. "It won't hurt, Mr. Sab?"

He shook his head. "He'll not feel a thing."

"Then yes. That'll be fine."

"Mother, what have you agreed to?" Cami asked.

Sab dropped the earwig into the tonic bottle on his throne. Cami saw the thing kicking around in the bottle, swelling up by the moment.

"What is that, Mr. Sab? Why did you put that bug in there?" Cami asked.

"Another instrument of regeneration, Miss Meriwether," Sab said evenly, smoothing the sides of his glistening black hair.

"We're leaving now," Mr. Meriwether said, fussing with the buttons on his jacket. "Come on, Evelyn."

Max started to flick the switch on his wheelchair.

"Don't go. Not so soon." Sab closed the door with a flourish. "I have something intriguing to show you, Max. A boy like you enjoys surprises, yes? Let me share one with you; then you may all leave."

Fear overtook Max's face. "Don't worry," Andrew told him. "I'll carry you out myself if I have to."

Sab leaned over the tonic bottle, narrowing his eyes. "Ah, good and full."

He placed the blue-lacquered box next to the bottle's opening. Cami watched intensely as the bloated bug crawled up the neck of the bottle. The earwig seemed to be drawn toward Sab's box.

"What are you going to do?" Cami asked. Sab flashed his eyes at her but said nothing. That's when Cami began to understand exactly what he was doing. "Oh no you don't."

In a sudden move, she swatted the tonic bottle to the floor with the bug still scurrying inside. It shattered with a crash.

"You . . . you will regret this," Sab hissed in her ear.

"No, you will, Mr. Sab." Cami squashed the distended earwig under her heel, tonic oozing like gel from the sides. "You may have my mother fooled, but I know what you are."

Mr. Meriwether, Max, and the boys were already at the door. "Let's go, Evelyn," Mr. Meriwether commanded. Cami took her mother by the arm. Mrs. Meriwether kept apologizing to Pothinus Sab as she was pulled from the room.

Once the Meriwethers were gone, Sab furiously hurled the blue box at the wall, splintering it. Then a thought, like a thunderbolt to the back of the head, restored his good mood. He quickly snatched a handful of Ammit amulets from a basket near the door and ran down the hall after the Meriwethers.

"My dear children, before you go, take one of these amulets as my gift to you. So sorry for the misunderstanding. Please, please wear them always. Never be without them. They will mark you for regeneration in the days to come."

At Peniel, the afternoon sunlight shone through pastel windows, casting gentle colors over the exhibits in Bethel Hall. Lucille Wilder gingerly positioned a pair of large metal keys into an open glass case. THE KEYS OF ST. PETER the plaque on the front read. She nearly dropped them when Bartimaeus called her name.

"Luuuucille? Luuuucille?" he yelled out.

"I'm here, Bart. In the corner." She caught sight of him and Tobias Shen in their gray Perilous Falls city worker uniforms. Giggles followed. "And what have *we* been up to?" She removed her cotton gloves and locked up the case. "This'll be good."

"We have been spraying every house and park in town with holy water," Shen confided to her. "Twenty-four refills later, we got everything."

"*Almost* everything," Bartimaeus said, galloping toward her on his crutches. "There was one crazy woman who wouldn't let us spray her house. Maybe we'll try to get her later. We even sprayed down city hall during lunchtime. The security's pretty awful there."

"The sheriff's department was a different story. Lots of officers running around. We didn't want to get arrested, so we skipped a few buildings: the jail, the sheriff's office, the parking area. It was much, much too risky. Otherwise, we got most of the town," Tobias said, removing his hat with some satisfaction.

"Sounds like you had a productive day," Lucille said. "Things have been a bit weird here. You must know that the sleeve of Moses's staff was discovered in Baldwin's office."

"So the abbot told ya?" Bart said.

"He did indeed. When I quizzed Valens about it this afternoon, he was very sweet. He tried to make excuses for the vicar the whole time."

"Do you believe him, Lucille? Valens, I mean?" Shen's flat eyes pierced right through her.

"Why should I doubt him? Most of the brothers in this house would hang Baldwin out to dry. Not Valens. He kept insisting that there had to be another explanation and that the vicar would never do such a thing. I don't know what to believe."

"Lucille." The low, regal voice reverberated off the vaulted ceiling.

They all turned to find Baldwin approaching from the library in the front of Bethel Hall. He was as imperious as ever. "Where is your great-nephew?"

"I haven't seen him," Lucille said. "Though he should be coming around this afternoon."

"He has been strangely absent of late—skipping his training sessions. Just the sort of thing a guilty party would do." Baldwin moved with the determination of a tank down the center aisle of the hall. "He is either guilty as sin or too juvenile to understand how he is compromising this community."

Bartimaeus leaned toward Tobias. "Sounds like the stove calling the furnace hot," he mumbled.

"I know your feelings for your nephew, Lucille," Baldwin said as quietly as he could, slipping his hands inside the folds of his habit. "But you must admit the possibility that he may have taken the staff. When I discover why"—he eyeballed Bartimaeus—"I hope you will support me in bringing justice to this house."

Lucille violently crossed her arms. "Vicar, I am for justice, whoever might be in need of it."

Baldwin looked confused by her response. "Good. Do let me know when William resurfaces."

Baldwin turned his hawkish nose away from the group and followed it toward the rounded opening that led farther into the museum.

When he was out of earshot, Tobias whispered, "He has a serious problem with Will. He is always after the boy. Bitter, bitter all the time."

"Keep your eyes on Baldwin. He may well be our man." Lucille stared coldly down the empty hall that swallowed the vicar. "He had access to the exhibit case keys, time to hide the staff, and the gold wrapping was found in his office. Though why would he steal it and for whom?"

"No idea. But I don't like the way he hates on Will." Bartimaeus cracked his knuckles. "Vicar or no, he'd better back off if he knows what's good for him."

Lucille laid her hands on Bart's. "Never you mind, dear. Baldwin will have to get past this Wilder before he touches a hair on my nephew's—"

"Lucille Wilder?" It was an official-sounding voice with a slight drawl. It came from one of the two officers standing in the entry of Bethel Hall. They wore tan uniforms and held their hats at their sides.

Lucille's eyes filled with worry. But Bartimaeus spoke before she could. "How can we help ya, Officers?" Tobias Shen inched behind a case, hoping the deputies would not spot his city worker uniform.

"I'm sorry about this, ma'am." The officer ignored Bartimaeus and directed his comments to Lucille. "We have a warrant for your arrest. You're wanted for questioning about your involvement in some odd events around town. You'll have to come with us."

Though Lucille's lips tightened in anger, she maintained

her composure. "Bart. Tobias." She locked her blue eyes on theirs. "Call Dan, tell Brother Amalric what's happened, and do keep watch over Will. He's in great danger."

She walked toward the tense deputies, tugging at the collar of her powder-blue silk jacket. "All right, gentlemen. Let's get this over with."

CHAPTER 14

GNATS

A hairy paw clenched the sapphire staff while a single talon scraped the third set of letters engraved on the side of the rod. The Hebrew letters instantly burned with a white glow. After it was raised toward Perilous Falls's purpling sky, the staff was suddenly driven into the dry dirt. Dust swirled around the rod. A filthy funnel of debris spun upward. Aside from the rushing wind, all that could be heard in the expanding cyclone of dirt was the deranged yowling of some unearthly creature.

Will tentatively approached Bobbit's Bestiary. He pressed his face to the front glass, cupping a hand around his eyes to see if Mr. Bobbit was inside. He spotted Ann Hye at the rear of the store, tending to the cages. He pulled open the front door and ran smack into Crocket, the old storekeeper who pointed a broom handle at Will's chest.

"What d'ya want, son?"

"I, uh, need to talk to Mr. Bobbit," Will said, sliding the broom handle away with a finger. "I only need a few minutes."

"He ain't here," Crocket croaked, stepping aside. "You best be getting on your way."

Will slipped past him. "I'll talk with Miss Ann for a minute instead."

"Miss Ann?!" Crocket shot a look over his shoulder toward the back of the store, his expression confused. "You shouldn't be here. When Mr. Bobbit's away, you shouldn't be in the store. Don't touch anything—and if Mr. Bobbit isn't back soon, you're going to have to go." Frustrated, Crocket gave up and went outside to sweep the walk.

The geese began to honk and hiss madly.

Crocket eyed him warily through the front glass.

"Miss Ann. I need to talk."

"Oh. Will Wilder." The willowy woman seemed shocked as she whirled around. "I didn't think you'd make it back." She frantically returned to petting the heads of the geese in the cages. "Poor things are in a state. They're all going to die. All my beautiful friends are going to die." She pulled the tangle of black wiry hair away from one eye. "Mr. Bobbit is sending them to their slaughter."

"How? Why would he want to slaughter them?" Will asked.

"He's up to no good," she sang in a warbling tone. "He means to kill them. Mr. Sab wants every one of them." She folded her arms hatefully and glared at him. "Where are your manners, silly?"

Will self-consciously checked his shirt to see if he had left it untucked or had possibly spilled something on himself.

"Hats shouldn't be worn indoors. And why are you carrying that bag around?" With agitation, Miss Ann flicked a finger in the direction of the front door. "Put them over there on the table. You're disturbing the geese."

Will did as he was told. "Where is Mr. Bobbit now?" he asked, alarmed by the black raven feathers hovering over the floor. They had increased in number since his last visit.

"Mr. Bobbit said he had business. He was just here with that horrible little man. They're taking all my geese. . . . They spoke of the staff too—the one you asked me about." Her head bobbed up and down, causing her great tangle of black hair to quiver. "He has the staff. He has it!"

"Mr. Bobbit has it?"

Ann Hye slapped two tiny hands over her mouth and lowered her head. The birds clawed at their cages. "I shouldn't be telling you this. Mr. Bobbit told me to be discreet, to never talk with strangers, and here I am chittering on about—"

Will checked the cage where he had seen the raven earlier. It was still there; at least that's what he thought at first. Only the raven seemed half dissolved. It was nearly transparent. Will crouched close to the bars and realized there was no bird. Only a large tooth glimmered in the back of the cage.

"Miss Hye, where is the raven?"

"You don't see it? Oh, Mr. Bobbit must have taken it. He has taken so many of the birds."

Will closed his eyes, cleared his mind, and thought of the gold coins he had seen in his great-grandfather's office. When his eyes popped open, a pile of gold doubloons occupied the cage.

"What are you doing there, Will Wilder?" Ann Hye asked, reaching for a goose's head. It recoiled into the cage to avoid her touch. "Mr. Bobbit mentioned that Lucille woman today. He did. He did."

Will rose to his feet, his hands balled into fists. "What did he say about her?"

Ann yanked the frazzled hair surrounding her face forward, as if she were too embarrassed to answer without being veiled. "He said she was dangerous—told the little troll that the old woman was dangerous," Ann chirped quietly. "Said she had to go."

Will's chest pounded and his palms got moist. He wished Bobbit were in the room so he could challenge him . . . tackle him.

"I need you to tell me one more thing. Is Bobbit 'feeding on the fattened geese'?"

Ann Hye said nothing.

"Miss Ann, is he 'feeding' on 'the fattened geese'?"

"All the time. Yes. He's sampled my precious friends. EVEN THOUGH THEY ARE NOT HIS TO HAVE." Ann Hye scrambled very close, her tiny, irritated black eyes locked on Will's. She steadied herself. "Mr. Bobbit's a cruel one. After he visits Sab next, track him. Stop him. There's no telling what he'll do to that woman—what's her name? Lucille. Do you know Lucille?"

Will twitched with fury between the cages of the store. He couldn't speak. He had to stop Bobbit, but he wasn't sure what his next move should be. Driven by pure adrenaline, he charged the front counter, grabbed his pith helmet and backpack, and reached for the door. "Miss Ann, I'll be back tomorrow. Try to find out where Mr. Bobbit's keeping the staff."

"I'll try. I really will." Ann scurried to the back of the store, picking up the feed bowl in the corner. "Keep our talks secret, Will Wilder. He can't know that we spoke. Not a word, not a word." She busied herself running the little gold spoon around the feed bowl.

Will pulled at the store's front door but tiny pinging noises on the window stopped him. Teeny bugs smacked into the glass. Thousands of black flecks with wings darkened the big window as well. Outside, Crocket was nowhere to be seen, which Will found odd.

He threw open the door and started running toward Peniel. It was only a few blocks down High Street. Aunt Lucille could help him make sense of all the new information he'd gathered. She'd know what to do.

Will heard a slight buzzing in the distance behind him. It grew louder as he ran.

Over his shoulder, he discovered a swirling wall of gnats bearing down on him. He didn't stop to think but ran from the bug cyclone, taking a sharp left on Phosphorous Way. He hoped the buzzing mass would continue moving down High Street. The swarm had other plans. It came spinning around the corner as if chasing him. Seeing what was headed their way, people along the street scurried indoors. Shutters on storefronts slammed and some folks jumped into their parked cars along the curb.

One elderly woman slowly walking her dog was mobbed by the gnats. They covered her in seconds. She hit the pavement, writhing, hopelessly trying to fend off the bugs. Her dog barked until he, too, choked on the creatures.

This is the third plague! Will thought.

With no one to help the old woman on the sidewalk, Will turned back, running headlong into the swarm. He could barely see, but like the frogs, the gnats avoided him. It was as if an invisible cone deflected the bugs surrounding him. *What's going on? Why aren't they all over me?*

He knelt down to help the old lady to her feet. As he touched her, the gnats flitted away from her body. Will removed his helmet to swat the winged horde. That's when he realized: It was the pith helmet repelling them. He put it over the old woman's head and even though the gnats got in his eyes, he delivered her and her dog to their front

door. Just before it closed, Will reclaimed his helmet and sprinted down the block.

The street took a sharp turn to the right, but Will dashed straight ahead into the woods that ran behind his neighborhood. The thick overgrowth dispersed the gnat swarm but didn't stop it.

He scaled the fence into his backyard and headed onto the deck. Gnats by the millions were everywhere, speckling the trees and even the fence. But he was surprised to see that none of them had landed on the houses in the neighborhood, including his own. He banged on the glass sliding door as he watched the lawn turn a jittery, rippling black.

His mother opened the door in the middle of a loud conversation with Dan Wilder. "You should be down there trying to get her out. How long have they had her?" Deb brightened her aggressive tone for a millisecond. "Hi, Will."

"Deb, I spoke to the sheriff deputies. They . . . they had a legal warrant. She's being held without bail!" Dan said, pacing in the middle of the kitchen. "It'll all work out. We have to just try to keep our heads . . ."

Will glanced from his mother to his father. "Who are you talking about? Have you seen all the gnats outside?"

"Gnats?" Dan sprang toward the sliding door. He ran his hands up and down the back of his head, a certain sign that he was about to lose it. "Oh my . . . Where did they come from? The sky is filled with them!"

Deb removed Will's pith helmet and gently put an arm

around his shoulder. She was acting really strange. "Your aunt Lucille . . ."

"What about her? I need to see her now. I think I know who has the Staff of Moses," he whispered so Dan couldn't hear. "Mom? What's wrong?"

Deb's lips were tight, her expression confused. "Your aunt Lucille was arrested this afternoon. She's in jail."

"They got her? Aaaah!" Will seethed. He threw his backpack into the corner. "It's Bobbit."

"The man who owns the pet store?" Deb asked.

Dan spun around. "These gnats . . . are they all over town, Will? This is not good." He ran to the TV under the kitchen cabinet and clicked on the remote. He found a report on Sidon Eight News, Deb's prime TV competitor. A blond reporter was unsuccessfully trying to swat gnats away from her face.

". . . They're bombarding the town of Perilous Falls. People we spoke with said they saw them fall from the sky. My cameraman and I ducked into this High Street doorway to try to get away from the . . ." *PUH . . . PUH.* She spat the gnats from her mouth and began pinching her lips with her fingers. "They're all in my lipstick. Holy cow." Her huge eyelashes fluttering, she stumbled back a little. The tiny black bugs were overtaking her neck and face. "I think one of 'em's under my contact. Bob, Bob, I can't see. A gnat's in my eye! This is an e"—*PUH . . . PUH . . . PUH*—"mergency. I've gotta get these things OFF ME." She swung the micro-

phone at the gnats and started screaming at the cameraman. "I know, Bob! I can hear the control room. I just can't
see." *PUH.* "Okay, we're going to take you now to a live press
conference at the Perilous Falls city hall. Rachel Riker Rut-
ledge, Sidon Eight News, reporting from a"—*PUH*—"bug-
infested High Street." *PUH . . . PUH . . .*

In the Wilder kitchen, Deb deadpanned to her family:
"She actually never looked so good." Deb rolled her purple-
flecked eyes and turned up the volume as Marin and Leo
wandered into the kitchen.

Will tried to watch the TV, but Leo pulled him into the
hallway leading to the den.

"With all these crazy gnats outside, do you think it's
time for me to *ignite*? You know, turn my light on?" Leo
asked excitedly.

"I'd keep it under wraps." Will craned his neck to see the
TV in the kitchen. "You don't know what you're doing yet,
Leo."

"I do. Aunt Lucille and I trained the other day. It was
short, but she showed me how to breathe and control my
illumination—"

"She trained you?"

"Yes, Will. You're not the only Wilder in training." Leo
jumped in front of Will, trying to hold his attention. "Should
I go outside and try to *ignite*? I think it could help."

"You've got to be careful with this—you don't
understand."

"I do. I might be able to zap the gnats."

"It's not a good idea," Will said, staring past him toward the TV.

"Maybe I'm supposed to do something."

"No, you're not." Will was annoyed. "Look, I need you to stay put. Someone is using Moses's staff to attack the town and now Aunt Lucille is locked up. I've got to figure this out, and I don't need your help right now, okay, Leo? Remember, I'm the *chosen one.*"

Leo looked as if he could kick Will in the shins. "You might be the chosen one, but you're not the *only one,*" he growled, and stomped upstairs. Will was about to chase after him, but the image on the screen in the kitchen held him in place.

The camera cut away to city hall, where Mayor Lynch, a strange smirk on her face, clutched her official podium. Pothinus Sab and Heinrich Crinshaw stood on either side of the mayor. Sheriff Stout sheepishly played with his hat in the background.

"Thank you all for coming on such short notice. I first want to urge all the citizens of Perilous Falls to stay indoors and off the streets for the remainder of the night. Only emergency workers and law enforcement officials should be on the roadways. There are confirmed reports of an insect invasion. We are investigating its source—though we have our suspicions . . ."

The mayor was oddly untroubled by the crisis befalling her city. The picture of composure, her right eyebrow rose slightly as she continued. "I have a bit of timely news to report. Owing to an extensive investigation launched months ago by a select committee of the city council, we have apprehended a suspect whom we believe may be responsible for many of the strange happenings in our fair town. This afternoon, Sheriff Stout's deputies arrested Lucille Wilder for alleged activities that could be related to the many disturbances we have experienced—including this insect business. There will be a formal court hearing tomorrow."

Grumbling and yelled questions rose up from the press corps.

The mayor raised a hand to the sky and closed her black-lined eyes. "Please, please, control yourselves. This investigation is beyond reproach. Why, even Councilman Dan Wilder, the suspect's nephew, reviewed all the evidence. Dan is himself a prominent member of the investigative committee."

Will pounded his fists on the countertop. "Dad! How could you do this to Aunt Lucille?"

"You don't understand . . . She is exaggerating," Dan protested. "I . . . I . . . Do you think I would—"

Marin put her hands on her hips. "You're being a very bad daddy."

"Aren't you going to even try to get her out on bail?" Will asked sadly. "I need to talk to her. This is serious. I could die."

"Stop being so dramatic, son." Dan fussed with his tortoiseshell glasses. "One of her friends at Peniel is an attorney. He's filed a motion to get her out. We'll see if that works."

"But what are *you* doing, Dad?" Will asked.

"Exactly what I was thinking," said Deb, turning angrily back to the TV.

In the community room at Peniel, some of the Brethren stared dejectedly at the old '80s-era console TV in the corner. This was definitely a low-def set. The TV seemed completely out of place in the stone room, surrounded by oil paintings of preoccupied monks, faded tapestries, medieval chairs, and leather couches. The lamps and wrought-iron chandelier overhead were at half-light.

Brother Baldwin sat on a high-backed chair against a wall, reading a newspaper. Other brothers attempted to play chess, their eyes fixed on the TV screen across the room. Bartimaeus, Tobias, and Abbot Athanasius were on the edge of the couch nearest the television, riveted by what they saw unfolding.

On-screen, the mayor stepped aside and introduced Pothinus Sab as the city's "spiritual consultant." Sab bowed slightly and took to the podium. "My dear children, we have witnessed amazing things, have we not? Blood in our water, a vicious frog invasion, and these horrible flying creatures. Only now we have an answer." He lifted the amulet of Ammit that dangled on the front of his white jacket. "Ms. Mayor, you have yours? Of course you do. Mr. Crinshaw?

Very good." Except for Sheriff Stout, all those on-screen held up their amulets.

"Now, some might ask, why must we wear these golden baubles? Why is this preferable to other signs and symbols? I will answer with one word: *regeneration*. This little creature is a sign of regeneration—hope for all of Perilous Falls. It has proven its effectiveness already. Isn't that true?" The mayor and Crinshaw nodded. "I want to share a video with you that the news people just recorded." Sab joyously raised a hand to a large screen in the chamber.

It showed the gnat swarm approaching a neighborhood. People slipped on the gold amulets as they exited their homes. While the gnats descended, they completely avoided the houses and the amulet wearers. A black haze of bugs behind her, a woman on-screen proudly announced, "This little medal is like a miracle." She kissed the hippo-like Ammit figure hanging from the chain around her neck. "It has spared us. Not one gnat has approached our family. Not one. I just feel safer wearing it."

A wide shot showed the entire family standing in the middle of a yard frosted in black bugs. Not so much as a single gnat landed on any of them.

"Is that amazing? Isn't it AMAZING?" Pothinus Sab asked. Tepid applause broke out in the city council chamber. Sab pulled a handful of chains with Ammit figures from his pocket. "The mayor and I—all of us—want you to enjoy the same protection these people have experienced. I know what some of you are thinking: Is this some sort of religious symbol? Noooo. Those things hold us back. This amulet is an act of communal spirituality—a sign of our shared commitment to one another and to this town. By wearing this, we are channeling our positive energy and saying 'I belong here. I am a citizen of Perilous Falls and I crave true regeneration.' That is what you want, yes? Now you can have it. The city has generously purchased free amulets for every man, woman, and child. Come to the Karnak Center at your earliest convenience and we will give you a personal amulet for your own safety. These are uncertain days. Why would you want to be without the connection and protection that your neighbors already enjoy?"

Abbot Athanasius stood, scratching at his beard. "This man is a deceiver, Brethren. We must find a way to convince the populace to reject these glittering idols."

"How are we going to do dat? We don't exactly have a TV station, Abbot," Bartimaeus said, shaking his head.

Several brothers offered ideas, from making posters to going door to door begging people to give up the amulets. Valens sauntered into the doorway of the common room and visibly felt the tension in the air.

"What's happening?" Valens warily edged his way into the room.

"This charlatan is forcing his amulets on the people," Tobias said toward the TV with contempt. "There are many, many swarms of gnats attacking the town."

"Gnats?" Valens asked.

"Yes, gnats, gnats. Bzzzzzz," Bartimaeus said, fluttering his hands impatiently to make wings. "Flying gnats. Weren't you listening to the radio in your room?"

Valens hesitated. As his lips began to move, Baldwin interrupted, "There are no radios in our rooms. The only radio is here in the common area."

Bartimaeus's eyes narrowed and he shot Tobias a look. "Hmm, must be my mistake. I could have sworn Valens told me he was listening to the radio in his room when—"

"Gnats are one of the plagues of Egypt, aren't they?" Valens cried, his blue eyes dancing. He turned to Tobias Shen. "Do you think this could also be connected to the Staff of Moses?"

"Your powers of deduction are extraordinary, Mr. Ricard," Tobias pronounced sarcastically. "In moments of confusion, the ability to see the obvious when it presents itself can be a gift."

"Tobias," Abbot Athanasius said in his most serious tone. "Send word to Will. I want him here tomorrow morning for training. His hour is coming and he must be ready. Now let's get to evening prayer, Brothers." He gathered up the stiff material of his black habit and moved to the door. "We will pray for the liberation of our sister Lucille and that peace might once again reign in this house."

Bartimaeus mounted his crutches and followed the procession of brothers through the doorway. Valens stepped aside to let Bart pass in front of him.

"No, you go first, Brother." Bartimaeus trained his milky pupils on Valens. "I'm thinking you might need those prayers a little more than I do."

CHAPTER 15

A MASSIVE DEFENSE

"**Y**our Honor, these charges are completely *bay-th-lis*," the rotund Brother Amalric Fulk bellowed in the courtroom that Wednesday morning.

"What did he say?" the judge whispered to his bailiff, waving off a few stray gnats that had made it onto his bench.

"Here sits an *up-th-anding* woman—a pillar of the *communi-th-y*." His already bulging eyes bugged out even farther as he gestured to Lucille Wilder, who sat uncomfortably in the witness box. "Your Honor, how could *th-th* little *per-thon po-th-ibly* control alligators, cause a river to run red, and compel frogs to overtake a town? These are *un-th-erious* charges and my client denies any and all *rethpon-thi-bility*."

Judge Blabbingdale and the entire courtroom stared at the attorney in wonder. Not only were they unsure what

Lucille Wilder's lawyer was saying, but also his figure was so gargantuan, his black suit so enormous, that the whole picture dumbfounded them.

Brother Amalric Fulk was a lawyer by training who spent most of his days in the filing room at Peniel. As the Brethren's community bookkeeper, he rarely left his desk and spent his spare time studying languages and the law by his lonesome. Some of the Brethren blamed his public withdrawal on the tongue thrust that marred his speech.

Only a crisis like Lucille's could have ever forced Amalric beyond the monastery walls. His prolonged solitude made him awkward and uncertain around strangers, as the fixed death stare he gave the judge demonstrated.

"Are you going to keep staring at me like that, Counselor?" Judge Blabbingdale asked.

"Was I th-aring? I didn't mean to th-are," he said, eyes popping.

"Are you quite done?"

"I believe tho, Your Honor." Amalric blinked oddly, buttoning his jacket as he lumbered toward the table facing the bench. Then like an elephant hitting a tree, he halted suddenly. "Oh, Your Honor, we humbly petition the court to *dith-mith* all charges and allow my client to return home. She *po-th-es* no threat to anyone. She *i-th* not guilty. We thank you." He accidentally backed into his defense table, sending it sliding against a nearby railing.

Mayor Lynch rose, fingers flexed on her tabletop across the aisle. "We believe she *is* guilty, Your Honor. Until there is a formal trial, there is no way the city council can permit Lucille Wilder to roam free in our town. We believe she is somehow manipulating the climate and releasing bizarre wildlife on the populace. Most recently gnats. After discovering convincing evidence, our committee believes Lucille Wilder is a danger to the people of Perilous Falls. She should remain in custody pending a trial." A slow smile developed on Mayor Lynch's face as she eyed Lucille. "Your Honor, our investigative committee makes this request—*unanimously.*"

"Not . . . not unanimously, Ava," Dan Wilder sputtered from the front row. Deborah squeezed his arm in support, while Marin and Leo glared at the mayor.

"Dan, that's enough. I will have you ejected from this courtroom," Judge Blabbingdale cautioned.

"But she's lying, Your Honor. She is bending and twisting reality to fit a . . . a . . . narrative. . . ." A red-faced Dan stood, struggling for words. "She will stop at nothing until my aunt Lucille is—"

"Dan!" the judge yelled. "This is my last warning. Now, Mayor Lynch, I will review the evidence such as it is." He ruefully looked down at the photos and reports before him. "For the time being, Ms. Wilder will remain in custody—"

A rumble of displeasure rolled through the courtroom. The judge pounded his gavel on the podium. "Ms. Wilder will remain in custody until I have finished my review. The concerns of the city council shall be taken seriously. We'll reconvene on Friday and I will decide then if a trial is warranted. That is all." He struck the gavel again.

Lucille Wilder did not so much as flinch or offer any emotion. She closed her eyes as if napping.

"Dad, what can we do?" Leo asked his father, his cheeks flushing. He stomped into the aisle, heading for the judge's bench. "Let my aunt Lucille go. You let my aunt GO!"

Mayor Lynch blocked Leo's path to the bench. Her dewy, skeletal face held a crooked smile. "Oh, sugarplum, we're *going* to let your auntie go." She pulled Leo close to her. "Together we can watch her go . . . with the police right now."

Sure enough, over the mayor's left shoulder, the bailiff placed Lucille in handcuffs and took her from the witness box.

"Bye, Auntie Lucille," the mayor brayed, waving her gnarled fingers next to Leo.

"Deborah, rescue your son from that dragon in red heels before she unjustly incarcerates him as well," Aunt Lucille called out, steel in her blue eyes. "Don't you worry about me, Leo. I'll be fine, dear. Justice will prevail."

"Looks from here like justice is doing just fine," the mayor said. Deborah Wilder plucked Leo from her grasp, pulling him down the aisle.

Judge Blabbingdale opened his mouth to say something to the mayor, but the moment she turned to him, he grimaced, stormed into his chambers, and angrily banged the door behind him.

Will unhappily stomped up the path beside the river toward Peniel. Simon, Cami, and Andrew surrounded him. More than anything he wanted to be at Aunt Lucille's hearing. But Mr. Shen had ordered him to come to Peniel first thing in the morning for some "very, very, very important training." Since he had to cancel a bike ride with his friends, he asked that they meet him at the St. Thomas churchyard. He was watering his blooming walking stick when his pals appeared. Together they proceeded up the path, shooing away the last remnants of the gnat swarm.

"Can't believe the city had your aunt arrested," Andrew said, trying to be supportive.

"Your father's deputies arrested her," Will said, staring straight ahead.

"He had to do it, Will-man. He's gotta follow the law. He's the sheriff. I know he wasn't happy about it."

"That makes two of us." Will kicked a rock on the ground, sending it spinning into the river.

Simon rushed ahead, waving his plague list. "We've got to talk about the plagues, Will. I've noticed something. There're only a few plagues left until . . . you know *who* gets you know *what*."

Will cut his eyes at Simon, raising a fist. "Your father had better release my aunt Lucille or I'm going to give *you know what* to you know *who*!"

"I'm sure my father will rule properly," Simon snapped.

"He judges according to the law. As he always says, 'Justice is blind.'"

"You're going to be blind if he doesn't free my aunt," Will growled.

"Could you all please KNOCK IT OFF." Cami stopped walking, forcing the boys to stand still. "They can't be blamed for what the city council did to your aunt, William. Listen to Simon for a minute." She walked in front of Will and lifted the brim of his pith helmet. For the first time she could see how angry and troubled he was by the arrest and the unfolding plagues. She looked deep into his hazel eyes. Then, unexpectedly, she wrapped her arms around him. Will was totally caught off guard by the hug. But it did calm him and felt better than he ever imagined. Will's scowl soon melted into a half smirk.

"I'm all right, Cami," he said, still in her embrace. "I've got to get to Peniel, so let's . . . keep moving." He awkwardly separated himself from her and marched onward.

Cami fluttered her fingers like agitated butterflies as a signal for Simon to start talking.

"I've been working on an updated plague list. I put a line through the plagues not caused by the staff. Here's where we stand." Simon handed the list to Will, who read it warily.

The Plagues

- ✔ 1) The Nile turned to BLOOD! SO DID THE PERILOUS RIVER.
- ✔ 2) Frogs! SHARP-TOOTHED AMPHIBIANS EVERYWHERE.

✔ 3) Gnats. STILL OUTSIDE.

4) ~~Swarms of Flies.~~ NOT CAUSED BY STAFF.

5) ~~Plague kills livestock.~~ NOT CAUSED BY STAFF.

6) ~~Boils.~~ NOT CAUSED BY STAFF. THANK GOODNESS.

7) **Hail, thunder, and fire!** "Moses stretched forth his rod toward heaven: and the Lord sent thunder and hail, and fire ran down to the earth." People and animals in the field died. Only the Israelite lands were spared. WHERE CAN I GET A TEFLON UMBRELLA?

8) **Locusts.** Moses lifted the rod, causing locusts to cover "the face of the whole land." They ate all the plants and all the fruit on the trees. NEED TO GET LOCUST SPRAY.

9) **Darkness.** Moses lifted his hands to heaven and there "was thick darkness in all the land of Egypt for three days." CHANGE FLASHLIGHT BATTERIES. STOCK AT LEAST THREE DAYS' WORTH OF BACKUPS.

10) **Death strikes the Egyptians.**

Will felt sick to his stomach. Somewhere in town, a demon with a weaponized staff wanted to exterminate him, and his protector, the person he needed most, was behind bars. With each passing hour, with each passing plague, death moved a little closer.

"Well?" Simon's shrill voice wavered as they walked through Aunt Lucille's backyard up the winding path to Peniel. "Any day now, hail, thunder, and fire are going to hit, then locusts and then—if we survive that—three days of darkness. How are we going to stop the plagues?" He snatched back the list and slipped it into his pocket.

"Let's not get hysterical, Simon," Cami said, rubbing his back as if he were a frightened cat.

"You'll be hysterical in a minute too. When we saw the prophecy the other day, I felt awful because I thought, 'Oh, my friend Will is going to die and that would be terrible.' Then last night I read the Bible again and do you know what it says?" He was jumping like beans on a hot griddle, turning colors with excitement. "After the three days of darkness the angel of death came for the Egyptian's FIRSTBORN. All the firstborn! It's not only Will that dies, but you, me, Andrew . . . we're all GONERS. Aaaaaah."

Andrew was so irritated by the display, he smacked Simon on the arm, hard.

"What'd you do that for, moron?"

"To bring you back to earth. We need to stay calm so we can stop the last plague from coming," Andrew said. "What do ya think we should do, Will-man?"

Will paused at the gates of the museum. "I'm not sure. Miss Ann, the woman who works for Bobbit, told me *he* had the staff. But there's no telling if he still has it."

"So you think Bobbit is the guy, not Sab? I mean, the dude has a picture of Amon in his office." Andrew smacked himself on the forehead. "But they're both eating the geese, right? So it could be either of 'em? Maybe both of 'em?"

"We should check up on Mr. Bobbit," Cami offered.

"Andrew and Simon and I can stake him out at his store. We'll let you know if he has the staff."

"Have you seen anything out of the ordinary, Will?" Simon pointed his index fingers up to his wide glasses as a visual aid. "Have you *seen* any of your strange, shadowy, imaginary friends?"

"Keep this up and you'll need some imaginary friends," Will said. "To answer your question, no. I haven't seen any demons with sapphire walking sticks—and no shadows either. Just those feathers—and they're all over the place."

The carved door on the front of the museum, the one with the image of a knight driving a lance into a dragon, swung open. From behind the door, Bartimaeus squinted at Will's friends, giving them a wave. "Will, you're late for your training. You kids come up in here for a sec." He disappeared back into the large structure that appeared more Byzantine monastery than museum.

The kids walked into the vast, dimly lit outer library. Bartimaeus threw his crutches out, propelling himself to a bookcase on the left side of the room. Like the other cases, it was fronted by a brass grill. He opened the grill with his key and pulled on one of the brass pelicans attached to the grating—which looked just like the one on Will's pith helmet. Bartimaeus opened the cage and reached for the middle shelf. He shoved a red volume into the shadows. He did the same to a blue book on a lower shelf and finally gave a black leather-bound diary a shove. He then stood back and leaned on his crutches, tilting his head as if pondering something weighty.

"Is he okay?" Simon asked after several seconds. "What are we waiting for?"

"We waitin' for you to get some patience. That's what we waitin' for," Bartimaeus said derisively, looking Simon up and down. "This place is old, young man—and old things take time. Sometimes the things we have to wait for are the ones we appreciate the most. So enjoy the anticipation."

Half of the entire bookshelf creaked backward, sliding into darkness, creating a passageway.

"What'd I tell ya? It might be old, but the action's reliable." He ambled into the dark space. "Can't find this kind of stuff at Ikea, I'll tell you dat." Moments later, he emerged from the darkness clutching a handful of twelve inch candles. "So put these in your bags and take 'em home," Bart said, handing out the candles.

Cami studied the white wax work as she took it. "Do they have some purpose?" she asked.

"You'll find out soon, miss. When we're in the middle of the three days of darkness, you won't be able to see ya hand in front of ya face. The electric lights'll fail—ya flashlights, ya phone. You'll be outta luck. In a supernatural darkness, the only thing that might provide a glimmer of light is a blessed candle. That's what these are. So keep 'em close and give 'em to ya friends and family. We gotta be defensive here."

Simon, on the verge of tears, stared at the candle. "Does this mean you think all the other plagues are coming? The hail, the locusts?"

"Son, I get sensations every now and then, but I don't get to see the whole picture." Bartimaeus pulled the books forward to their initial positions and hobbled out of the way as the shelf returned to its place. "I do know one thing, though: As long as there is breath in us, we gotta have hope—and we have to keep fighting for what's right, no matter the cost." He momentarily glanced down at his twisted right leg, the one a demon had shredded so many years ago. Bart's lower lip trembled. He quickly shifted his weight on the crutches and spun himself around to avoid saying anything further.

Will huddled near his friends and whispered, "Cami, I think you're right. Watch Bobbit today. See if he has the staff and let me know where he goes. Text me if you see anything."

Cami, Andrew, and Simon nodded.

"Tomorrow morning, if we can, let's meet at Bub's Treats and Sweets at ten o'clock. Okay?" said Cami, gripping Will's hand for a second.

"You've got it," Will said, squeezing back.

"So you kids stay indoors, ya hear?" Bartimaeus warned, locking the bookcase tight. "If this flamin' hail is as bad as advertised, this town's going to have burn marks before it's over. Best if those marks are not on you. Let's go, Will. The abbot's waiting for ya."

"Mr. Bartimaeus, if the days of darkness start, how dark do you think it's gonna get?" Andrew asked earnestly.

"Dark as the hearts of the people. Darker than you ever imagined, son."

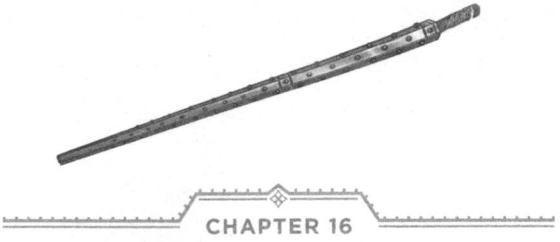

CHAPTER 16

THE PURGATORIAL COURSE

Will found Abbot Athanasius at the end of a hallway, in the rear building of the Peniel complex. The abbot was staring out a leaded Gothic window lost in thought, his back to Will.

"Abbot, I'm sorry I'm late. I have something I need to—"

"It's fine, Will. I have made a decision, or rather these wretched plagues have forced one upon me." He turned to face the boy, his eyebrows nearly touching, his mouth stern. He seemed almost apologetic. "Will, I must accelerate your training. Normally, I would have waited a year or two before even introducing—"

"Sure, Abbot." Will started searching through his backpack, his mind elsewhere. "But first I need to show you something I found at the Karnak Center."

"Why have you been in that place?" the abbot asked, hiding his hands beneath the black folds of his habit.

"Aunt Lucille thought I should go with my friend Cami and her family, so I did. The guy who runs the place has pictures of Amon all over the center. Then I found this." Will held up the Ziploc bag with the wax figurine. "It was in a weird room with food and feathers all over the floor. These little guys were stacked in a corner."

"Tell me you didn't touch this."

"I stabbed it with a knife and bagged it."

The abbot smiled for the first time since Will arrived. "At least you are paying attention." He eyed the wax figure shaped like Will. Whenever he was forming a thought, the abbot made a sound like a tiny locomotive gaining speed, which he did then. "I told you the *Sinestri* knew you, Will. This is proof that they do. The Ancient Egyptians would deface images of their god's enemies. The temple priests would cut the heads off the figurines, impale them with pins, snap off limbs. They thought they were assisting the god to achieve a common goal; the death of their enemy."

Will went pale but managed to keep his balance. "I need Aunt Lucille! We've got to get her out of jail."

Athanasius laid the Ziploc on a chair in the corner of the hall and addressed Will calmly. "Your aunt Lucille is fine. Brother Amalric has been working to secure her release. She would want you to focus on your training now, Will."

"I'll ask her when she's free. I need her. This demon

is trying to kill me. Sab is snapping little Will dolls in his crazy center. Bobbit has the staff—Mr. Timothy Bobbit. A woman at his store told me he has Moses's staff."

"A woman at his store told you this?" The abbot looked as if he smelled something foul.

"Yes, Miss Hye! She works for him. I think she'd know!" He adamantly stood eye to eye with the abbot. "Look, my friends are tracking Bobbit now. We might be able to get the staff back. Can you help us or not? With every minute—"

"Shhhh." The abbot placed his hands on Will's shoulders. "Whatever the hardship, it can best be overcome with silence."

Steam was practically leaking from Will's ears. "A demon is targeting me with Moses's staff and it's—"

"Silence." The abbot's blue eyes widened. "Your anger over the past is blinding you in the present. This demon, this Amon, has worked its way into your head. Once it lodges hatred and wrath there, you will see nothing. Silence and deliberate action are your best weapons against this beast."

Will wanted to scream. He wanted to kick and wail and thrash about on the floor. *Why won't he ever listen to me?* Will yelled inside. Air rushed in and out of his flared nostrils. And though he said nothing, he couldn't mask his rage and frustration.

The abbot, with a hint of pity, said, "Stillness will dispel your anger. Release it and follow me."

"Where are we going?" Will hissed as he followed the abbot.

"To a place I thought I could spare you until you were older."

They walked down a wide stone staircase, a place where shadows and light wrestled. As they reached the bottom, the shadows eventually won.

"Your great-grandfather created this chamber for his personal training. Later your grandfather, Joseph, and your . . . Many of us were trained here." They came to a dank passageway of slick stones, with cobwebs lining the edges. The abbot pulled a torch from the wall and led Will to an arched door that blocked the entire passage.

"Remain here," the abbot said. Will held the torch several feet away from Athanasius, who fished a key from a hidden pocket in his habit and approached the door. Black metal bands etched with flames crisscrossed the old wood. There were at least twenty keyholes along the main band at the middle. The abbot inserted his key into the second to last hole on the right. He quickly dashed back to join Will.

The massive door rumbled and shuddered. To Will it was as if some ancient animal were inhaling for the first time in eons. That's when the top of the door started pulling away from the stones framing it. Just as Will realized that the hinges were at the base of the door, the whole thing suddenly flopped forward, sending dust, cobwebs, and moisture into their faces.

"Jacob's idea of a precaution. Your great-grandfather never liked unexpected guests." The abbot walked over the flattened door, which resembled a varnished boardwalk, and slipped a key into a newly revealed slender metal door. "Here we are. You may enter." The abbot took the torch and jammed it into an iron holder inside.

"What is this place?" Will asked, removing his hat to get the wide view.

The enormous cavern rose up for several stories. From the platform where he and the abbot stood, three wooden suspended catwalks reached across an expanse of murky water. The railless, winding walkways terminated at another platform about forty yards away. But it was hard to see that far since the isolated pools of flame on the water's surface below provided the only illumination.

"Jacob called this the Purgatorial Course," the abbot said, closing the metal door behind them. "It approximates combat with a major demon. You might call it a demon fighter's conditioning center." He pointed a long finger upward. "Your great-grandfather constructed a network of ropes and ladders up above. It's a most challenging course. Some of the Brethren use it as Jacob did: to prepare ourselves for sudden combat. I believe you will be facing another demon soon, Will. We thought it best to bring you here now."

"*We?*" Will glanced around. "Who is *we?*"

"The council members. We discussed it as a council and even your aunt Lucille agreed that it was time. Brother Baldwin is there." He pointed up to a nook on the right side of the rocky cavern, about twenty feet up.

"Hello, William." In the flickering light, he nodded. Just the beak of Baldwin's nose was visible from below.

Will grimaced and slammed his helmet back on his head. "What is he doing here? And how does this help me?"

"It will help you to be vigilant outside and in. This coming battle is principally inside of you. To succeed, you will have to see the external while guarding your thoughts— guarding your heart! Do not allow anger or hatred in. Leave no room for the devil, Will. Only love and faith will save you." He raised a knowing eyebrow. "I've chosen Baldwin specifically to assist us. I'm aware of your *fondness* for one another."

Will stamped his foot and stared at the ground, trying to control the bubbling volcano he felt inside. Next to his feet, chiseled into the stone platform, were the words *Though a host encamp against me—my heart shall not fear.*

"Look at me." The abbot spoke intensely. "Unless you obey my instructions, you will not survive. The danger is very real. On the far platform, there is a staff. Your task is to secure it. Choose a path. Keep your eyes and *all* your attention fixed on that staff. Don't be afraid to use your instincts and improvise—"

"Why *him*?" Will sputtered in a quiet voice, pointing up to Baldwin. "He hates me. He probably stole the staff in the first place and now you're letting him join me for some kind of war games."

"Sometimes the people we most dislike are our paths to self-mastery. Use this challenge. Push yourself. The gifts are already within you." Abbot Athanasius was practically at Will's ear. "Baldwin will attempt to impede you. Do not be distracted. This course demands dexterity and calm. When you reach the staff, shove it into the hole on the stone at your feet and Baldwin will be blocked."

"What exactly is he going to be doing?" Will nervously shifted his lips from side to side.

"There is a cannon up on that ledge. He'll be shooting fireballs at you. Calm down. They can't kill you, though they might burn a little. Move quickly and maintain an inner silence. Try not to fall off the walkway and do not allow the circumstances or whatever is spoken to influence you. Just secure the staff." The abbot ran a thumb over Will's helmet and hid himself in a rocky niche near the door.

Will took a deep, uncertain breath, pulled his helmet strap under his chin, and made a run for the faraway platform.

He chose the middle path. Seconds later, a spinning ball of fire came hurtling toward him from above. "Keep moving," Baldwin taunted him. "Don't you dare look at the fire. Keep your eyes trained on the goal."

Out of the corner of his eye, Will could see the fireball getting close. He danced back six steps. The fireball hit the path just in front of him. He turned his body away to avoid the fiery backlash. The moment it dissipated, he sprinted forward, the path trembling beneath him. It started to weave back and forth. To avoid panic, Will forced himself to breathe deeply.

He paused and stood stock-still in the middle of the pathway.

"Don't stop. You're not allowed to stop, William!" Baldwin barked. "I told you he was not up to this, Abbot." Two fireballs rained down on Will in rapid succession.

In the inner quiet he had carved out amid the chaos, Will saw what he had to do. He would somersault the way Aunt Lucille had been teaching him for months. He would land on his feet, drop to his knees, and grab the edges of the catwalk.

Just as the fireballs approached him—as if he were moving in slow motion—Will flipped forward, evading the spinning infernos. His somersault carried him three-quarters of the way down the quaking catwalk. Falling to his knees, hugging the edges of the pathway, he was ten yards from the platform. Immediately, the whole thing tilted to the left, tipping him sideways.

Will screamed, wrapping his legs and arms around the narrow planks of the pathway. Shimmying forward, his goal in sight, the path unexpectedly flipped the other way. He dangled over the fiery water below, barely hanging on by his left arm and leg. Will froze. Fear overwhelmed him. He considered letting go of the wooden bridge and dropping into the water. He might be able to avoid the flaming part of the pool below. Maybe it wouldn't be so hot . . .

"I knew he couldn't do it," Baldwin wailed, firing three more fireballs directly at Will. "He's a boy, Abbot—an obstinate boy. Just like his father!"

Will felt the heat rising in his body. He wished he were the one behind the cannon, firing at Baldwin. As his fingers lost their grip of the catwalk, he envisioned Baldwin burned

to a crisp begging for—Then he recalled the abbot's instructions: *Guard your thoughts . . .* and the words on the platform: *My heart shall not fear.*

A newfound courage gave him the strength to pull himself up onto the edge of the tilted walkway. He regained his balance just as another fireball landed low, missing the path entirely. But a second ball of flame closed in on Will. He rose to his feet and did his best high-wire impression. Arms out, dancing across the narrow edge of the wooden planks, he barely dodged the second fireball. By the time he hit the platform, a third flaming ball smashed into the walkway behind him.

Will casually reached for the staff while Baldwin leaned over his ledge above yelling, "Dumb luck. You are far from ready, Will Wilder. Keep your guard up! Keep it up!" Baldwin violently pulled on the cannon lever, attempting to unload another volley of fireballs. But nothing happened and the rumbling sound of the cannon engine died.

Baldwin was pounding his fist on the underbelly of the cannon when Brother Philip stepped out of the shadows. "It works best when these are inside the engine," Philip confided out the side of his mouth. He held two fuses in his open palm and slammed the iron grate on the side of the cannon shut.

"Put those fuses back immediately," Baldwin barked.

Tobias Shen emerged from the darkness behind him. "Vicar, this was intended as a test for Will, but it has revealed much more."

"What does that mean, Tobias?"

"You were to help train the boy, not hurt him. The abbot thought we should be here—in case your emotions got the best of you," Shen said calmly.

"My emotions are completely in check. I was trying to train that—" Baldwin glanced over the ledge and began laughing. "Look at your great leader-in-waiting. Even with your assistance he's struggling."

When Will grasped the staff, the stones of the platform began to sink. He didn't know where to stand with stones disappearing into the flaming water by the second. One of his feet descended toward the pool while the other remained on a high stone. He quickly shifted his weight and stepped up—placing one foot atop the other. Spotting the stone with the hole in it, near the rear wall, Will lunged.

He drove the staff into the cavity on the floor with great force and used it to keep himself from falling backward. All at once, the wooden catwalk at his rear straightened itself, the stones surrounding him moved back into place, and the cannon on the ledge before Baldwin disappeared into the ground.

Will did a little dance on the platform, throwing punches into the air. "What happens now?" he asked jubilantly. "Do I get a prize? A trip to Hawaii?"

"You win a first-class trip to a true demonic battle," the abbot said, walking across the wooden path. "For your first time on the Purgatorial Course, it was not an embarrassment."

"Gee, thanks," Will muttered, shaking the water from his red high-tops.

"Very, very good, Mr. Wilder." Tobias Shen applauded, appearing at the bottom of a staircase hidden by a stalagmite. "Why don't you head up to Bethel Hall? We need to speak privately with the vicar for a moment." From Mr. Shen's face, Will could tell the chat was not to be a friendly one.

"Can't I stay?" Will asked, hoping to watch Baldwin get a good dressing-down.

"It would be best if you went upstairs," the abbot said, directing him to the metal door where they had entered.

"I miss all the fun," Will said, shuffling out.

The dying sun threw pink light on the piles of gnat carcasses and dead frogs surrounding the Perilous Falls city jail. A deputy swept the remains into neat piles on the edge of the front walkway. Heedless of his work, two swift figures tromped through the stinking mounds.

"Hey, watch where you—" The deputy changed his tune when he recognized one of the stompers as the mayor. "Oh. Sorry, ma'am."

Ava Lynch slowly turned her head in his direction. "Are you guarding the prisoner this evening?"

"Yes, ma'am."

"Take us to her, Deputy," she said imperiously, removing her gloves.

The mayor and her companion were escorted down a hallway of empty cells.

"Miss Lucille, you've got some guests to see you," the deputy announced loudly.

"Thank you, Deputy," the mayor whispered. "We can take it from here. Give us your keys and some privacy."

The young man hesitated for a moment, tugging at the sides of his belt. Then in a rush he mumbled a "yes, ma'am," handed over the keys, and vacated the lockup.

Lucille Wilder sat on a metal bed attached to the wall of her cell. Her wrists were bound in chains fastened to the floor. At the approach of the visitors, she bolted upright. "Who's there?"

The answer came in the form of keys clanging against the lock of her cell door.

When she saw the mayor enter, Lucille darkly asked, "What do you want?"

"Now, is that any way to greet an old friend?" Lynch loosed a throaty laugh, striding to the center of the cell. "Thought I'd come by for a little visit."

"Ava, you've got to free me for the sake of the town." Lucille took a jagged breath and hung her head. "There are dark forces at play and they have to be stopped—now! I know we've had our differences, but you have no idea what is out there. I can help."

"Oh, I bet you can. That's why you're in chains, sugar. Didn't want those little hands of yours getting too close to-gether. You're responsible for all of this."

"You know that's a lie. We may not agree on much but I—" Lucille stared at the Ammit pendant hanging from the mayor's neck. "Do you even know what that is, Ava?"

"It's protection from people like you. It was given to me by my friend and our town spiritual advisor." The mayor wrapped a bony hand over the amulet, clutching it over her heart.

Lucille smiled knowingly. "Pothinus Sab is a deceptive con man, and you have become so bemused by the *Darkness* that you can't tell day from night." She pulled at the chains in frustration. "Let me out of here."

"Oh, stop being so ornery. With all your chatter, I almost forgot. I came here to make an introduction." She raised her bangled arm in the air. "Pothinus, honey, come in and meet Lucille Wilder."

When Pothinus Sab stepped into the cell, Lucille's mouth dropped open. She physically recoiled, steadying herself against the cinder blocks behind her.

"Miss Wilder, I have been so looking forward to our meeting," he said, his black eyes glinting. He placed a weathered leather bag on the floor and bent at the waist, his hands on his knees. "You must be very thirsty, no? Are the guards hydrating you properly?" He didn't wait for an answer. "How about a nice refreshment?" He reached for his bag.

"I would rather drink sand than whatever you're offering, Mr. Sab," Lucille snapped.

He emitted a stifled giggle. "Aren't you amusing?" He lifted a flask of green tonic from the bag. "But charity demands helping those who won't help themselves. Isn't that true?" His voice suddenly flattened, and its usual music disappeared. "We have many methods of administering our tonic, Miss Wilder."

He drew a lacquered box from his white suit. Opening it, he delicately pulled out an insect that could have been an angry centipede with pincers. "Miss Mayor, if you would hold Miss Wilder's head to the side, we can share this specially brewed refreshment with her immediately." He dropped the earwig into the tonic bottle and held it directly in front of Lucille's eyes.

"It won't be long now," Sab said with a sympathetic smile. "You will be the first to taste the regeneration that Amon intends for all." Then he whispered, just for her, "You are ready for death—I mean regeneration—aren't you, Miss Wilder?"

Mayor Lynch immobilized Lucille Wilder's head, holding it to the side. Lucille yelled, but no one could hear her. She fell into silence and shut out the horror of the assault to come by closing her eyes tightly. Sab, as if administering a lifesaving drug, pressed the mouth of the tonic bottle to Lucille Wilder's ear.

She struggled, yanking against the chains. All the while the earwig, swollen with green liquid, its pincers snapping, climbed up the bottle's neck toward its final destination.

CHAPTER 17

MALLEUS DIABOLUS

After clobbering the Purgatorial Course and proving himself to Baldwin, Will resented being sent upstairs to Bethel Hall. He trudged up the broad staircase of the north tower. Making his way through the training wing, he could hear the Brethren's best tumbler, Brother Pedro, flipping off the padded walls behind one of the closed doors. Will's pace slowed as his glance fell to the floor. Levitating black feathers were strewn across the hallway.

Just as he approached the door leading to the courtyard garden, a "pssst" struck his ear.

He turned around. Not a soul in the hall, just the black feathers.

"Psssst."

It came from a nook in the wall several steps back.

A small potted tree filled the alcove. "Who's there?" Will asked.

"It's me." Valens parted the branches of the tree with his hands and poked his head through the leaves. "I was hoping you'd come by. I didn't want Baldwin to see us talking. I don't trust him at all."

"Me neither," said Will.

"Has Tobias or Bart or Lucille ever mentioned the *Malleus Diabolus*?"

"The what?" Will said.

"It is a book your great-grandfather rescued from a burned-out monastery in England. I was thinking that it could be of great assistance to you. I'm sure Lucille would want you to see it. It supposedly describes scads of demons—a very ancient text. Bart thought that Jacob might have made his own notations in the book."

"Where is it?" Will asked, fascinated.

"That's the problem. None of us have ever seen the *Malleus Diabolus*. Bart or possibly Lucille would know better than I—but the legend is: when the chosen one lays hold of an angel's leg, the book will present itself." Valens had mischief in his eyes. "Now, I have been all over this museum. There are only a handful of stone or marble angels. One of which is that statue over there." He pointed across the hall to a tall white marble angel, her wings at rest, standing atop a pedestal.

Without so much as a breath, Will marched over and grasped the angel's leg.

"It's probably not this one," Will said, releasing the statue after several seconds. "Where are the others?"

Valens ran two hands over his longish hair, parting it in the middle. "There is a much better candidate. See those columns?" There were six pillars on each side of the hall. Capitals at the top depicted saints and smiling angel heads with no bodies. But one capital featured a roughly chiseled devil, its arms held back by an apprehensive angel.

"It's kind of high up, but that one seems a good possibility." Valens pulled a wooden high-backed chair from the wall. "Do you want to have a go at it?"

Will leapt up on the chair and reached for the angel's leg. "How long have you been looking for this *Malleus Diab—* whatever it's called?"

"It's just a hobby of mine. You know how the mind sometimes fixates on things, then you're lolling about and "

Will clutched the angel's leg and the entire column turned on itself. A hollow passage opened.

"Hullo! That was easy," Valens said. His blue eyes scanned the hallway. "Shall we go exploring, then?"

Valens and Will climbed down a very tight staircase, which gradually widened as they got lower. With his flashlight, Will could see a desk piled with books and a large solitary shelf behind it. A blanket of dust covered everything. There were crossbows, spears, swords, and other instruments of warfare leaning against the walls. Others teetered off the edge on the uppermost shelf.

Valens found a switch that lit a large gas lamp in the center of the room. He immediately ran to the cluttered corners of the octagonal space.

"Look on that shelf, Will. Do you see a heavy book with a metal cover? I think it's silver with a series of crosses carved into it." Valens madly tossed weapons and canvases aside, hastily scanning the artifacts.

Will rubbed away the dust from the book spines. There were multiple cracked leather tomes and papers bound in twine, but nothing metal. Then in the middle of the lower shelf, his finger ran along a black book. The paper on the spine tore away. Silver glittered beneath.

He yanked the book off the shelf and peeled away at the black cover like he was unwrapping a gift. The heavy volume had one large cross and a smattering of smaller ones cut into the silver cover. "This must be the *Malleus*," Will said excitedly.

The discovery did nothing to slow Valens's search. "Put it on the desk. It should open at your touch," he ordered, preoccupied.

Will hesitated, holding the book at arm's length. "Don't you want to see, Mr. Valens?"

"I'm trying to help you, Will," Valens said with an edge in his voice, still ripping through the objects scattered about. "Has your aunt Lucille said anything about Aaron's staff? It belonged to Moses's brother."

"The prophecy said I needed to find—" As the words escaped his lips, Will immediately wished he'd said nothing.

"I need to find Moses's staff. What's Aaron's staff got to do with anything?" Will faked ignorance.

"Aaron's staff is supposed to be more powerful than Moses's rod. Your great-grandfather definitely had it. I saw Aaron's staff on one of our old inventory lists. But it's nowhere in Peniel. I've looked." He was now on a chair, going through the items on the top of the bookshelf.

Will carried the silver volume to the other side of the room. It had book spines on each side and no visible pages. As he laid the book on his lap, he absently glimpsed the ring he wore, the one Aunt Lucille had given him earlier. Inside the sealed glass capsule, the crimson-red blood of St. Januarius bubbled as if it were boiling. *Am I in danger or is Aunt Lucille?* Before he could really ponder the question, one of the spines of the book on his knees unlatched and the volume opened. Tall calligraphy announced *Malleus Diabolus* by Martin Del Rio. Will flipped the page and saw this:

· LEVIATHAN ·

Leviathan

A great wriggling serpent with seven heads and tentacles rises from the depths . . .

Will was too frightened to read any further. Visions in his mind's eye of the horrid creature riding the waves of the Perilous River forced him to quickly turn the page. A wooziness ambushed him. He licked his dry lips and made himself read on:

Amon

This demon is the hidden one. Amon is known as the local deity of Thebes, an Egyptian god venerated since the Old Kingdom. Exulted in the 11th Dynasty, the plumed regal figure in statuary and throughout the Egyptian empire is not Amon's reality but a cunning mask of evil.

In its true form, Amon appears with a raven's head, its large beak baring canine teeth. The creature vomits flames, spitting wrath upon all who encounter it. It has the body of a wolf and the slithering tail of a serpent hatched in the bowels of hell . . .

· AMON ·

There was much more, but Will's eye went to a note scratched in the wide margin of the parchment paper. It was Jacob Wilder's handwriting. Will recognized it from having read his great-grandfather's diary. The note read:

From the moment I arrived in Egypt, I began seeing paranormal raven feathers invisible to the others. The demon sheds them wherever its power is most intense.

Wily and loath to reveal its true face, Amon comes in many guises. The Staff of Moses had been temporarily lost and a host of plagues was loosed upon the Brethren here in Cairo. Following my arrival, we successfully used holy water, oils, and relics to defuse the plagues. Though there is no protection from the last plague; the coming of the so-called angel of death. According to an ancient scroll the Brethren showed me, the last plague when called forth by a demon is an event "outside of nature." Unlike blood, frogs, or gnats, the thing that comes to claim the firstborn is not of God. It is a denizen of the pit that ascends to strike its victims.

While battling the plagues, the Brethren in Cairo and I uncovered a plot by some priests of Amon. Clinging to the old ways, they attempted to physically summon the major demon into the world. They believed they could raise Amon from hell by ritually offering him one of his own: the possessed Pharaoh Tuthmosis II.

Tuthmosis may have been the pharaoh who barred Moses and the Israelites from leaving Egypt. That would make him the same stubborn pharaoh God delivered the plagues upon.

Using both the staffs of Moses and Aaron, I finally repelled Amon. The Brethren stopped Amon's priests from executing their plan and we secured the mummy of Tuthmosis II. This mummy, the staff of the Prophet, and that of his brother should be closely guarded and never allowed to leave our care. The disciples of Amon may

attempt to raise the demon again at some future time. The *Sinestri* never sleep. Neither should we. *Deus Vult.*
JW
September 1955

That's why my great-granddad stored the mummy at Peniel—to keep the Sinestri *from using it!* Will tried to turn the next page just to see what other demons might be described. When he tugged at the page, it felt as if it was glued to all the others. He couldn't pry them loose. In frustration, he slammed the volume shut.

"So what did it say?" a sweaty Valens asked, dabbing his brow with a silk handkerchief from his vest pocket.

"Nothing much. Some stuff about Leviathan. It didn't make much sense."

From the worried expression on Will's face, Valens could see he was withholding something. "Did it say anything about the Staff of Aaron? Where it might be found?" Valens closed in on Will, opening his graceful hand. "Might I see the book?" He licked his lower lip.

Will pulled the *Malleus* close to his chest. "You're not supposed to see it, Mr. Valens. It's meant for me."

"Why are you being so ungrateful, Will? I took you here." He smiled tensely, flashing his pearly teeth. "Let me have a look." Valens reached for the volume. The whole room suddenly shook. Dull explosions could be heard in the distance as the walls rocked back and forth.

Valens tumbled over the desk. Will stumbled sideways

into the staircase. From the shocks, it felt as though bombs were falling on Peniel. Will pounded up the slim staircase to see what was happening aboveground.

"Will, come back here! WILL!" Valens yelled, staggering to his feet.

The bulging earwig crawled onto the lip of the tonic bottle in Pothinus Sab's hand. Mayor Lynch held Lucille Wilder's head tightly against the bottle, anticipating the moment when the bug would slip into Lucille's ear and end their decades-old rivalry.

"Goodbye, Lucille," the mayor murmured, staring down at the strangely serene woman.

Lucille Wilder, her eyes closed, paid no heed to any of it. She continued silently mouthing something under her breath as she had since the mayor first laid hands on her.

"Regeneration comes swiftly, Miss Lucille," Pothinus Sab said.

Whatever he said after that was lost in a terrible noise.

A tremor hit the jail, causing the ground to shift violently. The mayor was hurled against the wall while Sab and his tonic bottle crashed against the cell bars. Had Lucille Wilder not been chained to the floor, she might have hit the ceiling. Instead the jolt threw her high into the air and she used the chains to land on her feet.

The dazed mayor was the first to see the hail, like flaming

charcoal briquettes, falling from the sky outside. "Pothinus! Pothinus! There's fire! Fire's coming down!" She pointed at the small window above Lucille, her skeletal face contorted in anguish.

Instantly understanding that the seventh plague was upon them, Lucille pulled the chains to their full length. She pressed her back against the cinder-block wall behind her.

The structure rumbled and a sizzling sound overhead made it clear that the roof had caught fire.

The mayor, whose leg and arm were bloodied, crawled across the floor to an unconscious Sab. "Get up, Pothinus." She struck his face. "We've got to get out of here." On his green-stained jacket, she spotted the fat earwig from the tonic bottle. The thing waddled north onto Sab's lapel, bound for his head. The mayor removed her shoe and clumsily whacked the earwig with it. Her aim was off, so she kept trying.

A moaning squeal of twisting metal echoed from the ceiling. Lucille watched in horror as flaming fissures cracked through the plaster surface.

"Stay still, you bugger," the mayor screamed, smashing her heel into Sab's collar. Green goo and bits of the dead earwig oozed down the front of his jacket. The blow startled Sab, who jerked upward just in time to see the ceiling cave in.

A clanging cascade of metal, bricks, and fire pounded onto the floor of the cell. To avoid the falling debris, Sab and the mayor backed into the hall. They peered through the dust and flames. "Lucille? Did you make it, Lucille?" the mayor yelled.

Only the crackle of burning wood and tumbling bricks replied.

"We've got to go. Come on, Pothinus," the mayor screamed, a hand over her bleeding arm. She hobbled down the hall.

Pothinus Sab did not immediately follow her. He lingered for a moment to check for any sign of Lucille Wilder. "Are you there, Miss Wilder?" he asked in a singsong voice. On the other side of the flaming rubble, a red flash ignited. It only lasted a moment. *Probably the main electrical lines snapping,* Sab thought.

He shouted into the inferno, the burning hail raining down through the open ceiling. "On the off chance that you survive, there'll be no running away. We wouldn't want that, would we?" He slammed the cell door shut and took the keys, sealing Lucille inside. "You and your Brethren can do NOTHING to stop the rising of Amon. Can you hear me, Lucille Wilder? The people will welcome the *Sinestri*," he taunted her through the bars. "They are already ours."

CHAPTER 18

FLAMING HAIL AND LOCUSTS

Unable to find Will in Bethel Hall, Tobias Shen searched Peniel's training wing. "Mr. Wilder? Mr. Wilder?" Shen cried, walking briskly down the columned hall. Minor quakes rattled the tower as he neared the courtyard door. Outside, clumps of fire dropped into the garden. Shen worried that Will had used the courtyard as a shortcut and might have been struck down by the hail. Slightly panicked, the old man doubled his pace and ran smack into Will, who exited the column's secret chamber carrying the *Malleus Diabolus.*

"Mr. Wilder. Thank the Lord you are in one piece," Shen said, uncharacteristically embracing him.

"We need to talk, Mr. Shen," Will said, checking over his shoulder. *"Alone."* He didn't wait for a response but sped up the staircase to the north tower. Shen noted the open column in the hallway with a troubled frown but didn't stay to investigate. Instead he charged after Will.

Despite the tremors, none of Peniel's buildings suffered major damage. Climbing the tower, Will surveyed the rooftops of Peniel through the small windows in the stone and realized the hail was deliberately avoiding Peniel's structures. Continuing to the top of the staircase, he opened the door to a spacious communal room, which overlooked all of Perilous Falls. Tobias Shen came heaving through the doorway moments later.

"Why do you run so quickly? What is wrong with you, Mr. Wilder?" Shen threw himself into a chair. He raised his faint eyebrows and grunted when he saw the book in Will's hands. "Explain!"

Will closed the door before responding. He told Shen about the secret passageway in the column and how Valens had led him to the *Malleus Diabolus*. "Once it opened, Mr. Valens wanted to see the book and started asking all these strange questions about Aaron's staff. He wanted to know if I knew where it was."

"What did you tell him?" Shen looked past Will, through the expansive windows at the town below.

"I don't know where Aaron's staff *is*. What do you think I told him? But I'm sure he was searching that secret room for it." The sight of fire raining down on Perilous Falls pulled Will to the window and broke his concentration. "Is the city going to burn? I'd better get home—" He started for the door.

"No need, Mr. Wilder," Shen said. With two fingers, he indicated a leather chair. "Bartimaeus and I pretreated most of the houses and buildings in town with holy water. It should shield them from this demonic attack. The town seems to be holding up well." Shen nodded contentedly, observing the hail burning trees and striking roadways but missing most of the houses and businesses.

"Mr. Shen, the prophecy and this book said I had to get two staffs. Bobbit may have Moses's staff, but what about Aaron's?" Will pushed his pith helmet back and stuck his chin out, demanding an answer.

"Our power resides in what is small, Mr. Wilder . . . in obedience," Shen said, watching Will's reaction closely.

"I have been obedient. I have done everything you all asked. But there is a demon out there trying to kill me and I need to know where Aaron's staff is. Do you *know*? Where *is it*?"

Oblivious to his tantrum, Shen dispassionately changed the subject. "Have you been attending to your tree at the St. Thomas churchyard, Mr. Wilder?"

"Yes, yes. I have watered it every day. Obedient Will has watered that dumb tree every day since you first told me to—"

"Good. Good. Good. Obedience is the shortest path to perfection. Where there is no obedience, there is no virtue. Where there is no virtue, there is no good. The devil fears the obedient, Will." He smiled, igniting the starburst of wrinkles around his eyes. "I am very, very pleased."

Will rolled his eyes in exasperation, wanting to press him about the location of the staff. But a suddenly agitated Mr. Shen was on his feet, walking to the window. Smoke plumed from a building behind city hall.

"The jail," he said, fear in his voice. "Bartimaeus and I skipped a few of the government buildings: the sheriff's office and the jail. It was too risky." He craned his neck to see over the trees of the park. "We didn't protect the jail. I hope Lucille is safe."

Will checked his ring. The blood roiled inside the ampule. "The burning hail looks like it's stopping. We should go check on her now."

"Yes. Yes. I'll take you home. Then I will visit Lucille myself." Shen maneuvered past Will and pushed open the door.

"Mr. Shen, wait up," Will said. "This *Malleus* book had a note from my great-grandfather about a plot to raise Amon using *the mummy*. The one downstairs. Kinda freaky, huh?"

"We must share all of this with the abbot," Shen said, descending the stairs. "In the meantime, I will tell the Brethren to keep careful watch of Valens."

Unbeknownst to Shen and Will, Valens had been keeping careful watch of *them*. Had they returned to the top of the stairs and checked behind the door of the communal room, they would have found Valens standing exactly where he had been for several minutes. It was the perfect spot to overhear their conversation and to plan his next move.

Before Will went to bed Wednesday night, Mr. Shen called to tell the family that Lucille Wilder's jail cell had burned in the fiery storm. By the time Mr. Shen arrived, the rubble still smoldered, though Lucille was nowhere to be found. Dan Wilder, in his robe, sped to the jail to get answers from the firefighters. "No one's seen her," he was told. "She might be buried in the wreckage. We don't know for sure."

Will had just changed into his pajamas when his mother knocked at his bedroom door.

"Can I come in?" she asked.

He opened the door and affected a brave face but said nothing. Deb, in her nightgown, walked over and sat on the edge of his bed while Will avoided facing her, rearranging figurines from Peniel on his bookshelf.

"Everything has a beginning and an end, Will. Even our time with those we love." She spoke gently and waited for him to respond. When he didn't, she continued. "Your aunt Lucille loved you very much. More than anything, she wanted you to use your gifts and to make sure you were safe."

"I know," Will said without turning around.

"If you want to continue your training, I'll support you. I know Lucille was very adamant about the prophecy and your role in it."

"Uh-huh." His voice cracked and he said nothing else.

"She felt the same way about your sister and brother. She started training Leo, too, you know. He's scared and coming to terms with his gift. He was in his room today practicing breathing and . . . I don't know what he was doing, but he needs your support, Will."

"I'll try."

Deb rose and placed her hands on Will's shoulders. "You're not the only one who feels the world is closing in on him. And you're not alone."

Will spun around, his eyes brimming with panic. "Do you think she's really gone, Mom?"

"I wish we could know for sure, but I can tell you one thing: No matter what danger she faced, your aunt Lucille would have fought to the bitter end. We've got to do the same." She kissed him on the head. "Go to sleep. We'll probably know more tomorrow." She left, noiselessly closing the door behind her.

Will hit the light switch, plunging the room into darkness. Life without Aunt Lucille was unimaginable to him. Lying on his bed trying to sleep, he couldn't envision facing Amon or whatever lay ahead without Aunt Lucille's guidance . . . her protection . . . her love. He angrily punched at the mattress.

Aunt Lucille's gone and I'll be next. Then everybody . . .

To mask his sudden sobs, he buried his face in his pillow, soaking it with tears. The emotional toil and the physical trials of the day eventually dragged him to sleep.

It was nearly half past eight in the morning when he was awakened by a droning noise outside his window. To Will's ear it sounded like a thousand tiny maracas being constantly shaken in the yard.

Did all the neighbors start up their Weedwhackers at the same time? What the heck?

His head and an arm hung off the edge of the bed, his legs knotted in the sheets. Will kicked free of the bedclothes and lifted his blinds. "Those aren't Weedwhackers," he said. "They're weed EATERS!"

Thousands of winged lime-green grasshoppers filled the air. They feasted on the trees, which were broken and burned by the hailstorm in the backyard. The front lawns and gardens were spared—at least those Will could see. *Mr. Shen and Bartimaeus must have hit the lawns and the houses with their water treatment.*

He quickly dressed and ran downstairs.

"Locusts have descended upon Perilous Falls with inexplicable fury," the reporter on TV blared into the Wilder kitchen. "It is nothing short of biblical. Though I have to say, the swarm has thinned from a few hours ago. . . ."

"At least people won't have to cut their grass for a few years," Will said, tucking his shirt in. Getting no reaction from his father, he turned serious. "Dad, do we know anything else about Aunt Lucille?"

Dan Wilder took a swig of coffee and turned from the TV. "Nothing yet. I'm going back to the jail now if I can get through. . . . Just look at this . . ." His palm trembled as he raised it to the television. "Where are these things coming from?"

Will was too upset to debate with his father. "You know where they're coming from, Dad. A demon has the staff. I know you don't want to hear it, but I'm not the first Wilder they've attacked." He tied his red sneakers, watching his father closely.

Dan said nothing, sipping from his coffee mug. Then looking up, he asked, "Where are you going? You can't go out into this . . . this swarm."

"It's not as bad as the gnats or the frogs. At least these things only eat leaves." Will grabbed a raincoat from the hall closet. "I have to meet the guys at Bub's. Where's Mom?"

"She's upstairs getting ready for a shoot. You know she loves supernat—events like . . . this." Dan abruptly wrapped his son in a bear hug, speaking urgently. "Don't do anything dangerous, Will. Keep your distance from the Brethren. Their old stories can only hurt you, son. Look at your aunt Lucille." He held Will close, tears forming in his eyes. "If we rationally focus on real things . . . on the here and now—the *present*—maybe we can survive. But when we dwell on . . . other things . . . old fables . . . we can bring them into our lives. I don't want that for you—for any of us. I only want to keep you safe. Do you understand?" Dan held Will by the shoulders and studied his face with worried eyes.

Will broke away from his father, placing the pith helmet on his head. "This is the *here and now*, Dad." He opened the front door, pointing to the swarms of locusts swirling on the street. "This is the *present* that I have to deal with. If I don't, there may be nothing left for you to *keep safe*."

"Don't say that."

"It's the truth," Will said, stepping outside. "These things aren't natural, Dad, and they're not old fables. Why won't you admit it?"

His father looked pained, wanting to say something more. But he stopped himself. Finally, over the buzz of the insects clouding the street, Dan yelled, "Be careful, son."

"Sure thing." Will waved, skipping into the locust haze, his raincoat flapping behind him. For a split second Dan almost ran after Will. Instead, he white-knuckled the door frame, reminding himself of all the possible explanations for the locust storm. Conflicted and miserable, he watched his son disappear from sight.

There were fewer bugs in the sky than when he awoke. Like the frogs and the gnats before them, the flying grass-hoppers never approached Will. It was as if he were wearing some sort of insect repellent.

Catching sight of a house on the corner of Falls Road, he slowed his run. The place looked like it had been target practice for a couple of bomb squadrons. The smoking roof had caved in and locusts coated every inch of the home. The swarm greedily munched the grass, trees, and bushes out front. Will did a double take because all the houses sur-rounding it were pristine—not a locust on them.

The bedraggled owner, a large woman covered in soot, defended her front doorway with a broom. The locusts were clearly winning. Will walked up the path to the house. "Are you all right, ma'am?"

"Sure! It's a laugh a minute around here." She never stopped swinging at the incoming locusts. "The city came through a few days ago spraying the houses and ol' big mouth here told them she didn't want any poison in her yard. 'Let nature have its way,' I thought. That worked out great." She jumped a little and reached into her blouse, pulling two locusts out by their wings. Snarling, she tossed them into the air.

"Let me see if I can help," Will said, removing a holy water vial from his backpack. He scattered the contents near the front door and the locusts took flight, clearing the entryway.

"Hey, hit me with some of that too," the slack-jawed woman demanded.

Will sprinkled her with the water. She dropped her broom to the ground. "Thanks a lot, kid," she said, amazed by the suddenly bug-free zone.

He gave her a wave and wondered how the dilapidated house was still standing. Backing away, he hoped that it wouldn't collapse until he cleared out.

"Kid, if you see an Asian man in a city truck, tell him to swing by. He offered me a treatment a couple of days ago. I think it's time," the woman bellowed. "Tell him it's Alveda Bruckburger's house. He'll probably remember me."

Will smiled in a "this is weird, so I'm leaving" kind of way and ran up Main Street. Before reaching Bub's, he took a short detour to the jail, which was only steps from city hall. Crackling sounds, like toothpicks snapping, came from the locusts gnawing shrubbery on either side of Will, but the buildings seemed fine. He was not prepared for what he found at the sheriff's office.

CHAPTER 19

POSSESSED BY AMON

Police tape sealed the collapsed, smoking jail. Every wall had fallen in. Even so, Will wanted a closer look. He lifted the police tape and started to duck under it.

A cop jumped out of his squad car, flicking locusts away from his face. "You can't go near the jail, young man," he announced.

"My aunt Lucille was in there last night, Officer. Why isn't somebody looking for her?"

"You've got to ask?" The cop held his arm out, covered in locusts. "These things are coming out of our ears. Wildfires are burning in almost every public area. We did a pass through the jail and there's nobody in there—alive or otherwise." He shooed away the bothersome bugs and jogged back to his police car.

Will mumbled a "thanks" and unhappily stomped to

Bub's. Oddly, the usual collection of cats, dogs, and even a few birds congregated along the front of the sweet shop, transfixed by the locusts. The full bowls of milk and dog treats seemed to keep the pets in place. The flies that usually hung about the alley couldn't be seen through the locust blur. As if frightened, the animals yowled, chirped, and purred at Will's approach. Or maybe they were reacting to Simon, who strolled up wearing a full beekeeper outfit.

"Don't stare at me!" Simon said defensively to Will. "You're wearing a raincoat and there's not a cloud in the sky. At least I'm dressed appropriately for interacting with winged threats." He shook a finger at the bellowing animals outside. "You all can shut it too," Simon brayed, opening the door to Bub's Treats and Sweets.

Andrew and Cami were already seated at one of the shiny chrome tables inside. They were the only patrons. While Simon peeled off his beekeeper apparel, Cami tried to keep from laughing in his face. "I already ordered you a Puffer Fluff, Will," she said, lightly smirking. "You too, Simon."

"We staked Bobbit out most of yesterday," Andrew said, buttering a muffin. "Nothin' doin' there, Will-man. He's sick. But he never ate a goose."

Simon took his seat and jumped into the conversation. "Here's the full report of his activities." He smacked a notebook, scribbled with entries, onto the table. "Mr. Bobbit delivered a couple of cages to the Karnak Center. But they were covered, so he could have been delivering monkeys for all we know—we're assuming they were geese. He then stumbled home, grabbing his stomach twice. Once he got there, he watched TV and never left. We saw everything."

"I have to give Beekeeper Simon credit," Cami chimed in, sipping from her milkshake. "It was his idea to observe Bobbit from the rear balcony of the Blabbingdale house. It gave us a perfect shot of Bobbit's front window."

"We also had a bathroom to use during the stakeout, which was a lucky thing," Andrew said through a mouthful of muffin. "And when the flame balls started falling from the sky, we had a place to hide. Had we been outside, it could have been a bad scene."

Will stared off in the distance, not really listening.

"William. What's wrong?" Cami could read him better than the others.

"My aunt Lucille. She was in the jail when it burned last night. They can't find her. She's probably—" He pressed the backs of his hands to his eyes.

Nobody said anything. Cami lightly touched his arm.

The waitress, Miss Ravinia, a brawny lady with clown-red hair and a voice like a bugle, dropped a plate on the table. "Here's one Puffer-Fluff for the young man." When none of the kids reacted, she turned serious. "Did I interrupt something? I'm so sorry, y'all."

"It's all right, thank you," Simon managed, focused on Will.

But Ravinia didn't move. Instead, her heavily lined eyes roamed beneath the nearby tables. She spoke distractedly, "Let me know if y'all see a beige cat. Mr. Roberts has been coming around lately, but with all the bugs and hail, we can't find him. Bub's really worried about that little tabby."

All three kids stared at her in disbelief. "If we see a beige cat, we'll let you know," Andrew said curtly.

Once Miss Ravinia left the table, Cami leaned over to Will. "Do you want me to come with you to find your aunt Lucille? The sheriff's office might have moved her somewhere else."

"I don't think so. She was in her cell."

"Andrew can ask his dad to help us," Cami said, nodding toward Andrew. "Come on, I'll go help you look." She started to get up.

Will grabbed her by the arm. "We've already spoken with the police. She's gone."

Cami would have insisted, but the way Will shook his head made it clear that he did not want to discuss it further. So she quietly sat back down.

To change the subject, Simon pulled out his plague list. "Long story short, none of us think Bobbit is your demon. It's not plausible," he whispered to Will. "The real problem is: with the arrival of the locusts, there is only *one more plague* before death comes."

"Tell me something I don't know!" Will said, a trace of fear in his voice. "It doesn't matter what you all saw. Bobbit has the staff. He had a partner-in-crime at Peniel, he hated my aunt Lucille, and he probably had a hand in getting her locked up. I say we go to his place and confront him."

"Confront him with what?" Andrew challenged. "Tell him

that the woman who works for him thinks he's a demon who hates your aunt?"

"You all do what you want to do." Will forcefully pushed away from the table, slipping his backpack on. "I'm going to Bobbit's. He's not getting away with this."

Cami and Andrew called after Will, but he bolted into the street without even touching his favorite pastry. They ran after him. Simon tossed a few dollars on the table, slipped into his beekeeper outfit, and hopped into the street like he was running a sack race.

"Strange kids," Miss Ravinia said toward the kitchen. She picked at her red bouffant with a pencil. "Just like our furry friends. More trouble than they're worth."

In the front window of Bobbit's Bestiary, Will saw Crocket cleaning a display case that normally housed puppies. He burst into the front door, sending the attached bell flipping loudly in all directions.

"Where's Mr. Bobbit?" he fumed at the old man.

"You'd better pipe down, kid," Crocket said, leaving the window display. "Get control of yourself. You shouldn't even be here."

"I need answers!" Will yelled out, "Mr. Bobbit? Are you here?"

Bobbit, looking gray with droopy red-rimmed eyes, stumbled from the back of the store. He was slightly stooped. "What do you want?" he heaved.

"I want to know where the Staff of Moses is. I want to know why you hate my aunt Lucille."

Bobbit looked confused, disoriented. "Staff of what?" He leaned against the wall, pressing a hand to the side of his ample belly. "Get out of here. I can't talk to you now. Crocket, make him leave."

Will cut his eyes at the old assistant, who remained where he was. Will got in Bobbit's face. "Why did you say my aunt Lucille was a threat?"

"I never said—" Bobbit barked. "You mean the woman at the museum up the hill? Lucille Wilder?"

"You wanted her in jail, didn't you? So you and Pothinus Sab could use the Staff of Moses. WHERE IS THE STAFF?"

"I don't have any staff. I've never had a staff." Bobbit was desperate, like a cornered animal, his eyes rolling around.

"You're lying. You're cruel and you're a liar," Will bawled.

"Easy, boy. Stop that now," Crocket counseled from the side.

Cami, Simon, and Andrew barged into the shop. Crocket raised two thin arms to hold them back.

"Why are you asking me these things?" Bobbit whimpered. "I'm not a well man. I don't know what you're talking about."

"Miss Ann told me everything! Miss Ann? MISS ANN?" Will looked around the store. "Where is Miss Ann?"

"I don't know a Miss Ann," Bobbit said absently, pulling at the fat of his neck. "There's no Ann here."

Will stared the man down. "She works for you. Now you don't even know your own employees? Mr. Bobbit, you're *lying.*"

"I am not lying! I don't know . . . I'm so confused." He buried his head in his hands. When he lifted it, he seemed a different man, hatred filling his eyes. "Get out of here, boy. All of you OUT!"

In a flash, Will saw something he had never seen before. For a few seconds, Mr. Bobbit's face took the shape of a furious raven. He might have been wearing a semitransparent mask, only this beak moved and was filled with sharp teeth. *Amon! It's Amon.*

Will scuttled backward, frantically reaching into his backpack. He fingered the flat reliquary holding the Veil of the Virgin, which he had taken from his great-grandfather's office. If ever he needed a relic that dispelled anger, this was it. He pulled the relic out and pointed it toward Bobbit.

"Nooo! Nooo!" Bobbit screeched in a voice not his own. He grabbed at his stomach and staggered against the wall. "Get it away from me!"

After several seconds, Crocket called out to Will in a deep voice, "William, that is enough!" The old man stood straight up, his hunchback disappearing. He clawed at the skin under his nose and around his mouth—ripping the flesh away.

A horror-stricken Simon squealed, "I think I'm going to throw up." He grabbed Andrew and Cami, pulling them to the doorway.

Crocket dropped his shredded face to the floor. "William, step away and calm yourself," he said.

Will knew that voice. He turned to find Abbot Athanasius in Crocket's clothes, bits of latex hanging from the side of his face.

"*You're* Crocket?" Will asked.

"I have been watching Mr. Bobbit for weeks. Had you not been so blinded by anger, you might have recognized me. I'll explain later," the abbot said. "Since he may be possessed—or at least oppressed by the demon—you should step away, William. The relic has done its work." Athanasius glided toward Bobbit.

"That's one cool dude," Andrew said, nodding in admiration as the abbot passed.

Though a bit calmer, Bobbit was still bewildered. "Crocket? What are you going to do?"

"I'm going to help you." Athanasius handed him a small vial of water. "Drink this. It will combat the foul contents of that tonic Sab has been feeding you."

Bobbit swallowed the whole vial. His mouth stretched sideways in pain. "It hurts. It hurts so."

Athanasius crouched next to the shattered man. The abbot closed his eyes and began intensely reciting something in a low voice. Will only caught a bit of it: "*Adjuro te, Amon, serpens antique, per judicem vivorum et mortuorum, per factorem tuum* . . ." Turning his palms up, Athanasius touched his forefingers and thumbs together, making an O with each hand. That's when Will saw a blue neon wisp of light move through the abbot's extended fingers to Bobbit's stomach. Bobbit writhed in the corner, unleashing a string of inhuman yowls.

"Exi ergo, transgressor," the abbot continued. *"Exi, seductor, plene omni dolo et fallacia . . ."*

A billowy purple fog spilled from Bobbit's gaping mouth, his arms fully extended. Will started to sneeze from the foul smell. After several minutes it was over. A spent Bobbit collapsed in the corner. He regarded the store with confusion, like he had just woken from a terrible nightmare and couldn't quite situate himself.

"I should never have gotten involved with Sab. His tonic made me worse. It made me hunger for things I never . . ." Bobbit caught sight of the empty cages lining the walls. "Where are all my birds? My macaws and finches—my geese." He placed two hands along the sides of his head, a vain attempt to hold back the horrible memories surfacing.

"Oh no, no, no . . . I delivered them all to Sab this morning. He wanted everything. Every last animal"—Bobbit began moaning—"and I gave them to him."

"You ate them, too, didn't you?" Andrew asked.

"Only once. In my whole life, I'd never eaten one of my animals. But I couldn't stop myself. I yearned for them— all the time," Bobbit said with shame. "I only gave in once, that's the truth. I ate only one goose."

The abbot whispered to Will, "It was probably the spirit of Amon within him. The demon entered and partially controlled him via the tonic."

"What about Miss Ann?" Will asked, shaken.

"There is no Ann," Bobbit said quietly.

"And the staff? She said—Do you have the staff?"

"I truly don't know what you are talking about," Bobbit said.

The abbot gently turned to Will. "This Ann—or whomever it was you spoke with—was visible only to you. I saw you here myself conversing with thin air. She was a spirit of some kind. There's no use fretting about it now. You'll figure it all out by the end." He straightened the tattered sweater he wore, turning to the kids. "I'll tend to Mr. Bobbit. I want all of you to return to Peniel straightaway. It's important that you go now." Cami, Andrew, and Simon (still in his beekeeper outfit) headed out the door.

Athanasius touched Will on the shoulder. There was a mischievous twinkle in his eyes, as if they held some wonderful secret. "When you arrive, William, go immediately to the Chapter House. There is something you must see there." His smile puzzled Will. But rather than press the abbot to explain further, he raced to Peniel to find his own answers.

CHAPTER 20

THE HIDDEN STAFF

The televisions of Perilous Falls were almost universally tuned to coverage of the locust invasion. After nine hours of continuous insect reportage, the viewers needed a change of pace. So the producers at Sidon Channel 8 broke away to an "inspirational special": a prerecorded interview with Mayor Ava Lynch and Pothinus Sab.

The unsuspecting might have thought that they had stumbled upon a very odd "home shopping" channel. Sab held up his now-ubiquitous amulet, touting its many virtues, "particularly in moments of crisis or strife." The mayor spent most of her time reinforcing Sab's pitch with an occasional "absolutely" or "that is so true." The duo weren't selling the Ammit necklaces. They were urging people to come down to the Karnak Center and pick up their own amulet, compliments of the city. For the homebound, a Sidon news van—by special arrangement—would be driving through Perilous Falls and adjoining counties, distributing the amulets as long as supplies lasted.

Over on WPF Channel 4, images of a farmer tearfully watching locusts devour his tomato crop were interrupted by a special report.

Deborah Wilder, looking glamorous and determined, teased viewers from the anchor desk: "Is it safe for you and your family to wear Pothinus Sab's free amulets? Or are they part of a dark pagan belief system? I spoke with Pothinus Sab himself and an expert to get answers."

The camera cut to an interview with a "distinguished professor of archaeology," an Egyptologist named Dr. Franz Xaver von Neuhaus. The man had a high forehead, heavily lidded eyes, and black half-glasses. He leaned back in his chair, dangling one of the amulets from his fingers.

"Zeese are most dangerous," he said in a rumbly German accent. "I would certainly not haffe ziz creature anywhere near my person and certainly not near children." He made a clucking sound, shaking his head.

"But, Professor, people in Perilous Falls claim they feel protected wearing it," Deborah Wilder said earnestly. "It has warded off gnats and frogs and kept them safe. What is the harm?"

The professor frowned, holding the amulet between his fingers. "Zeese people you mention, they must be ignorant of who Ammit—the creature on the necklace—is. In Egyptian belief, Ammit devours soulz. It is the destroyer. The bone breaker. Zis creature is not a means of safety, but of destruction. It bringz only death and judgment."

The camera then cut to Deborah chasing Pothinus Sab down Dura Street. "Experts say that Ammit is a creature of destruction and death. Yet you claim that your Ammit charm will bring regeneration. How is that possible? How is it protecting people?"

"It is drawing positive energy from the population. You have seen it yourself, yes? It is their personal energies that protect them," Sab said, dismissing her, moving fast.

"Then why is it necessary to wear the amulet, sir?"

Sab stopped abruptly, running a hand over his beard, his anger palpable. "Miss Wilder, have you a schedule? So do I. The schedule says that I must now tend to the many people who have made appointments seeking my help. If you have questions about our amulet, I would advise you, and all those watching, to get one for free. The Karnak Center offers them as a gift—without judgment or needless questions. Thank you." His broad smile didn't alter the spiteful look in his eyes.

Dr. von Neuhaus returned to the screen, laughing lightly. "If I were Mr. Sab, I would refuse to answer your questionz too. His is an object of evil. Hurl it into the trash bin. Burn it. Return it to Sab. But under no circumstances should anyone wear zis thing. The protection people seek will not be found in zis creature or in Sab's talk of regeneration. It is a lie."

Gathered around the TV in the community room of Peniel, some of the Brethren applauded von Neuhaus.

Brother Amalric, occupying a good two-thirds of a sofa, turned to Philip, who was fixing a watch with a tiny screwdriver. "I thought von Neuhaus was retired to *Au-th-tria.* How did Deborah *th-cure* an interview with him?" Amalric asked.

"Doctor von Neuhaus gave the abbot permission to impersonate him," Philip said through the side of his mouth, lifting his jeweler's magnifying glasses. "Remember how Athanasius used to get thrown out of class for impersonating von Neuhaus?" He narrowed his eyes, indicating "now you know."

"You mean that was the abbot on TV just now?!" Amalric wriggled in amazement. "His *imper-th-onation* was *th-pot* on."

"Yes, it was. Shhhh." Philip dropped the magnifying glasses back onto his nose and resumed his watch repair. "Who do you think made the glasses he wore for the interview?" Philip nodded proudly, pointing a thumb at himself.

Will and his friends rushed into the community room. "Where is the Chapter House?" Will asked, out of breath.

"Over in the east building, off the courtyard," Ugo Pagani said, rising from a leather chair. "C'mon, I'll take you there. What's your hurry? Trying to elect yourself abbot or sumpin'?"

Will had never been to the Chapter House before. It was solely reserved for the members of the archabbey. And though he was considered a *collaborator,* Will did not attend the morning chapter meetings or the routine votes that the order held there.

From the courtyard, Will and his friends walked past spiraled columns to enter the Chapter House. Stone arches exploded like fountains from squat pillars spread throughout the room. It was a bright place with a continuous stone bench running along the walls. Bartimaeus, Tobias Shen, and Baldwin were clustered in the rear of the room, their backs to the kids.

"Ya got some visitors," Brother Ugo announced. "I don't think they came to meditate on the Rule." He chuckled to himself and returned to the courtyard.

"The abbot said I should come here right—" What Will saw stopped him cold. His heart skipped a beat or two.

When Bart and Tobias parted, there stood Aunt Lucille. Aside from a bad scrape on her cheek and bandaged wrists, she looked fantastic.

Will ran over, taking her hands. "I thought you died in the jail. I can't believe you made it out. I mean, I'm *glad* you made it out."

"I'm rather glad myself, dear. For a few moments I wasn't so sure. Hello, kids." Lucille waved to Cami, Andrew, and Simon, who drew closer. She massaged her wrist, grimacing slightly. "Pothinus Sab and Ava Lynch tried to attack me in my cell. Sab's definitely in league with Amon."

"How did you escape? The jail was totally torched," Will said.

"When the ceiling caught fire, just before it collapsed, I

yanked at the chains attached to my wrists. That hailstorm might have been a plague for some, but for me it was a blessing. A piece of the ceiling fell and popped one of the chains. That allowed me to blast the other chain and blow through the cinder-block wall with my . . ." Her forefingers and thumbs touched, forming a triangle. "You know what I mean." She glanced over at the kids, smiling apologetically. "It's not necessary to get into everything, but I was just telling the Brethren here that Sab warned me that Amon would rise again."

Will wasted no time telling her about the plot to raise Amon mentioned in the *Malleus Diabolus*.

Baldwin interjected, "There is no need to worry about the mummy of Tuthmosis. It is quite safe. At Tobias's urging, Brother Pedro has been guarding it since this morning."

"I think we're too late," Will said gloomily. "On the way over, I kept thinking about the mummy. What if somebody already handed its remains over to a priest of Amon?"

"The mummy is *entirely secure* in its case and has not been disturbed, William," Baldwin snarled.

Bartimaeus sat on the stone bench along the wall. "Will could be right." Bartimaeus picked at his brow with his thumbnail. "You know, Baldwin, I thought for a while that you might be our staff snatcher."

Baldwin tilted his great hooked nose toward Bartimaeus and sneered, shoving his hands beneath his black habit.

"Even though they found that gold wrapper in your

office, it was all a little too pat," Bart said. "You wouldn't be stupid enough to leave that kind of evidence lyin' around."

Cami, Andrew, and Simon joined Bartimaeus on the stone bench, eager to hear the rest of his theory.

"So Tobias and I were talkin'. The night the staff went missin', Valens claimed he put the keys to the exhibit cases in Baldwin's office after he cleaned the mummy. . . ."

"Wait a minute," Simon said, slapping his knees. "Valens could have taken a piece of the mummy while he was cleaning it."

Will nodded in agreement.

"Lights go on for you, little man. Good thinkin'." Bart tapped a very pleased Simon on the leg with his crutch. "Valens also lied to Tobias and me. He knew about the water turnin' to blood as it was happenin', even though Peniel was untouched by the plague."

"That night he said he heard about it on the radio in his bedroom," Tobias said ruefully.

"Only there ain't no radios in the archabbey bedrooms. He knew what was goin' on because he had a hand in it." Bartimaeus pulled at the lapels of his tweed jacket. "So, Vicar, I want to apologize for thinkin' you nabbed the staff. Valens was our man all along."

"The cute guy?" Cami asked Will. "The one with the pretty blue eyes, the long hair? The muscular guy? He seemed nice to me."

"Darlin', muscles don't always make a hero. I know dat's true," Bart said, glancing down at his own lanky frame.

"Valens stole the staff; knew about the plagues; tried to pin it on Baldwin—and I think Will and Simon are right. He's already bagged some of that mummy."

Baldwin's face fell. He fled the Chapter House, ordering brothers passing through the courtyard to find Valens. Looking like a hungry eagle searching for a mouse in a field, Baldwin called back to those in the Chapter House, "I'll return once I find him." And he was gone.

Aunt Lucille positioned herself near the kids and Bart. A very troubled Will joined her. "It's time to lay your hands on Aaron's staff," Aunt Lucille told Will solemnly.

"If I knew where it was, I would be happy to lay my hands on it," Will sarcastically responded.

"Ah-ah-ah." Tobias raised a flat, lined palm to Will's face. "What did I tell you long ago?"

"Are we going to have another talk about obedience?"

"I am not ruling it out," said Shen stoically. "I told you: protect your tree and it will protect you." He stared at Will until his expression changed. "Aaah. It is now time for your tree to offer its protection."

"My tree—your walking stick—is the Staff of Aaron?"

"It is. The fruit of obedience, Mr. Wilder, is always goodness."

Amid the laughter and the joy of the moment, Andrew started making odd noises in the corner. "Uhhh. Guys, you'd better come see this." He slowly stood, pointing toward the pillar next to his seat. Low on the adjoining wall, a line of three blue ears hung from the stone.

"Look away, kids," Aunt Lucille demanded. She touched her fingers together and hit the ears with a blast of red and white light that turned them black. Under the heat of the ray, they withered until they looked like rotted fruit.

"You know Valens and his pals probably heard every word we said." Bart picked the shriveled ears off the wall with the end of his crutch. "So we better get to that tree double quick."

Baldwin ran into the Chapter House in a lather, eyes ablaze. "He's gone. Valens hasn't been seen all day."

Shen sped into the courtyard. "There is no time to waste. He has gone where we must. But he'll not get what he desires. Come, come, come." They all chased Tobias, past Baldwin, out of Peniel toward the St. Thomas churchyard.

On the way, intermittent shadows darkened their path. Looking up, Will discovered the cause of the blocked light. Ravens. A full sky of ravens like shifting clouds concealed the setting sun's beams. "What do you see up there?" Will asked Cami.

"Nothing. I mean it's a little hazy," an unconcerned Cami said, blithely walking along with the others.

It didn't matter. Will could see them. The ravens continued to circle overhead and the light thickened. He could feel the approach of the first day of darkness.

Mayor Lynch leaned over the desk in Judge Blabbingdale's chambers.

"I want a new arrest warrant," she demanded. "We need to turn this town over until we find that woman. Lucille Wilder is a fugitive from justice." She wore a sling around an arm and one of her legs was wrapped in bandages.

"Ava, we don't know where Lucille Wilder is. She may well have—forgive me, Dan—died in the blaze at the jail." Judge Blabbingdale removed his glasses, placing them on top of the folder before him. "I'm not issuing another arrest warrant. She's a missing person right now."

The mayor smacked the desktop with her good hand, staring firmly at the judge. The sound made Dan Wilder and Brother Amalric jump in their chairs. Amalric, who was called at the last minute, cleared his throat and spoke up.

"Your Honor, this might be a good time to *revi-th-it* the original charges." Amalric rifled through a pile of wrinkled papers on his lap, eyeing the mayor sheepishly. "These *prepo-th-terous accu-th-ations* are not *th-th-tainable*. Is the city *th-ill* arguing that my client *th-omehow* rained fire on the town while she was in chains? Can any *th-en-thible per-th-on* imagine burning down a jail while you're in it? I move for a complete *di-th-mi-th-al* of the charges."

The mayor's left eye began to twitch as she glared at the judge. "Perhaps Lucille didn't realize she'd burn down the jail when she . . . did whatever she did. We need a new arrest warrant!" she urged the judge.

Judge Blabbingdale pushed the folder away and laced his fingers. "These charges were always flimsy, Ms. Mayor. I gave you the benefit of the doubt. Aside from your very pronounced hatred of Ms. Wilder, you still have no real evidence. Given all of that, and the sad possibility that she may be deceased, I am vacating all the charges."

Mayor Lynch didn't react for a long moment. She hobbled behind the judge's desk and with a big smile on her face, embraced him. "You will regret this," she whispered in his ear.

"Keep it up, Ava, and I'll throw you in jail for contempt and coercion of a court official," he whispered back, kissing her on the cheek.

The mayor narrowed her eyes at Dan Wilder and Brother Amalric. "If you see Lucille again, tell her this is far from over." She pounded out of the office without awaiting a response.

Aunt Lucille was the first member of the traveling party to speak when they reached the churchyard. "Let me approach Valens first. I might be able to win him back from the *Sinestri.*"

She walked into the open field to find Valens insanely yanking on the sapling nearest the riverbank. He threw his back into it, bending the trunk to the ground in an attempt to uproot it. The little tree could have been a steel spring given the way it bounced back.

"COME OUT, YOU BLOODY THIIIING. Come on now!" he yelled at the tree.

"Valens." Aunt Lucille was calm, her voice tinged with sorrow.

He shamefully unhanded the tree, speechless. After several seconds of running his hands through his long locks, he regained his composure. "You're alive? Out . . . out of prison. Free. That's nice— good to see." He nodded uncomfortably.

"What are you doing, Valens? What have you done?" Lucille seemed disappointed in him, slipping her hands into her jacket pockets. "It's not too late. You can come back to us."

Valens looked beyond her to Bart, Tobias, Will, and his friends at the edge of the clearing. "And let Will win? I can't do that, Lucille." His eyes were as pale as arctic ice. "The master is counting on me." He grabbed the tree by its trunk and pulled with all his strength, cursing under his breath.

"That will do you no good." Tobias Shen approached him, assuming a wide stance. "It is not meant for you. It will never yield to you, Valens."

"Why not? WHY BLOODY NOT?" He angrily kicked the tree, his wet hair falling into his face.

Shen motioned to Andrew, who, according to plan, grabbed one of Valens's arms. Shen held the other. Though Valens flailed, Andrew and Shen managed to overpower him and bring him to his knees.

"Take it now, Mr. Wilder!" Shen commanded, gesturing toward the tree with his head.

Tentatively, Will wrapped his fingers around the faint

Hebrew inscriptions along the tree shaft. He gave it the lightest tug. Will's heart did flip-flops as the thin branches and roots retracted into the trunk. Within moments, he no longer held a tree but the knotty walking stick he had planted with Mr. Shen months earlier.

"The Staff of Aaron," Shen said. "Holding that, you look just like your great-grandfather." Shen's mind flooded with images of Jacob Wilder wielding the two staffs against the Nazis in the fields of Axum a lifetime ago. "Throw it down, Mr. Wilder. Throw it with force and hold your ground."

Aunt Lucille wrapped Simon and Cami in her arms, pulling them back. Will hurled the staff away from him. It squirmed in the grass at first. Then like a balloon filling with helium, the crown of the staff enlarged into the head of an enormous yellow snake. Huge slits opened to reveal cunning eyes. Simon wailed like a girl at the sight. From the tiny staff, an enormous sleek body oozed out. The snake reared up, jabbing its head toward Lucille and the kids, then to Valens, Shen, and Andrew.

"Don't dat beat all." Bartimaeus laughed, backing into the underbrush. Then a look of concern spread over Bart's face. "Lucille," he called out. "Somethin' bad's coming. I'm feeling a chill . . ."

"Look at the tail, Mr. Wilder," Shen instructed. "Do not fear the snake. Remember your lessons. With great serenity and stillness, take hold of the tail."

The very end of the snake appeared stiff and wooden, as if the staff's tip had been glued to the serpent's backside.

Will reached for the tail. Shadows moving on the grass distracted him. When he looked up, thousands and thousands of ravens were flying in dizzying formations, blocking out the light.

Darkness. It's the first day of darkness. . . .

Will seized the tail of the snake. With a whoosh of air, the viper withdrew into the staff. His eyelids fluttered in amazement as he held the rod, his breath returning.

Across the clearing, Valens broke free of Andrew and Shen. "That staff won't help you, Will. My master already has the remains of Tuthmosis and I gave him the Staff of Moses." Valens darted onto Falls Road like a madman. "None of you can stop what's coming!" he screamed over his shoulder, spit flying from his mouth. "Look at the sky. LOOK AT IT! Darkness approaches and from that darkness the master will bring forth Amon. The great and mighty Amon comes to devour your 'chosen one' and all the Brethren." Valens was soon lost in the blackness of the trees.

Will seethed. He raised the staff, poised to hurl it to the ground again. *Let the snake chase Valens down,* he thought.

Aunt Lucille grabbed him hard by the arm. "Not now, dear. He's tempting you to vengeance. Valens told us more than he should have. For the sake of your life, Will, we have to prepare quickly for the real battle. There is not a moment to lose."

CHAPTER 21

AMMIT UNLEASHED

Darkness tightened its grip on Dura Street and all of Perilous Falls. Unlike a typical nightfall, the streetlamps failed to ignite and gloom spread like spilled oil.

In the lengthening shadows of the de Plancy Cemetery, four figures crouched behind a huge statue of a graceful woman. Flowing marble robes nearly concealed her delicate foot crushing the head of a snake.

A city truck rumbled onto the curb in front of the cemetery. The engine quickly died. A woman with thick glasses in a gray uniform abandoned the truck, followed by a small boy. Her blond ponytail swished as she walked. She carefully searched the shrines and gravestones of the cemetery until she spotted the veiled statue.

With no fear, she and the boy approached the four dark

figures gathered near the pedestal. "What do we know?" she asked crisply.

"I know dat's one of the worst costumes I've ever seen," Bartimaeus said, slipping off his glasses. "Lucille, you'd better leave the disguises to the abbot." He winked in Athanasius's direction.

"It's the only wig I could find—Oh, never mind that. The disguise worked. I had to find a way to get Leo here undetected. Thank goodness Dan wasn't at home." The blond wig washed out Lucille's features. "Is Valens inside?"

The abbot fixed his gaze on the side door of the Karnak Center. "He is inside, and about half an hour ago he carried out several bags of feathers. They've killed all the fowl."

"Been getting bad vibes since we got here," Bartimaeus said, extending his hands. "They're performing some kinda ritual inside. These vibrations are different. They're cold, deadly."

Will anxiously rapped the Staff of Aaron against the statue base. He missed having Simon, Andrew, and Cami with him. But the adults thought it best to leave them safely behind and not expose anyone else to the danger of Amon. "Shouldn't we rush the place?" Will blurted out. "This 'firstborn' kid would like to rush the place. We can't let them offer Amon the mummy's remains."

Tobias Shen laid a thick hand on Will's arm. "Abbot, perhaps you and Mr. Wilder should go inside. I'll show you to the back entrance. Then Bart, Lucille, Leo, and I can post here." He turned to Will. "If you need assistance, holler. You do remember how to holler, Mr. Wilder?"

Will scrunched up his face. He adjusted his pith helmet and held the staff with both hands. His little brother suddenly gripped the staff as well. "Be careful, okay, Will?" The younger Wilder could not have been more sincere. "We don't want to lose *the chosen one.*"

Will blushed, feeling slightly guilty about what he'd told his brother earlier. "You've been chosen, too, Leo. You might have to *ignite* after all. It's pretty dark out here. Are you ready?" Will asked.

"Yep. Aunt Lucille's been giving me more tips."

"Good. We all have our *thing* to do, right?" Will said, tapping his brother on the head.

"We do indeed," Aunt Lucille said. "In this horrible darkness, Leo's light might permit us to see and perhaps weaken any *Fomorii* we encounter. As for you . . ." She turned to Will, her eyes like billiard balls behind the costume glasses. He could sense how serious she was, so he did his best to keep from laughing.

"Remember what the prophecy said: 'forsake all anger' or it will blind you."

"I remember."

"When you face the beast, be silent. Strike it with everything you have, dear. Find Moses's staff and once it's in your possession, turn both rods on the demon." She pulled him close to her, which made Will feel uncomfortable given her crazy getup.

"I promise to do my best if you promise never, ever to wear that wig again." He gave her a half smile, nodded at Leo, and followed Mr. Shen and the abbot to the rear of the Karnak Center.

Shen pried open the window to the storage room and held it so the abbot and Will could crawl in. Once they were inside, the abbot lit a blessed candle. He and Will ventured out of the cramped room into a grimy hallway. At the end of the hall, to the right was a narrow wooden staircase and to the left, a sandstone wall with a six-inch-wide slit at the bottom. Athanasius motioned Will toward the stairway. En route, they passed the opening to the largest room of the basement. The rapid clinking of heavy chains moving sounded along the ground. A growl, low and unnatural, stopped their advance.

"Up the stairs, William," the abbot instructed. His troubled face lit by the flame, Athanasius quickly scanned the big room for the source of the snarl while Will scrambled upstairs. The abbot finally decided not to tarry with whatever sheltered in the darkness and chased Will up the staircase.

The small door at the top of the stairs opened to the entry hall of the Karnak Center. They emerged behind one of the bloated columns flanking the rectangular pool. Torches starkly lit the room. From behind a column, the abbot peeked at the surroundings.

The double bronze doors at the back of the room were open. Inside the chamber, Sab stood before a massive statue of Amon, two stone plumes atop its head, white linen swaddling its body. The abbot barely recognized Sab in the firelight. He was now completely bald and dressed in an elaborate pleated white linen outfit that circled his waist and covered half his torso. Sab held the Staff of Moses topped by a golden ram's head in one hand and a metal vessel billowing incense in the other. Valens knelt beside the statue, his face to the floor.

"Rise beautifully in peace, Amon, Lord of Karnak, Prince of the Temples of the Gods and Goddesses that are in it!" Sab intoned. "Be on watch and be in peace. You watch in peace, Master of Fear, Great One of the Terrors in the Hearts of all Rekhitou."

A grooved onyx block before the statue was laden with assorted dead birds, two jugs, flat bread, and fruits. Sab laid the staff on a pile of plucked geese.

Will whispered to the abbot, "Is this the deity buffet? What's going on?"

"I suspect Sab's offering nourishment to the *ka*—the spirit of Amon that he thinks resides in the statue," Athanasius said.

Sab lifted both hands in the air, the incense creating a fog bank. "Oh great Amon, accept these offerings and use them to bring your enemies low. These things, true and pure, are established for Amon, Lord of Karnak. Take these divine offerings and fuel your wrath with them."

With a nod from Sab, Valens placed a small stone jar at the edge of the offering block, next to the fowl pile. He withdrew, pressing his face to the ground and reciting:

"Amon-Ra, Lord of Karnak, adorned with his mantle so he can walk on the earth in the form of a mummy . . . walk the earth in the form of a mummy . . ."

"What should we do?" Will hissed.

Athanasius had already drawn a vial of holy water from his habit. "We have to disrupt the offering."

"I have Brother Philip's Super Soaker in my backpack. I'm ready!"

The abbot returned the holy water bottle to his habit. "Give me the soaker. You just hold on to that staff and follow me."

"Shouldn't I face Amon alone? I'm supposed to face him alone."

"Do you see Amon?" the abbot asked. He waited a moment, and when Will shrugged, he spun the boy around. "Until he appears, you'll follow me." Pulling the large water gun from Will's backpack, Athanasius flipped a switch on its side and raced toward the inner sanctum of Amon.

Something reflective and metallic on the front steps of the Karnak Center drew Tobias Shen's eye. The two torches on either side of the front door made the metallic objects twinkle. Darkness had conquered the sun and all along Dura Street, no light shone in any window—which only made the sparkling metal more mysterious.

Against Lucille's protests, Shen went to investigate the

shimmering objects. He left Lucille, Bartimaeus, and Leo behind in the cemetery, promising to return shortly. Stealthily creeping past the sandstone rams out front, he neared the front stairs. Strewn along the steps and the walkway were Ammit amulets by the hundreds. Some people had obviously seen Deborah Wilder's TV special and had come by earlier to discard Sab's hippo-like charms.

Watching from behind a great Celtic headstone, Aunt Lucille whispered to Leo, "I need you to concentrate on your inner light. I know we haven't had much chance to practice, dear. But simply think of the light filling your body. Like you did at my house the other day. Breathe in, push the light out and you'll do fine."

Leo shoved his wire-framed glasses up the bridge of his nose. "It's veeery dark out here. I have a question: When can we go home?"

"Hopefully soon. Have patience now. We can't have you going off unexpectedly. If we need your light, I'll tell you, okay?"

Bartimaeus's fingers moved through the air as if he were playing some invisible piano. "Oh, I think we're gonna need that light for sure. The *Darkness* is descendin', Lucille. It's stirrin' something fierce now. You'd best get Tobias away from that door." His brows pulsed weirdly. "We got a battle comin'."

"Tobias! Tobias!" Lucille half whispered, motioning for him to retreat. "Come back here. Come here!"

But Tobias waved her off, scooping up amulets from

the steps. "We should dispose of these. They should be destroyed," he said, collecting the charms by the handful.

The speed with which Athanasius invaded the inner sanctum and attacked the offerings to Amon stunned Sab and Valens. With a flying kick, he toppled the small jar on the edge of the offering stone. As Tuthmosis's ashes scattered onto the floor, he used Will's water gun to spray them while still in midair. Once he landed, he splattered holy water on the birds, the produce, and the blue staff heaped on the hieroglyphed block.

"SARSOUR!" Pothinus Sab screamed in fury, his hands spread wide. "Release Ammit. RELEASE THE DESTROYER!" Sab madly lunged for Moses's staff, but Will was too quick for him. The boy had already slid along the floor, as if stealing third base, and snatched the staff from the pile of offerings while Sab was focused on the abbot.

Valens rushed Athanasius, who threw down his water gun. Touching his index fingers to his thumbs, he extended his arms toward Valens. A pair of thin blue rays streamed from Athanasius's fingertips, causing Valens to bend backward. It looked as if invisible hands held Valens by the collarbone and lifted him slightly off the floor. One of the few exorcists in the Brethren, Athanasius had the power to not only draw demonic spirits from humans, but also bind the demons themselves.

Pothinus Sab turned to Will, who now wielded the two

staffs. Sab's hair was gone, as was his goatee. Hairless, he was even creepier than usual. "You will die this night, Will Wilder. The hour of regeneration has come."

Let's hope it regenerates your hair, Will thought.

A clanging of chains and a terrible growl rumbled outside the room. "Sarsour! Is Ammit free? RELEASE HIM NOW!" Sab yelled.

The sweaty and frightened little man struggled with a rusty chain in the outer chamber. "I'm trying, Master. He is fitful. Ammit!" Whatever was at the other end of Sarsour's chain, hidden by the wall, had a mind of its own. "NO, NOT THAT WAY!" Sarsour screamed.

With a screeching thud, the stone wall of the inner sanctum that hid the thing bulged inward. The chained creature repeatedly smashed into the wall nearest the bronze doors. Will's body convulsed when he felt the force of the beast on the other side of the shifting stone blocks.

Is that Amon? Is that the demon?

Transfixed by the dust flying from the breaks in the wall, Will braced himself for the next crash. Athanasius maintained his focus on Valens. In Will's confusion, Sab yanked the Staff of Moses from Will's hand and threw it on top of the plucked geese.

"You want the staff?" Sab taunted Will. "Then you'll have to go after it. It belongs to the great Amon." Sab pulled a lever on the wall and the entire offering stone flipped, sending the fruit, the birds, and the staff plunging into a dark hole that had opened in the floor.

Will dove for the rod, but it was gone before he could grasp it. Sab cackled as a stone slid into place, closing the hole in the floor. "The *Darkness* will soon consume you. Are you afraid of the dark, Will Wilder? You should be." For an instant Sab's head elongated into the snapping hateful raven Will had seen on Mr. Bobbit's face. The demon's spirit was alive in Sab.

A ferocious roar and the clinking of iron snapped all heads toward the outer chamber. In a blur, an enormous creature galloped around the rectangular pool of the entry hall. Bashing into columns, it moved so quickly Will couldn't make out its features. He only knew it was huge and loud.

"Is that Amon? Is it?" Will poked the thick end of Aaron's staff at Sab. "Tell me!"

Sab cocked his bald head to the side, a toothy smile cracking his face. "It is nice to see you so angry. Amon is surely with us." He pointed a finger toward the entry hall. "But Amon is far, far worse than that."

Will jammed the staff into Sab's belly, causing him to double over. "Is it YOU? Are you Amon? What is your true name? Do you feed on 'the fattened geese'?" Will was at once scared and enraged, sweat pouring from under his pith helmet.

"How ridiculous you are, Wilder," Sab wheezed. "The sacred geese of Amon would never pass my lips. They are his alone."

In the outer chamber, Ammit began smashing through

something wooden and hard. The noise of wood splintering fell like a sharp pick on Will's ears.

Across the chamber, Valens passed out against the wall under the force of Athanasius's rays. The abbot now turned to Will and Sab.

"Tell me where Amon is." Will raised the staff high, ready to crush Sab's head with it. "Tell me! TELL ME!"

"*Self-mastery*, William," the abbot whispered sternly. "Forsake wrath and you shall find the truth."

Will's face relaxed. With some shame, he lowered the staff. The crashing of wood in the outer room grew more intense.

"Do you hear that? Do you?" Sab asked, gasping for air, holding his bruised abdomen. "That is the sweet sound of regeneration. Ammit shall seek out all who wear the amulet and devour them. Then . . . peace shall reign, yes?" He coughed out a ragged laugh. Before he could speak again, Abbot Athanasius hit him with the wispy blue ray from his fingertips and began mouthing Latin words.

CRRRRAAACK!

The main door of the Karnak Center buckled.

CRRRRAAACK!

Ammit's relentless pounding and scratching created a hole. Sarsour yelled from the outer chamber, "He is nearly free, Master! Nearly free!"

Sab could not respond. Purple plumes billowed from his open mouth, his head tilted to the sky. Sab's limbs jerked violently as the spirit of the demon escaped his body.

Will ran to the doorway of the inner sanctum, watching what appeared to be a super-sized hippopotamus demolish the front door. In the limited light, he could only see the rear end of the creature.

"Wh-what should we do?" Will asked the abbot.

"A scream for help might be in order," the abbot said, coolly blasting away at Sab. "Let me finish with this one and then we'll root out the demon."

Will understood his meaning. Running toward the side door to alert Aunt Lucille and the others, Will caught a glimpse of Sarsour struggling to control Ammit's chain in the entry hall. The little man was so preoccupied with the creature that he completely missed Will.

"Aunt Lucille!" Will shouted out the side door into the cemetery. "Ammit is coming—through the front door." Not that she needed the warning.

The front doorway of the Karnak Center had been spitting wood chips and metal for several minutes while Ammit pounded it from the inside.

Tobias Shen, his hands filled with amulets, ran into the street to create some distance between himself and whatever was coming out.

"Get ready," Bartimaeus said, his face pinched, his fingers still straining at the air. "So it's a *Fomorii*—a big one. The hatred of this thing is *intense*."

Aunt Lucille squatted down, locking eyes with Leo. "All right, now I need you to focus. Breathe, and let your light shine."

Leo, clearly worried, puckered his thick lips. "Do I throw my arms out or keep them tight?"

"Throw them out as wide as you can and let 'er rip, dear," Aunt Lucille said, pulling back the sleeves of her silk jacket. "I'll be ready for him too. On my signal, okay?"

Leo gave her two thumbs-up.

The beast burst through the shattered doors of the Karnack Center. The sheer size of the thing shocked Tobias Shen. The front of its body looked to be that of a gargantuan lion with massive claws, but its haunches were those of a prehistoric hippo. It had a red reptilian face with an elongated snout surrounded by a great mane of unruly hair. Ammit stood on the top step growling in fury. Each time it opened its crocodile-like mouth, irregular razor-sharp teeth flashed in the torchlight. Nostrils flaring, it turned its massive head left to right.

Sarsour tentatively sidled up to the creature. "Time to feed, Ammit. Crush the bones of those who wear your image. Devour their souls." He frantically pulled a pin on the metal collar at the creature's neck, releasing it from the chain. Then he backed away fearfully. "He is free, Master. The great servant of Amon is free," Sarsour rasped into the broken entryway.

Tobias Shen remained completely still in the darkness of the street. He stared down at the hundreds of amulets in his hands, knowing that holding them sealed his fate. He considered casting them aside and running, but he feared it could jeopardize the safety of his friends. Motionless, he

held his ground—offering himself as a willing decoy for Ammit's rage.

"All right, Leo, ignite. NOW," Aunt Lucille urged her great-nephew in the cemetery.

Leo drew a deep breath and tightened his eyes in concentration. He shook from the effort.

Ammit lowered its snout, two beady green eyes locked on the amulets in the street. The creature's front legs bent low, preparing to spring at the victim it could sense in the darkness.

"Concentrate, Leo," Aunt Lucille begged, her voice higher than usual. "Show us your *light*."

Leo strained, but his body did not illuminate in the slightest.

"Come on, Leo!" Aunt Lucille said, slapping her thighs in frustration.

The beast was off the front steps and tearing through the reflecting pool out front. Shen did not wait for the thing to reach him. He dropped a few of the amulets, clutched the remainder, and sprinted onto the lawn toward the Karnak Center.

Ammit hit the street, stopping suddenly, its claws ripping into the asphalt. After sniffing the amulets on the ground, the great reptilian head popped side to side. Spotting Shen, the *Fomorii* pursued him with astounding speed, crashing into one of the sandstone rams in front of the building.

Tobias serpentined between the other statues out front,

Ammit close behind. The weaving disorienting the creature. Repeatedly zigzagging after his prey, Ammit lost patience and just demolished the three statues nearest the front entrance. By the time the last statue toppled over in pieces, Tobias had somersaulted onto the top step of the Karnak Center. But as he neared the wrecked door, Sarsour pulled a knife on him.

Hunching down in the cemetery, Bartimaeus told Leo, "I can't see nothin' in this darkness. But I know Tobias is in trouble and unless you start to glow, little man, this is gonna get reeeeal ugly. So TURN YA LIGHT ON!" he yelled.

Leo was so startled by Mr. Bart's tone that he could feel the glow surging into his hands and face.

On the front porch of the center, Tobias elbowed the knife out of the tiny henchman's hands. In one swift movement, he necklaced Sarsour with hundreds of amulets before bounding off the porch toward the graveyard.

Horrified, Sarsour ripped at the charms around his neck. He popped a few of the chains, throwing them as far as he could. But Ammit rose up from the edge of the porch like a tidal wave, falling on him all at once. The creature's jaws viciously chomped on Sarsour, finishing him in seconds. With broken chains and crushed amulets hanging from its stained teeth, Ammit searched the darkness for the next victim.

Leo's skin shimmered in the cemetery. He pressed his small palms together tightly, just as Aunt Lucille had taught him.

Ammit spotted the gleaming light between the headstones and sprang from its perch. Roaring like a T. rex entering a steakhouse, it charged toward the glow.

"Lucille, you may have to blast the beast," Shen said, crouching next to his friends.

"I don't think I can hold it. This is not your average *Fomorii*."

After nervously watching Leo illuminate from penlight to lamp wattage, Bartimaeus turned to the creature. "Somebody better do somethin' 'cause that thing's hungry and it don't look like the appetizer satisfied him. He's fixin' on having a *main course*."

CHAPTER 22

THE WRATH OF THE DEMON

Ammit swiftly covered the lawn of the Karnak Center and closed in on the de Plancy Cemetery.

Aunt Lucille couldn't let the creature get any closer. Leo was still not at his full radiance and if she waited any longer, it might cost a life or the lives of the whole town—something she could not permit. "Tobias, when I hit Ammit, you run around back. Strike it from the rear," Lucille ordered in her rat-a-tat style. "Leo, Bart, behind me."

She made a triangle with her index fingers and thumbs, holding her hands against her chest.

Ammit leapt into the air to pounce upon all four of them. The huge lion paws splayed open, its reptilian mouth agape. While the creature was in midflight, Leo's skin lit up with such intensity that everyone had to shield their eyes.

He opened his arms, unleashing a white radiance, like a hundred stadium lights in all directions. The incandescence paralyzed the creature, suspending it in midair. Protected by his sunglasses, only Bartimaeus could see Ammit floating before them.

"I've heard of keeping someone dangling, but that is ridic-u-lous," Bart said with a laugh. "Keep it comin', boy."

Lucille released a red-and-white ray from the triangle of her hands that seared into Ammit's furry chest. "Stay right there, Leo. Just a little longer," Aunt Lucille said through tight lips. Her red beam cut into the creature. Still, Ammit clawed at the air, its hippo hindquarters kicking in a desperate struggle to break free. A look of fear, then utter confusion filled its green eyes seconds before it exploded into a murky olive mist.

Leo gently touched his hands together and his inner light dimmed. A smile of satisfaction lingered on his round face. "Did I do good?" he asked.

"Oh, you did better than good, Leo," Aunt Lucille said, hugging him hard. "You not only dispelled the darkness, but you also managed to turn your light off."

Tobias Shen did not join the celebration. "I'm going inside to check on Will and the abbot. You all remain here."

"Uh-uh," Bartimaeus said, throwing his crutches out. "If you go, we all go. That's the way this team rolls, right?"

"Right!" Aunt Lucille and Leo said in unison.

Abbot Athanasius proposed that he and Will hunt the demon in the basement of the Karnak Center. He figured if Sab dumped the offering to Amon through the floor of the inner sanctum upstairs, something must be beneath.

Will sneezed as they descended the rickety wooden steps. In the damp hallway of the basement, leading to the space directly under the inner sanctum, they were confronted by a fairly new sandstone wall. A crude etching of Amon with his plumed crown was carved into the center. A thick, yard-long slit along the bottom of the wall seemed to be some kind of air vent. Small bones and browned meat were scattered near the opening.

"We've got to"—AH-AH-CHOO!—"get in there," Will said, indicating the wall.

"And how do you propose we break through stone?" the abbot asked nonchalantly, holding his candle.

Will shrugged, scratching the side of his head with Aaron's staff.

"There's an idea," Athanasius said, tapping his index finger on the rod. "You could give the staff a try. Moses used his to liberate water from a stone—why not a demon?"

Looking at the petrified wood in his hands, Will twitched his lips sideways, consumed by doubt. "It might snap the rod in two."

"There's only one way to find out."

Will clutched the knobby end of the staff, projecting the point toward the wall.

"Not that way, Mr. Wilder," a voice bellowed behind him.

It was Tobias Shen, who had just stepped into the hallway followed by Aunt Lucille, Bartimaeus, and Leo. "Turn it around. Your great-grandfather broke through stone using the thick end. Of course, he used Moses's staff, but . . . hit the figure on the wall there. Be very, very gentle."

Will flipped the rod around and pressed the thick end to the Amon carving. The entire stick began to radiate with dim amber light.

"Now shove it at the wall firmly, but not in anger," Shen instructed.

Will shot Tobias an irritated look, but since everybody was watching, followed directions. In his hands, the staff vibrated like the power drill his dad used to repair the deck or build Boy Scout projects with him. The staff pulsated and under its own power, punched through the image of Amon. It actually penetrated the wall.

Will swallowed hard, turning to Shen. "Should I pull it out?"

"Keep hold of it and be still," Tobias advised.

From the staff, cracks like black thunderbolts started moving in all directions along the face of the wall. Everyone, including the abbot, stepped back.

"Wait." Will worriedly looked over his shoulder. "Why are you all backing up?"

"Because the wall is coming down," the abbot said flatly.

"Uh, I kind of figured that out!" Will said, still holding the amber rod.

In the detached voice he used when he was sensing

something out of the ordinary, Bartimaeus started to speak. "When you see what's on the other side of that wall, ya might want to back up too. That is one baaad dude in there."

The velocity of the traveling cracks made the wall look like a mosaic.

"Mr. Wilder, it is time to pull the staff out," Shen said, pushing Lucille, Leo, and Bart back into the room where they had entered.

Will yanked the staff from the wall and ran to join the abbot. Chunks of sandstone, starting from the hole in the middle, crumbled away, filling the corridor with debris and dust. Soon the whole wall had collapsed.

Will grabbed an unlit torch from a stand in the hallway. He touched it to the flame on the abbot's candle and ventured through the thick haze into the crimson red chamber. Squat columns hugged the circular walls. In the smoggy firelight, Will detected a figure, its back to him, sitting at an ancient bronze table. A rapid snapping sound, like castanets clicking, was the only thing he could hear. Then silence. An awful eerie silence. The *click, click, clicking* resonated once more. Will slowly approached the table. It was littered with mostly geese carcasses and bones, as was the floor.

The figure eating at the table wore off-white linen and had a familiar dark tangle of wiry, shoulder-length hair.

"You came at feeding time," the airy voice of Ann Hyc said without turning around. "Aren't you lucky."

At that moment, from the table and the floor, all the dead geese and fowl sat up, honking loudly at Will. Their cries and hisses were shrill and unnatural.

This could be a problem!

He instinctively fled the room to the safety of the hall.

The abbot caught Will by the arm. "What did you see? You can stay out here. Just tell me where to go and I'll confront it."

Aunt Lucille stuck her head out from the side room. "You know you can't do that, Athanasius. The prophecy was very clear: Will has to face the demon *alone* with the Staff of Aaron."

The abbot reluctantly agreed with her. "What was the line in the prophecy about silence?" he asked Will and Lucille.

"Silence and trust shall be his strength," Lucille said as Will mouthed the last words along with her. The abrasive hissing and honks echoed in the hallway.

Athanasius placed a long hand on Will's helmet. "Remember what you did on the Purgatorial Course. Guard your thoughts, permit no anger in, and remain silent. Move quickly and take back Moses's staff." The abbot's voice fell into a harsh whisper. "Do not converse with the demon."

"What do I do if it comes at me? It supposedly spits fire! My great-grandfather said it—"

"TRUST. Trust in the grace you've been given. Improvise the rest. What you do in that room is less important than the state of your heart when you do it." He clapped Will on the shoulders. "Call me once the demon is restrained and I'll finish it off."

Will took a deep breath and nodded sharply. Carrying the torch and the staff, he stepped over the broken wall and into the smoke-filled chamber. It was chilly inside, more like a walk-in freezer than a stone room. Will tossed the torch to the middle of the floor and held the staff with two hands, like a lance. The geese and macaws fell silent, appearing lifeless once more.

A shadowy figure familiar to him stood facing the far wall. Ann Hye threw a gnawed, bloody goose onto the table before her. In the torchlight, Will realized she no longer had hands but gargantuan gray paws with dirty talons.

"Isn't it interesting . . . I told you Mr. Bobbit lied. Yet you believed him over me. He knew me all too well, Will Wilder. My spirit was in him. Oh, the time I spent with that cruel, cruel man," Ann said, her voice darkening into a low growl. "AND STILL HE TOOK MY PRECIOUS GEESE. THEY WERE NOT HIS TO TAKE. HE DARED TO FOUL MY OFFERING—AS YOU AND YOUR FRIENDS HAVE!"

The table and its contents flew into the air and collided with the metal door on the far wall. Pained, ghostly honks and hisses rang out in the chamber.

Will breathed hard but did not move.

"I know why you've come, silly boy." Ann's high musical voice was back. "You want this, don't you, Will Wilder?" A gray paw held out the Staff of Moses, tapping it on the floor. "Well, do you want it or not? You can tell us." There was no sound. Will wrestled with whether to lunge for the staff or ask the demon for it. He finally opted to shut his mouth and stay put.

"If you want the staff, Will, you can have it." Ann lifted the sapphire rod above her head. "Or rather, it can have you." She threw the staff to the ground and retreated behind a shadowy column near the ruined table.

Will was too busy tracking Ann to notice that Moses's staff had started to squirm and balloon on the flagstones. He reached for it, but as he bent down, the expanding face of a blue snake, big as an elephant, rushed at him.

In self-defense, he cast Aaron's staff to the ground and hid behind the nearest column. From the rod rose an amber snake larger than the blue serpent filling half the chamber. The two snakes reared back and sprang at one another. The yellow one, defying gravity, slithered along the ceiling to avoid the blue snake's fangs, which struck the wall. Will tried to stay off the battlefield in the shelter of a pillar. All the while, he worried that Amon might attack him from the side.

Lucille and the abbot craned their necks for a view of the snakes flipping and flailing, striking at one another in the next chamber.

"Aunt Lucille." It was Leo, tugging at the side of her jacket. "I need to go to the bathroom."

She glanced away from the battling serpents for a

millisecond. "You'll have to wait, dear. I don't even know where the facilities are."

"I don't need a facility. I need a toilet," he said, scowling.

Aunt Lucille ignored him, returning her attention to the action. The blue snake's fangs were sunk deep into the floor opposite Will. It writhed to extract itself from the flagstones. That's when the yellow snake coiled itself around the blue one. Disengaging its jaws, it began to swallow the blue snake whole, from the tail up.

The amber tail, with a rock-hard tip, wriggled near Will. Without hesitation, he clutched the snake's tail just as it consumed the blue viper. Instantaneously, the great serpent trembled and started to shrink. The scaled body was absorbed into a single emerald staff webbed with blue fissures. Will gripped the newly combined rods in amazement.

"Abbot, I've got it—I mean them. I have the staffs," he called out toward the hallway.

"They've all lied to you, Will Wilder," Ann Hye said in a reverberating sweet tone. She remained hidden by a column. "Did they tell you that those staffs would stop me? It's not true. They sent you here as a sacrifice. Athanasius and Lucille knew that only a healthy offering would satiate me. You must be it."

"I don't believe you," Will sputtered without thinking.

Ann came out from behind the column, her hair shielding her face from Will's glance. "Thank you for talking, Will. The truth can be upsetting. But you know I speak the truth, don't you?"

Will angrily shook his head, the luminous staff at the ready.

Ann edged closer to him, her arms behind her back. "What did I tell you when we first met? Oh, I remember." A gray hairy arm shot up, one paw pointing to the sky. "If you only see the outside, you miss a great deal." The paw pulled back her weedy black hair to reveal a hideous raven's face. Shiny, coal-black eyes glared at Will and a sharp yellow beak stuffed with rows of serrated teeth snapped. Ann then jiggled the rats' nest atop her head, and it transformed into sleek black feathers. In the smoldering torchlight, she seemed to grow larger as she advanced on him. The wolfish arms and chest, covered in filthy gray hair, swelled with each step. And then inexplicably, her two paws hit the ground and her legs disappeared. From beneath the torn linen around her midsection, the gray-green tail of an immense serpent emerged.

Undulating slightly on its massive tail, the monstrosity stood upright and roared in a deep voice, "Jacob Wilder had that same expression when I came for him. They told him lies as well. Told him he could restrain me. HAAAAAAA. As long as there is anger in the world and willing servants, Amon will never be restrained."

The demon had gotten too close to him. Will had to move. In an awkward somersault, he flipped past the beast and ducked behind a column.

"Oh, you are playful. I like games," Amon said, wriggling around. "Let's try one in the dark." The beast raised its tail and smothered the torchlight in the center of the room. "I can feel your fear, Will Wilder. Or is that your rage?"

Will could hear its talons scraping across the floor and the scuff of its slithering tail as the demon moved. He used the sound to help him locate new hiding spots. At one point, the tail slid only inches from where he stood.

"William, are you all right?" the abbot yelled into the chamber.

"GO ON, ANSWER HIM!" the demon fumed.

Will said nothing.

"William?" the abbot called again.

"Why don't we turn the light up," the demon said. A flame spewed from the open beak of the creature. It shot upward, setting the edges of the ceiling aflame. "Ah, that's better," it said.

From his hiding place, Will could see the abbot approaching the room. He silently motioned him back. But Athanasius had already started mounting the rubble.

"There will be no assistance! Each one faces us alone," Amon raged. At the demon's command, broken sandstone hurtled down the hall, colliding into the staircase behind the abbot. Athanasius ducked into the side room with the others just in time to avoid the airborne avalanche of debris.

"Now where is my little *Seer*?" The demon spun in a circle, the huge raven head poking behind the pillars. "I'll flatten every wall and post in this building to find you, Wilder."

The serpent's tail crushed a column it imagined Will to be hiding behind. "Show yourself, Jacob—AAAH—Will!"

Will stood in the rear of the room near the mangled table and the sealed metal door. His shoulders pressed against a column, he knew he had to move quickly toward the entryway. With the fire spreading across the ceiling, it was his only path to safety. While the demon searched behind the columns on the left side of the room, Will ran along the opposite wall.

Amon caught sight of him and spat clumps of flame in rapid succession. But Will moved so fast the fireballs missed him. On the run, he concluded that if silence and trust were his great weapons, he would deploy them in the main doorway. Pointing the fused staffs at the beast, he would stand his ground and trust that the One who fashioned them, who gave them their powers, would know how to stop this evil creature.

"WHERE ARE YOU, WILDER?" the demon fumed. "We will consume you as we once devoured your great-grandfather. Did your daddy or Athanasius or Aunt Lucille ever tell you that? That even the great Jacob Wilder fell? Oh, how they've *lied* to you, boy. They all knew what awaited you—and *still* they sent you in here to die like the others."

Questions, anger, doubts clouded Will's mind. *Did my great-grandfather die at the hands of a demon? How could he have written so much about the Sinestri if they killed him?*

Maybe he died like this: alone with nothing between him and a demon but a stick. He forcefully banished the thoughts from his head and focused on his mission: face the enemy with silence and trust. Nothing else.

He stepped into the middle of the entryway, his back to the hall, and took a wide stance. His radiant staff pointed directly at Amon.

The demon slid down the center of the room toward the boy, flaming bits of the ceiling falling around him. "No, Jacob had no staff when he faced us, but it would have done him as little good as it will do you. Resign yourself to the fate of your ancestors. This is the time of the *Sinestri*, Will Wilder. Give us the stick and submit. Without you the Brethren will be—"

The beady eyes of the beast dilated as a surging emerald beam from the staff struck its body. Its tail decomposed before Will's eyes. The wolfish arms and torso flailed on the ground. Its raven head thrashed about in hatred, cursing and squawking. Minutes later the glow of the staff dimmed and Amon lay moaning in the middle of the chamber.

"Abbot? Abbot?" Will called over his shoulder.

A wary Athanasius bounded over the stones in the hallway and ran into the chamber. "Where is it?" the abbot asked, studying the room.

"It's there." Will pointed to a spot near the middle of the room, though the abbot saw only a wobbling goose carcass, bruised fruit, and cascading ceiling embers hitting the floor.

Trusting Will's sight, Athanasius laid a purple sash over

his shoulders, which he only wore during major exorcisms. He pressed his index fingers and thumbs together and projected the wispy blue rays Will had witnessed earlier. Amon cried in anguish under the punishment of the beams and the forceful words spilling from the abbot's mouth. It finally yelped mournfully as if finishing an argument, "Amon. AMON! Are you happy now, Athanasius? We are AMON!" With those words, a black hole opened up in the center of the creature and it collapsed in on itself. Amon was no more. Within seconds, the coldness in the room lifted and only the crackle of the burning ceiling could be heard.

Aunt Lucille and Tobias watched from the hallway. "You'd both better get in here before that ceiling falls in. I know what that's like and it isn't pleasant," she said, massaging her wrist. Will and the abbot heeded her warning.

"Aunt Lucille!" Leo groused, popping out of the side room. A hand on a hip, his lips in full pucker, he asked, "Can I use the bathroom *now*?"

CHAPTER 23

BLOODY QUESTIONS

The fire set by Amon destroyed everything but the Karnak Center foundations. Tobias and the abbot managed to pull Valens from the blaze, but the floor gave way before they could reach Pothinus Sab. Had Sab remained against the wall of the inner sanctum, where they left him, he might have survived. But the self-help guru awakened at some point and crawled toward the statue of Amon. The weight of the stone figure dragged him into the inferno created, ironically, by the beast he worshipped to the very end.

For his role in the Sab affair and for stealing artifacts from the museum, Valens was sentenced to a long prison term. By a unanimous vote, the Brethren expelled him from the community. Still Athanasius and occasionally Aunt Lucille would visit him in jail, offering their support and prayers. Valens was remorseful and eagerly talked about returning to Peniel someday. But not even Lucille could ever see that happening.

Days after his confrontation with Amon, Will still wrestled with questions seared into his mind by the demon. Once sunshine returned and the strange wildlife had fully receded from Perilous Falls, Will stopped by Peniel to seek the answers only Aunt Lucille could provide.

Hard at work in the depths of the museum, Lucille had just locked some artifacts in the vault when Will located her. He shadowed her upstairs to Jacob Wilder's office like an unfed, eager puppy.

"I need to know what happened to my great-grandfather," Will insisted.

"It's a complicated story. Why so curious all of a sudden, dear?" Lucille asked, opening the elaborate door of the office.

"Shouldn't I know what happened?" The clinks and clamor of the great door unlatching nearly drowned out his voice.

Aunt Lucille briskly stepped into the office, Will in pursuit. "I don't have all the answers, Will. There are some things . . ." She fluttered her eyelids, running her fingers through the strawberry-blond curls on the back of her head. "You're not prepared to hear all of that history."

"I already know it," Will said, throwing himself into the chair in front of the desk, his eyes steady. "The demon told me."

Lucille laughed lightly, sitting in her father's high-backed leather chair. "Well, that's hardly a reliable source. You know how they distort and deceive—"

"He was devoured by the *Sinestri*. A demon killed him."

Aunt Lucille's face turned crimson. "You have no idea what you're talking about."

"Are you lying to me?" Will asked, laying his hands flat on the desk. "The demon said you were lying—and I think you might be."

She leaned over the desktop. "Listen to the *Sinestri* long enough and you won't be able to distinguish truth from lies. You have no idea how my father perished and neither does that demon."

"Were you afraid that I wouldn't help the Brethren if I knew that demons killed him?"

Aunt Lucille rose from the chair, hiding her suddenly moist eyes from Will. "He *offered* his life—sacrificed himself for the people he cared most about. He did it out of love—"

"But the demons killed him?"

"The demons *tried*. Love, Will, is stronger than any plot of the devil." She clenched her quivering hands, trying to ground her voice. "I will not discuss this further."

"I need to know what happened."

"You will KNOW when the time is right. NOT BEFORE!" she thundered. Will was about to speak back, but given Aunt Lucille's passion, he reclined in the chair and crossed his arms in silence.

Moments later he asked quietly, "When will you tell me the whole story?"

"When you need it." Lucille arranged some items on the desk and took a book from the side shelf. She lingered on a framed photograph of her father wearing his pith helmet, hanging on the wall. Ever so tenderly, she reached up and touched it. "He was a great man, Will. He built this fortress against the *Sinestri* and repelled every major demon."

"So why are we still fighting them?"

"Because he didn't finish his mission. But he ensured it was left to us. He gave his life so we could have ours. The *Sinestri* come for each generation. During this time, it is up to us to resist and destroy them if we can. As you know better than most, we live in occupied territory, dear. And though there are demons lurking outside and within, there is also much good that needs protecting."

Will felt badly about upsetting Aunt Lucille. He could tell from the way she spoke that his questions had awakened painful, personal memories A part of him wanted to apologize, but he decided to change topic. "So are we going to train today, or what?" he asked her, the old twinkle back in his crescent eyes.

Aunt Lucille had a distant look, still preoccupied with whatever was running through her memory. She took Will by the hand and squeezed it. "No training today." She hastily turned from him, retreating to the mantel behind the desk, emotion choking her voice. "Go spend time with your family—see your friends. That's what we fight for, Will. Love them and savor the day."

While Lucille wasn't looking, he gingerly pulled the Veil of the Virgin from his backpack and reunited it with the larger reliquary on the side table. He then walked behind his aunt, gave her a hug, and promised to see her later.

As he padded down the hall, Aunt Lucille shouted to him, "I figured that's how you broke the wrath of that demon. The veil also probably strengthened you during the battle. I was wondering when you were going to return it. Thank you."

Will scooted down the spiral staircase with only one thing in mind: joining Cami, Simon, and Andrew in the back room of the Burnt Offerings Café.

In the late afternoon, a man in a black hood and cloak rowed a small boat into the shallows of the Perilous River. The boat ran aground under a thicket of dead trees. It was a wasteland across the river from town, a swampy place on the outskirts of Wormwood where few ever ventured.

The hooded figure left the boat and trudged through the dark forest until he came upon a small cabin. Tangled in vines, the door and outer walls of the hovel were covered in a green veneer of mold. The man pulled at the rickety door and entered.

He threw back his hood. "Is anyone here?"

"Oh, yes, I'm here," a woman's smoky voice announced from the corner near a smoldering fire. "Come sit by me." She wore a tattered hooded cloak and sat in a stiff-backed chair, facing the fireplace.

Baldwin considered leaving. But he had come this far, so he obediently shuffled over to the woman.

"Sit." She half turned her shadowed face toward him. "I thought we would *both* be in hoods today, honey. You are bold to reveal yourself." Her bony finger pointed to the stool at her side. "Sit!"

Baldwin took his place. The prolonged silence rattled him. "My cousin, Lilith, told me I should see you. She said you were easy to speak with . . . could see things."

The woman greedily grabbed his big hand and turned it to the soft light of the fire. "You are a leader. But someone blocks your path."

"Yes! I can't speak to my brothers of this. They lack understanding," Baldwin stammered. He started to pull his hand away, but the crone's fingers were like a vise.

"I can't help unless I see your palm."

"I'm not interested in getting tied up with the *Darkness*. I don't want a reading! Only advice."

"It's the young Wilder boy, isn't it?" The woman groaned, running a finger over a faint line on his palm.

"Who told you that?"

"Oh, I know all about him. I know his family well . . ."

"He's impetuous. Untested," Baldwin spat in his superior tone. "You should hear my Brethren. They praise him day and night. 'He is the chosen one, Vicar. We must follow Will, Vicar. He is the fulfillment of the prophecy, Vicar.' I have trained my whole life to fight the *Darkness*! I, too, have faced demons and been victorious time after time!"

The crone stroked his palm, which had a strange calming effect on him. As he looked down at her hand, the knobby fingers straightened and the wrinkled flesh was suddenly smooth and plump. "You are strong," she said, "and you have earned the right to lead your community." Before he knew what was happening, she drew a knife and slit open the fatty part of his palm beneath the thumb. His blood dripped into a gold saucer at the woman's feet. Baldwin struggled to pull his hand away, but she held him fast, the blood continuing to flow. Then she released her grip.

Baldwin jumped back, knocking over the stool. "What have you done? Who are you?"

"I'm a friend with a common interest." She reached her two hands toward him. They were once more knotted and shriveled with age. Baldwin checked his own hand and the cut had closed. He rubbed at his eyes. Perhaps the stinging smoke had obscured his vision. He was so confused.

"You are stronger than the boy. Wiser," the woman said. "Win his confidence. When you have him alone, overpower him. Finish him. I know you have it in you."

Baldwin shook his head in a panic. "No, witch. I do not have it in me. I am a man of honor. I should never have come here." He reached for the door, but it would not yield to him.

"Know this, Baldwin—a mighty, cunning one will soon rise against Will Wilder and those nearest him." She picked up the golden saucer pooled with blood. "Even a *Seer* can doubt his eyes. Wilder will not see this one coming. While he is bewildered and preoccupied, use your strength to smite him. This chance will not come again for you." The door of the cabin flew open and a cold wind whistled through the place.

Baldwin, flushed and disoriented, ran from the cabin into the darkness, searching for his boat and the way back home.

Will was in the backroom of the Burnt Offerings Café half joking with Andrew about trying out for the middle school football team next season.

"I think you're a little light for that, Will-man," Andrew said between forkfuls of pancakes. "I mean, you could be a kicker or somethin' but . . . it's a tough game. Of course, Simon could show you all the moves." He laughed, nudging Simon's chair.

"I'll do that right after you show us your academic moves, moron." Simon adjusted his rectangular-framed glasses and smirked. "I've always liked your repeating pattern—as in repeating *the year.*" Simon instantly got up and ran to the other side of the round table to avoid contact with Andrew's hand.

Cami was about to add her two cents when Will lifted a biscuit to his mouth. She made a strange face when her eyes caught his hand. "William, what's going on with your ring?"

Will turned the biscuit away and checked the ring's face. He lost all expression as he watched the deep red blood churn beneath the glass.

"Are you okay, Will?" Simon asked.

"I'm not sure," he said, looking sick. "Either Aunt Lucille is in trouble or I am."

He lengthened his arm, warily staring at the frothing blood in the ampule, hoping it would stop. His friends exchanged worried glances and gathered around to offer support.

Cami finally broke the long silence with a whisper. "I was going to tell you later, but . . . Max had another nightmare last night. You were in it."

❖ ACKNOWLEDGMENTS ❖

Since Will and I always receive a great deal of assistance on these adventures, some thanks are in order. For their abiding affection, I must first thank my children, Alexander, Lorenzo, and Mariella, and their mom, Rebecca. Their unfiltered feedback saved me from many a wrong turn in Perilous Falls. And without Rebecca I would never have had the time for this return trip. I love you all so very much.

To my team at Random House, your contributions and dedication to all aspects of this second book have been peerless. My editor at Crown, Emily Easton, has once again held my feet to the fire and posed important questions just when I needed them most. You are simply the best. Every writer should receive the support and wisdom that Phoebe Yeh, my publisher at Crown, and Barbara Marcus, president of Random House Children's Books, have lavished upon me. You have encouraged and bolstered my efforts in ways you will never know. I am in your debt.

I love working with creative people, and at Random House Kids, I have found them in abundance. To my pals Dominique Cimina and Mary McCue in publicity; John Adamo and Kim Lauber in marketing (who create marketing materials worthy of an art gallery); Ken Crossland, our designer (who has incredible taste and a rare eye for beauty); Isabel Warren-Lynch, our art director; Samantha Gentry, the ultimate editorial assistant (who is in charge of absolutely everything); and the entire sales force—each of you has contributed mightily to make this second book so special. Thank you for the gift of your time and talents.

Jeff Nentrup has once again captured the Wilder spirit with another boffo cover and truly spectacular interior illustrations.

Francis "Chip" Flaherty has been my constant wingman from the start of this series. He always ensures that everything goes according to plan. Thank you, my friend.

For their inspiration, friendship, and support, I must thank Dean Koontz, Reed Frerichs, Laura Ingraham, Pete Anthony, Jim Caviezel, Randall Wallace, Ron Hansen, Christopher Edwards, Umberto Fedeli, Monica and Kevin Fitzgibbons, Joe Looney, Stephen Sheehy, Shawn Sheehy, James Faulkner, Cristina Kelly, Peter Gagnon, Lee South, Mary Matalin, Ryan Milligan, Corey Frank, Michael Sortino, Doug Keck, Mother Angelica and her sisters, and my parents, Raymond and Lynda Arroyo.

To the kids, parents, teachers, librarians, and all those who have embraced Will's adventures, my sincere thanks. When I founded my literacy initiative, Storyented, in 2015, our goal was to help everyone "find your story and find your way." After countless school visits and signings, I am humbled that so many of you have chosen to make Will Wilder's story your own. A zeal for adventure and a sense of wonder are so needed today. I hope Will inspires both in all who encounter him.

Finally, I have long thought that we authors are only responsible for about 50 percent of any story. The other half of the tale relies on the imaginative generosity of readers who give life to our creations in their hearts and minds. Thank you for doing your part, and I hope you'll return to Perilous Falls very soon. . . .

❖ ABOUT THE AUTHOR ❖

Raymond Arroyo is a *New York Times* bestselling author, award-winning producer, and lead anchor and managing editor of EWTN News. As the host of *The World Over Live,* he is seen in nearly 300 million homes internationally each week. He is also the founder of Storyented, a large-scale literacy initiative. When not in Perilous Falls, he can be found at home in Virginia with his wife and three children (where there are absolutely no amulets of Ammit!). You can follow him on Facebook and on Twitter at @RaymondArroyo.